PAWS FOR REFLECTION

David Beeson

Mostly illustrated by Senada Borcilo but with a much appreciated contribution from Dana Mallon

Dedicated to the excellent household that supported me in bringing this book to completion: Misty, Luci and Toffee, and above all Danielle - or human/domestic number 1 - who even went so far as to proofread it.

My thanks also to my son Michael and friends Hazera Forth and Deb Breen, who read bits as they became available and provided me with precious feedback and encouragement.

Equally warm thanks also go to Senada Borcilo, who produced the cover design and most of the illustrations, as well as to Dana Mallon who contributed two more.

CONTENTS

Paws for reflection

The household with human number 1
By Senada Borcilo

How it all began...

"A bit overweight, isn't he, for a cat his age?" my wife suggested, as I was fumbling for the door key that night long ago. "Do you think we need to put him on a diet?"

I was distracted and may have been too casual in my reply.

"Perhaps you're right. He does seem a little fat."

As I said it, I knew I'd made a mistake. Misty, our far from anorexic cat, who'd been sitting patiently at our feet until then, spun on the spot and stalked off into the night, his tail flicking threateningly from side to side, his head held disdainfully high. We didn't see him again until the following morning.

That was no empty gesture. It meant giving up on his usual privilege of sleeping on the bed, or on top of us when the mood took him, a right he'd always cherished and protected. He was obviously offended.

Which was remarkable. It meant he'd understood us. He'd mastered English.

It was a while, though, before I realised that he didn't just understand the language. He knew how to write it too. That he was, in fact, keeping a diary.

To my further astonishment, when our toy poodles Luci and Toffee joined us, they decided to follow Misty's example. Three animals, three diaries. I sneak in to read bits of them when they're not around to catch me.

In fact, I've gone further and stolen some of the entries. It seemed worth sharing them with a wider audience.

After all, if I find them fun, so might you.

Misty taming the domestics

Christmas wasn't bad. A full complement of domestic staff – not just the usual two, domestics 1 and 2 as I like to think of them, but also the two young ones who were around when I was a kitten. It's always good to see them, but I don't understand why they don't just stay instead of clearing off after each visit. Aren't they ashamed to abandon us? Do they think we're not good enough for them? Do they imagine it's more fun somewhere else?

Still, when they show up, I'm always inclined to be forgiving. I just can't help myself. The prospect of curling up on those laps leaves me without the heart to show how irritated I am.

What's strange, though, is that it doesn't take long before they start getting all blasé again. Just a couple of days after they showed up, one of the young domestics got very casual about stroking me. Watching TV or something. Absent-minded with his hand movements. I can't abide that. So I bit him. Did he curse! A lesson he'll remember. Get offhand with this cat? Not good for your health, my friend. Offhand, bitten hand, I say.

Then things turned bad. After Christmas. They *all* cleared off. Both my regular domestics and the young ones. Without asking permission. Which I wouldn't have granted anyway.

To be fair, they got the substitute in instead, the one I think of as number 3, and she's OK. I've got her trained. She knows to open the front door when I ask, instead of sending me to the cat flap at the back. She lets me drink from the tap in the bathroom. And she checks that my food bowl's kept full, keeping me well fed, without calling me fat.

Still, it was a relief to see the others come back for New Year's Eve but, to be honest, the celebration was a wash out. A few loud noises and our dog, Janka, becomes a quivering wreck. A full firework display? She was like "is this Armageddon, or what?"

I'm no fan of dogs. Quite honestly, once you've smelled one, you've smelled the lot. Some are too big and a tad intimidating, some are small and just too wimpish. Apart from that – well, I hate to sound racist, but they're all just dogs with nothing to choose between them.

But our Janka's different. I mean, she's *our* dog. She lives with us. She may not be the sharpest knife in the drawer, but she's part of the family. So we get on. Even though she's terrified by any sound louder than a door slamming. And so yappy! On and on. Whenever anyone turns up, even if it's the domestics coming home. Yap, yap, yap. Tiresome. Domestic number 1 tries to do something about it, sometimes even spraying her with water. She even tries to get her sidekick, domestic number 2, to work on it too, but he's hopeless. Doesn't like the noise but won't make the effort.

Well, like I said, Janka was terrified on New Year's Eve. So I went and lay down with her. Least I could do, I felt. After all she's been around all my life, pretty much. That makes a bit of a bond, really. I owed her, I reckoned.

But, blow me down, as soon as domestic number 1 got up to leave the room, Janka jumped down and went trotting after her. Completely ignoring me. As though I didn't count for anything.

Well, I got her back. I sat on the stairs at bedtime and wouldn't let her go by. When I do that, she doesn't even dare to come up to where I'm sitting glowering at her, let alone push past me. That meant she couldn't go straight to the domestics' room to lie on the floor next to their bed – she's not allowed up like I am – but had to wait till I left for the night's mousing. It was a simple gesture on my part, but I certainly showed her who was boss, who was not to diss.

On the other hand, with the domestics, after they came back, I was the very model of generosity. Kind and tolerant. Very indulgent. Didn't take it out on them. Didn't show them my resentment. Came and lay on their laps as usual. I think they appreciated the gesture.

But domestic number 2's no good. I'd been lying on him barely ten minutes when he complained about the weight. Weight? Me? With the exercise I get? He should look at his own waistline.

Anyway, he pushed me off. After nearly a week away. And he thinks he can do that to me?

I didn't act immediately. I like to build the dread of coming punishment for a while before I administer it. I like him to stew a while. I got him the next day. He reached out to stroke me when we were both on the sofa. Got him with as neat a claw stroke as anyone might wish, if I say so myself. Right across the back of his hand.

That'll teach him. He seems pretty well untrainable but, hey, I'm not going to stop trying. After all, it's good to get a little practice with tooth and claw. And, you never know, someday the lesson *might* get through to him. In the meantime, I'm sure it does him some good.

It certainly does me plenty.

Misty's gaze
By Senada Borcilo

Misty contemplates
his claws

Aren't claws hell? I don't know how others cope, but I'm in a bit of a dilemma over mine.

Domestic number 1 used to try to cut them. But those very claws she was attempting to cut, she soon found out, I could use to fine effect as a deterrent to cutting. She learned that approaching *my* claws with a pair of clippers wasn't a smart move. Now, it doesn't happen anymore.

I mean, I need to keep them sensibly long. Or do I mean effectively long? Sensible to be effective, I suppose.

Most interlopers in my garden get the message when I just give them a bit of a reprimand – I have a fine caterwaul, deep and drawling – and they get the message in spades if the poor old dog Janka joins me.

It happened with that ghastly thug Napoleon, from a few doors up the street. Not a stray, of course, he's got a good home, and his coat and his physique aren't the kind you see on strays, only on cats with good domestics giving them plenty to eat. But he's a stray *at heart*. A bully. A hood. Arrogant, throwing his weight around, and his weight is considerable. Much more than mine. I have a fine, sleek physique, but next to him I'm positively thin. And he's not fat. On the contrary. It's powerful flesh that he's carrying.

He was in the garden the other day. Well, I had to challenge him, didn't I? I mean, you just have to. For the principle if nothing else.

"This is my garden," I told him. "You're out of your territory. Please withdraw to beyond the borders of my garden or, regrettable though it may be, a state of hostilities may arise between us."

It wasn't really that formal. And certainly not that polite. Basically, we were just howling at each other. I'm translating that into what we meant by it.

"I never withdraw. This is my territory," Napoleon countered, "It was mine long before you showed up, it's mine now."

"Maybe that's how things were. But then I moved in along with my domestics. Your time in possession is over. This is mine now. You need to leave before things get nasty."

"Nasty? You're going to make things nasty? You and whose army?"

Well, that's when the army showed up. Janka came flying out of the house and ran straight towards him. I don't know what she'd have done if she'd reached him. Probably licked him. But he didn't stay to find out.

Big, noisy and smelly – Janka has a powerful scent very much her own and not to everyone's taste – she represented a force that he had the sense not to want to take on. Instead, he raced for the fence, and the safety promised beyond it.

They all do that. They don't bother to find out what I don't intend to tell them: she's not the dangerous one of the two of us, not the sharpest tooth in the jaw, let alone the fiercest runner in the pack. She's frightened of her own shadow, however threatening she may sound with her crazy yapping.

However, if the ball of barking wool's not around, and my caterwaul isn't sufficient to frighten off an intruder, it's nice to know I can count on twenty finely sharpened weapons to back up my teeth.

On the other hand, and I know this is a weakness, I'm fond of a blanket. And the trouble with that is, if the claws are the right length for a scrap, they're the wrong length to avoid getting caught in cloth. Then, dammit, I can't get them out anymore.

That is *so* irritating!

All I can do is complain. Loudly. And hope one of the domestics comes over to help me out. Sometimes it's the doggy-friend Janka that comes. She's useless, of course, but somehow, and I can't explain how, she helps. A good caterwaul gets her going, and she's over like a shot. If I see something smelling canine and barking at the top of her voice coming straight at me, the claws just sort themselves out and withdraw without any help. Like they just decide it's time to go. Must be some deep instinct in me, I suppose.

The number 2 domestic says it's 'atavistic'.

No idea what that means but, hey, I don't expect he knows either. He likes to use complicated words. As far as I'm concerned, as long as he understands "dry food", "wet food", "water" and "no, not in a bowl you moron, dripping from the bath tap", that's more than enough vocabulary. But he likes to use obscure terms because he thinks they make him sound intelligent. He even said "apportion" the other day, and it didn't mean a bowlful of food.

In fact, he's always trying to be clever. When I got my claws stuck in the duvet the other day, what did he do? Did he get up and help? Did he heck. He laughed. And made some sarcastic comment. Like "teach him to let his claws grow so long".

He even said "Just let Janka loose on him. He'll soon withdraw them. It'll be stronger than him, the instinct to get away. No need for us to do anything."

I didn't react just then. I can bide my time. You see, I know him. He likes what he calls "playing". It means waving his hand vaguely in my direction, in the hope I'll attack it. Gently, of course, with velveted paws. Or so he fondly imagined.

I taught him. Velvet my paws? After he's laughed at me? Not a chance. I got him good and proper. And showed him how claws the right length combine perfectly with, if I say so myself, finely sharpened teeth. I wonder whether apportioning pain like that is atavistic in me?

Not that I care whether it is or it isn't. They say that he who laughs last laughs longest. They're right and boy, is it sweet.

Getting my claws caught on a blanket occasionally is a small price to pay for such complete satisfaction.

Misty on domestic staff

Who'd be a cat?

The domestic staff just appal me with their cheek. Why, you'll never believe what they did last night. They chucked me out of my room! The one where I let them share the bed with me.

I mean, getting chucked out is bad enough. What made it far worse is that they let the dog spend the night. All she does is lie on that silly mat of hers and snore.

When I'm in the room, they don't just get a presence, passive and dull, they get an *experience*. I'm genuinely affectionate, so I'm happy to let them lie in the bed next to me. Fairness is my middle name, so I make sure I give them both roughly equal time to enjoy having me lying on them, and I take trouble to make sure I lie on different bits of them at different times of the night. I move around on the bed too, so that the duvet gets a bit of a fluffing up every now and then.

You'd think they'd appreciate my thoughtfulness.

But no. They preferred to chuck me out. Unbelievable.

As it happens, I thought they'd missed their opportunity last night, as I hid the very moment domestic number 1 came up with a nasty remark about not being able to sleep, "what with the bloody cat moving around all the time." Bloody cat? Bloody impertinence, I call it.

I shot straight under the bed. Clever, I thought. They wouldn't find me there. But *obviously* I had to come out at some stage, and the number 2 domestic was waiting. He pounced on me.

He made this great groaning sound over picking me up. A big pantomime, like he was lifting some colossal weight.

Very droll.

If you don't like picking me up, I reckon, you can just stop. Pal. You think I like it? I haven't scratched you enough for you to get the message?

And that's when the number 1 domestic added insult to injury. Really stuck the knife in. So disappointing, so treacherous, seeing I think of her as a bit of a friend. Reliable, you know. A supporter.

"Careful of your back!" she called out to number 2. "He's quite a lump, isn't he?"

A lump? A *lump*? Me?

And the worst of it? They've put me on low-calorie feed! You can just taste the lack of calories in the insipid stuff. I mean, I eat it of course, because low calories are better than no calories, but boy it's offensive to put me on that kind of diet. It's not just cheek but downright insolence, in my not-so-humble opinion.

Now, I admit I'm not anorexic. I like to think of myself as sleek. Particularly compared to them: they're not exactly slim. How shall I put this? I don't want to call them lumps or anything – I don't do rude, or at least not the way they do – but well – shall I just say, "high BMI"? And when I go for food, I have to jump six times my height onto a shelf, where they sensibly keep my bowl out of the way of the vacuum cleaner dog, and I do that just fine, thank you. I'd like to see them make that kind of effort. It's about as much as they can do to slump onto the sofa with their heaped plates of food, to watch TV while they stuff themselves. Pathetic.

To top it all, when they do that, they can't even make a lap for me. They just sit there gobbling away and watching some bloody silly thriller with subtitles (do they think that a TV series has to be better for being in Italian or Danish? I suppose it *does* make it more mysterious but, hey, isn't that something that ought to be left to the plot?)

No lap means nowhere for me to lie. Which is pretty much

the same as chucking me out of the bedroom. How can I show my affection if they don't let me? And then domestic 2 moans on about me being anti-social. Because I occasionally scratch a bit.

Anti-social? He whinges about my weight. He chucks me out of the bedroom. He keeps me off his lap so he can stuff his fat face. And then he says *I'm* anti-social?

I like nothing better than company. Unlike him I have real manners. And I'm happy to blend in with others.

If he's not getting the treatment he wants from me, isn't it time he asked himself what *he* might be doing wrong?

Misty welcoming the domestics home

The domestics are back from their idea of a holiday. Just as well. These jaunts to strange places are just disruptive and ought to be discouraged.

And what a weird place they chose to go to this time! Some place far, far away. OK, it seems it's practically nothing but coastline and the fish is good, but I understand the cats are a mangy lot for the most part, leading a claw to jaw existence. Trust me, that's far from joyful for either the hunter or the prey.

I don't understand why the domestics don't just settle down and enjoy life at home. After all, so much is just as it should be here. There's a tray full of dry food, and however much I eat of it, it keeps filling up again. OK, I have to remind the staff from time to time to move some wet food from pouch to bowl, but domestic number 2's pretty smart – well, reasonably smart, for a domestic – maybe the right word's 'trainable' – and generally gets it if the reminder's hard enough.

But then they go away. I mean, don't get me wrong. I'm not complaining about the service when they leave. They get domestic number 3 in, and she's fun. It's true she tosses around in bed a lot, which is a pain in the backside, sometimes literally, and instead of learning to stop when I bite her feet, she just chucks me out, which is plain offensive. But mostly she's fine: she knows who's boss, and when I drive the bloody dog Janka off the sofa to reclaim my rightful place, she laughs – a good, sensible reaction.

Even so, it's nice to get domestics 1 and 2 back. So nice in fact that the morning after they came home, I was my winsome best with number 2. Not so much cat as puss, if you get my meaning. Pretty damn adorable, if I say so myself.

But he's hopeless. Clumsy oaf. Left my bowl empty all afternoon. I had to wait till evening to get a proper meal.

Domestic number 1 wouldn't let me on her knees while we were watching TV so I had to use his lap and, honestly, the guy is useless. Fidgeting. Moving his right foot over his left foot, then his left foot over his right. Practically throwing me off by moving his knees apart, then nearly squishing my fine food-filled stomach when he remembered and moved them together again.

I had to go and lie next to him on the couch instead. And even then he came up with some silly comment about "don't be so bad-tempered" when I drove the bloody dog away.

Bad-tempered? Does the dog honestly think she has the right to lie on the couch when I need it? What kind of entitled thinking is *that*?

Why, domestic 2's lucky I let even *him* share the couch with me.

He tried to make up for his tactlessness by stroking me. It was no use though. It was that cackhanded, hamfisted style of his, far too fast, far too clumsy, far too easily distracted. I let him get away with it in bed in the morning, when breakfast might be on the way, but by the evening I've had enough. And he'd made the mistake of wearing a short-sleeved shirt. A joy when you've got claws and jaws. Did I get him!

Winsomeness? Forget it. A puss? That's for the birds. I'm a cat. The birds are for me.

Normal service resumed, in other words.

You have some good reason for disturbing my rest?

By Senada Borcilo

Misty explores his catechism

Today I had one of those moments, as we surely all do, when we get to thinking about the nature of the universe, why we are here, and the relations between Catkind and the Godhead.

First of all, let me say at once that it's time to debunk the rubbish so many domestics talk. They have this quaint but outlandish view that they're created in the image of God. Laughable. They've got only two legs, no tail, barely any whiskers and a stupid vestige of hair instead of proper, sleek fur.

And they think this is the image of God?

It's as if they'd missed the point about the nature of the divinity. Or perhaps I ought to say, forgotten the point. Back in Egypt, when domestics were properly grounded, they knew better and understood the respect due to cats. Today they've lost a proper sense of awe before the great Cat above, the one that put the cat into catalysis, to say nothing of catastrophe and cataclysm. It's enough to make you want to fire them from a catapult until they're catatonic.

How could the divinity be anything but feline? How could one explain the existence of mice? They're certainly not placed on Earth for the pleasure of domestics, are they? Domestics mostly loathe them. But to us they're a source of hours of harmless pleasure with the prospect of a pleasant snack at the end. Harmless to us, that is. Not so harmless to them.

Only a Cat God could have created mice.

Think how enthralling they are. Some may imagine it's boring to sit next to a hole or a drain waiting for them. Nothing could be further from the truth. Sometimes the anticipation is as great as the pleasure itself. All the greater, if anything, for being prolonged. Gratification is just a brief concluding moment, following the joy of anticipation that can last hours.

I sit there, silent as the tomb, unmoving, alert, nerves aquiver and ready for the pounce. Meanwhile, the poor dumb creatures are gradually lulled into a sense of security.

Completely without foundation.

And then – they come sneaking out. And meet – me. Who put the cat in catch.

I know there are some cats that don't eat their prey but drop them indoors, as a kind of offering to the domestic staff. Poor saps. Wouldn't catch me doing that. There's nothing left when *I've* finished.

Well, to be strictly honest, *sometimes* I've taken the dead little thing into the house. But not often. Only if it's proved too easy to catch several of them and I've had my fill. And only if I can leave the corpse in a place where the domestic staff will step on it when they come downstairs still half asleep in the morning. Preferably barefoot.

Oh my! You should hear the language. Enough to turn my ears pink, if they weren't covered with elegant fur.

Otherwise, four or five bites and a chew or two, and the little thing's gone to a much better place. That's a place deep inside me. Leaving me replete and murmuring a little prayer of thanks to the great Cat in the sky. My catechism.

I'm the cat in catharsis.

What possible grounds can our human servants have to think the world was made by a God even remotely concerned with *their* pitiful satisfaction?

Misty on disciplining dogs and domestics

The domestics were away again this weekend. Well, they need their time off, of course they do, and I don't begrudge it. And I'm not complaining that they didn't take me: at least they've learned to stop carting me around in a car. Honestly, they used to coop me up for hours in that ghastly metal cage. Eventually, I had to take drastic action to show them. Not by peeing everywhere, or even getting the claws out, as certain other cats – and I mention no names – tell me they've done. Oh no, I find a constant prowl, interspersed with occasional growls and sustained low-pitched moaning gets the message across quite forcefully enough.

"Five hours and he hasn't stopped that intolerable racket," domestic number 2 said the last time he imposed car travel on me.

Well, yes. If he doesn't want me to complain for five hours, he shouldn't lock me up in that contraption that long. That's elementary logic, isn't it?

It's a mercy to be spared that fate these days. Though I admit a bit of me did feel just slightly put out that they didn't even ask if I wanted to come. I could have given them a haughty shake of the head, and a sniff, which would have been much more satisfying than just being left behind without a by-your-leave.

They took the bloody dog, Janka, of course. Great lump. She just trots along faithfully behind them, wherever they're going, and however long it takes. No mind of her own. No pride. No willpower.

That was a lesson the domestics had to re-learn, I understand, while they were away. She has no power of discrimination when it comes to food. "That's edible," she exclaims when she sees something that might just be. And she flings herself on it, vacuuming it up in two shakes of a shaggy head. Apparently, that's what she did with the bowls of the other two dogs who were there.

The results were apparently spectacular. What's it the medical specialists among the domestics call it? Output? Yes, that's it. Input's what you eat and drink, output's from the other end. Seems Janka's output went through the roof.

Well, not literally. Not even on the floor, as it happens. But since like all dogs, all Janka can do with her 'outputs' is wag her back paws at them instead of making a proper hole, they went into lots and lots of little bags. Evil-smelling little bags which the domestics had to deal with.

I suppose dogs just aren't civilised. Though to be fair, I've been tempted to behave that way myself, ever since domestic number 1 turned the perfectly comfortable garden we had into a terrible desert of gravel paths and vegetable beds protected with mesh I can't get through. Fortunately, the neighbour's decided to do nothing about her own garden, so I have alternative toilet facilities close by. But wanting proper facilities is only my delicacy anyway. Janka wouldn't care. She just makes her mess and leaves it for the domestics.

Honestly, there are times I can't work out what they see in her.

Although I've perhaps begun to understand why she's so popular with domestic number 2. The one who's basically the footman as opposed to the housekeeper. Or maybe the assistant scullery hand.

An event took place after they got home which made an important point.

I was generous as always on their return and came to lie on

domestic number 1's lap. No hard feelings, I wanted to say. And to show the footman nothing had changed with him either, I had a good pounce on his arm later on. But, would you believe it, before I could plunge the teeth and the claws in, Janka, who was lying right next to him, snapped at me.

Snapped at me!

Snapped!

At *me*!

What can she be thinking of? Does she feel *sorry* for him? There's nothing to feel sorry for. He enjoys it when I have a go at him. He may not say so. He may even complain about the minor superficial wounds I inflict. But he knows they mean I'm paying attention to him, and that must give him the kind of internal glow that's well worth a little pain. Yes, of course it hurts. A bit. But nothing he doesn't recover from quickly. And it also teaches him an invaluable lesson, about relative standings in the scale of things. By attacking me for my tough love approach to him, Janka is undermining his hopes of becoming civilised.

To say nothing of her being downright disloyal.

She should have learned by now that crossing me is not a smart move. She had her reminder the very same evening, when she tried to get back into the house after her evening pee. Brilliant. You should have seen that great lump cowering outside the back door as I – little me – just lay across the doorway, watching her whimper, too frightened to push past me. I'm not sure she has sufficient brains, but I hope she realised she was being taught a lesson.

As for domestic number 2, when Janka snapped at me, he told her "good for you, you show the vicious little beggar." Oh dear, oh dear. Doesn't learn his lessons any quicker than the dumb dog. But I don't forget. Especially not abuse like that. I know how to wait for my opportunity. He can expect his correction any time.

When he least expects it.

Misty says goodbye

"So it's just you and me, then," domestic number 2 said to me this afternoon. In a tone of some dejection.

Still, dejected or not, it had a funny side. I mean, why does he talk to me at all? After all he *knows*, he just *knows*, I don't understand English. So what *is* the point in talking? Poor sap.

As for "just you and me", I really hope that's wrong. I have to believe that before long we're going be up to strength, with domestic number 1 back among those present. It doesn't mean she's gone for good, just because she's gone right now. Again. Without any good reason I can see.

What's the point in gadding around so often? What's the point in having a house if you don't live in it? What's the point of taking a position on a cat's staff if you're not going to serve him properly?

Still, I reckon she'll be back.

I know she will.

She has to.

Doesn't she?

What domestic number 2 meant about being just him and me was that we wouldn't be seeing any more of the oaf dog, Janka. She, it seems, is gone. And I don't mean for a while. Unlike domestic number 1, with Janka this time, it's for good.

Now, I know she hadn't been well. She was having these fits. Nasty, violent, twitchy things. Drooling at the mouth with her tongue hanging out and all four legs jerking. Not nice to see. This morning, the domestic told me she'd been having them all night (you see, he *will* keep talking to me).

He was going to take her to the vet. It was far too late, though. Which I knew and he clearly didn't. I saw it all this morning. Something much more worrying than the fits.

I can't think how to put it, except to say that I saw her *go*. I was watching her and suddenly it happened. One minute she was ill but still there, and the next moment something in her eyes went out. There was still a dog, but there was no Janka.

Next thing there wasn't a dog either. The domestic hadn't realised he'd left the front door open. What was left of her walked out of it. He didn't see it happen.

I tried to tell him.

I put up a piteous mew and when I do piteous, I *really* do piteous. But he didn't get it. He was bustling around, in a terrible flap, getting ready for the trip to the vet. Which, if he'd woken up to what I was trying to tell him, was completely irrelevant since there wasn't even the shell of a Janka around anymore.

 Which rather made the point, actually. If Janka had still been inside the dog, she'd never have headed out at all. That she did was all part of the oddness. She'd never wandered off on her own in her life. But this time the dog that had been Janka had done just that. On her own. Proof if any were needed that the real Janka wasn't there.

For a moment, I thought it might be a good thing. Going for a walk without one of those silly leads of hers. Getting a breath of fresh air, that had to be good. Always works wonders on the canine soul. Perhaps it would get Janka's soul back, because it sure as hell wasn't there right then. But afterwards I thought, there was no point looking for that bit of her outside anyway. It was indoors that I'd seen the real Janka vanish. If that part of her was anywhere at all now, she was still indoors. Nowhere near the shell of a dog wandering the streets.

The domestic didn't get any of that. When he worked out that the dog had gone, he got into a panic. He started by phoning the police and rearranging his work so he could avoid going into the office. Then he wasted his time driving off in the car or going out on foot and walking around, calling out "Janka, Janka," not realising that there wasn't any Janka left in the dog he was looking for.

Somebody found the dog and took it to a vet. The domestic shot around there as soon he heard. I kept trying to tell him that there wasn't much point, but he went anyway.

It was quite a time before he returned. He was looking washed out.

"She's not coming back," he told me.

I'd been trying to tell him that myself. But maybe domestics need it confirmed for them by a vet.

He was all sad, poor fellow. He folded up the cloths the domestics used to put on the couch to stop it getting that distinctive Janka reek and said something pathetic like, "won't be doing *that* any more." He had chicken legs for his delayed lunch and I'd swear he was close to tears when he chucked out the bones instead of setting them aside for her. And when he caught sight of her lead – oh, Lord. You could practically hear the violins.

To be fair, I wasn't entirely unaffected myself. She was a noisy, clumsy, smelly old thing, but she was ours. Well, now she was someone else's. Or nowhere at all. We won't be getting the ridiculous cannonade of barking whenever anyone comes to the front door. That great lump won't go blundering around the place or trying to take my position on the couch. Even the smell will start to fade.

Strangely, and I'm a bit ashamed to admit it, I feel I'm going to miss that a little

But I'm not as broken up about it as the domestic, because at least I saw her go.

I've had to deal with friends leaving before. Usually it's because they've moved. Sometimes, though, their domestics are still there but the friend isn't. Gone from one day to the next. What I'd never seen was the moment of departure, which I did with Janka. It made me sad but I'm pleased I was with her right up to the moment she left.

Of course, domestic number 2 doesn't realise I can have that kind of thought. He *knows* cats don't understand those strange and inexplicable partings that happen around us. And I don't want to shatter his illusions. Especially when he's having to cope with losing the animal that was his number 2 owner.

Doesn't stop me thinking he's a poor sap, though.

Misty and variable weather

He's got a real cheek, that domestic number 2.

He keeps making what he thinks are smart comments at my expense, though they're not so much smart as smartarse.

Maybe he thinks I don't understand them. Maybe he realises I do and thinks this is a clever way of getting back at me for my judicious use of claw and tooth on him. Unwise, if that's the case. I still have my teeth and claws, and I keep them in good order.

His latest wheeze started when the weather turned rainy. He thinks it terribly funny that I don't like to go out when it's chucking it down. Well, who would? He doesn't. He grumbles about it all the time. And he's got jackets and umbrellas to protect him. All I have is fur and let me tell you, when fur gets wet, it stays wet a long time.

Why, both domestics comment on it.

"Oh, poor Misty," they say, stroking my damp back, "are you all wet?"

Yeah. Right. Duh. Very acute. I've just been outside in the rain. Can't hide anything from sharp observers like you guys.

That isn't what makes domestic 2 laugh, though. What he thinks is funny is when I try to go out, without a care in the world, and undergo the terrible shock of discovering rain on the other side of the cat flap. He watches me get half out and then come back. He thinks that's quite amusing. I suppose he thinks it's undignified, wriggling backside first into the house.

But what really tickles him is when I ask him to let me out of the front instead.

"What?" he says, "you think conditions might be different there? That it might be raining at the back but fine, warm, mousing weather at the front?"

Oh wow, he thinks that's *so* funny. He's just *so* caustic. *So* bloody superior.

But I ask you: how can he *know* the weather's going to be the same at both doors? I mean, until he's looked?

OK, sure, it always has been. I admit that. But who's to say it always will be? And wouldn't we look stupid if we missed out, on the one occasion it was just glorious at the front, though it was chucking it down in the back garden?

In the meantime, let me make one thing clear.

I don't appreciate being dissed, OK?

I'm off to sharpen my claws. And make sure the teeth are filed and ready for action when I need them. Just as soon as I get the opportunity.

Misty musing on mice

It's funny how little things can teach big lessons.

The domestics have this thing about animals. They talk about saving the planet. That means all sorts of high-minded things like "learning to share our world" or "maintaining biodiversity."

Now I don't have any fanciful ideas like that. I know the world is a tough place. The trick is to make sure you're the one making it tough, not the one on the receiving end of the toughness. No reason not to make it hard for the little critters who had it coming to them anyway. Or, putting it another way, keep well out of the way of any predator yourself, while making sure your prey doesn't keep out of you.

There's some domestic called Hannah Barbera who's come up with one of the least funny cartoon series anyone could imagine. It's called *Tom and Jerry* and it's just plain sick. When it comes to real life, I'm on the side of Tom. I mean, he's a *cat*, for Kibble's sake. Jerry's a grotty little rodent. But somehow that ghastly Barbera woman has made the cat really slow and stupid and tried to make Jerry the clever agile one.

They should try making *Misty and Jerry* instead. It wouldn't be a long series, let me tell you. But it would make up for its brevity in sheer gritty realism.

And the truth is, whatever they may say about sharing the planet, the domestics aren't that keen on rodents either. When it comes to mice, they're as anti as I am. Well, more really – they don't even recognise them as the tasty little snack packets they are.

The other day, they realised what I'd known all along, which is that there was a hole in the wall of the kitchen. If you're small enough – Jerry-small – you could slide your way through it into the back of the cupboard where the domestics like to keep their cereals.

There's nothing quite like a cupboardful of cereals to fascinate a rodent. As there's nothing like a rodent to make a mess of that cupboardful.

I cherished that hole. I used that hole. I tried to protect that hole.

I mean, there was no way for me to get through it, of course. But there was no way for a rodent to get back out of the cupboard except by using it.

Getting the picture? It's a dream for a cat. A single exit for mice, who have to come out sometime. Brilliant.

It meant any time I had a little leisure, I could lie down right outside the hole. I could relax, one of my favourite things, and wait for a prey, my favourite thing of all. I'm *very* patient. And I'm *very* watchful. Some mice escaped my grasp, but let me assure you, not many. Not many at all.

What could be better? A source of entertainment *and* snacks. I certainly wasn't going to mention the hole to the domestics. Why did they need to know about it? After all, if they wanted a mouse hole, they could find their own.

But then domestic number 1 noticed. And she didn't have any compunction at all about mentioning it. Mentioning it a lot and repeatedly.

"All the bread flour, ruined. The cereals gone. A filthy mess everywhere," she complained loudly. "I don't know what the previous owners were thinking of, making a hole right through the wall like that, especially as they never used it for anything…"

Domestic number 2 made some little soothing sounds, like he always does when he wants to express sympathy over a problem but is dreading being asked to do anything about it. I hoped his do-nothing approach would predominate over her more activist outlook. I feared, though, that it would be hers that would win the day. It turns out that I was entirely justified in my apprehension.

What they did was have someone come round to block the hole. With cement. Far too much for a rodent to gnaw through, or a cat to claw through, however determined.

The end of a perfectly good source of innocent fun and fine eatables. Gone. Just like that. In a flash.

I went out to sit by the now non-existent hole that once gave me so much fun and now only allows me to indulge my nostalgia. Sadly, I pondered the ending of a golden era. Domestics. No appreciation for the finer side of mice. Or of the good life. Well, a life that's good at the cat end of the business, at least.

Heyho.

Misty, the hunter caught

Well, well. It's been amusing watching domestic number 2 at work.

Or what he erroneously imagines to be work.

It all started when my cat flap – *my* cat flap – turned treacherous and viciously assaulted me. Oh, yes. You just try to imagine what that feels like.

A cat flap's a passageway, a means of getting into and out of a place. It's useful, and I made frequent use of mine. But then, when I was going through it in a perfectly normal way, it suddenly came off the door and ambushed me. There I was, innocently using *my* entrance to *my* house, when suddenly it grabbed me around the waist and wouldn't let go. A plastic frame, like nothing so much as a gaping mouth, with the flap bit still attached, like nothing so much as a ghastly tongue.

I'm not too proud to admit that I was a little perturbed for a moment. Not, I repeat not, panic-stricken as some slanderous tongues have suggested. Just worried enough to take appropriate action. What ought to have been a door had turned, without warning, into jaws that had me in their grip.

I went straight down on my back and let it have it with all claws drawn. I'd never been caught in a predator's maw like that before and, believe you me, it's no fun. I scraped it off fast and made a break for freedom.

Domestic number 1 was quite nice about it.

"Oh, poor Misty!' she exclaimed. "The cat flap's come right off the door and he's stuck in it."

Domestic number 2 just laughed. Rather distastefully, it

seemed to me.

"If he weren't so fat he'd have got through without difficulty. No wonder he was caught at the waist."

Honestly, the things he says. And he has the gall to get upset when I chastise him.

Just for the record, though I'm not anorexic, I'm far from overweight. A good size for my height. Just enough to inspire respect around the neighbourhood, but without exceeding any reasonable limits. Fat? Perish the thought.

Anyway, the domestic got his comeuppance straight away.

"I'm going to go and buy a new cat flap. I'll even buy you a jigsaw," said number 1. "Then you can put it in this afternoon."

He said something like "Yes, dear," but the fear in his eyes and his drooping shoulders told a far less positive story.

She turned up with the new cat flap and hour or so later.

"This one will do. It's for large cats or small dogs," she announced. As though we ought to be pleased. Let me just stress that the fact that other cats around here are feeble little creatures, doesn't make me "large". The new flap is just right for well-built, adequately proportioned cats.

You should have seen domestic number 2 setting to work.

"This illustration's no good. The screws can't possibly go there."

"Yes, they can," she explained in that tone of voice she adopts when he needs something simple clarified for him. You know, each syllable carefully detached from the previous one, all enunciated terribly distinctly, and a little slowly. "That's not an illustration, it's a template. Cut it out, pin it to the door, mark all the way round, then cut to your markings."

Well, he didn't. He cut a bit round the existing opening. And tried to force the cat flap in. Which didn't work. So he cut some more off. And failed again.

Every time he cut the saw made an appalling racket. The domestic who lives next door to us works nights and tries to sleep during the day. He must have cursed! My domestics used to say they had a neighbour from hell. She's gone, but the nice family who took her place must be wondering what sort of neighbours *they* have.

Domestic number 1 came to take a look.

"What you've cut is far too small," she said, "just take a look at the template."

"It's not a template," he replied but by then it was just a grumble, without conviction.

"Look," she said, "let me show you."

She took a pair of scissors and cut expertly for a few seconds. She then held a perfectly cat-flap-shaped piece of paper up against the door.

"See? You haven't cut enough."

"Oh," he said, in the tones of a smartarse who couldn't think of a smart response.

Ten minutes more cutting and he'd got it about right.

He'd cut a bit too much to be honest, so the plastic bit's a little loose in the hole. Still, it could have been worse. Even though it had taken him an hour and a half to do a twenty-minute job. He also bent the jigsaw blade beyond repair in the process. But hey, for domestic number 2 that's a triumph of engineering precision.

As for the flap, it works fine. Much quieter. Smoother.

And it doesn't try to make me look fat by suddenly jumping out and grabbing me around the middle.

Misty and the cold white stuff

It sometimes seems to me that domestic number 2 imagines I'm dumb. And sometimes I agree with him. Not for the reason he thinks, though. Only because I keep convincing myself that the moment will come, someday, sometime, when he fails to live down to my expectations of him.

I mean, he does just fine with serving me food and stuff. Let's give him credit for that. But that's pretty much the baseline for any domestic, isn't it? Just occasionally he could go, not the extra mile since I don't want to be too demanding, but just a few extra inches. Perhaps.

Well, at least, rise above the level of the buffoon which seems to be pretty much the limit of his aspirations.

Ah, well. I keep hoping, but then I'm the perennial optimist. Dumb of me. Or at least naïve.

We got a sad instance of this the other day. It was when that ghastly white stuff was falling out of the sky. Domestic number 1 always gets excited about these terrible moments.

"At last," she cries out, "snow. We can get the skis out again."

I couldn't believe my ears. Getting the skis out? They did that a couple of years ago. It was frankly embarrassing. They went skidding about on the streets on skis, making complete idiots of themselves. Who on earth skis in a town? If you have to do that kind of bloody silly thing, do it somewhere way out in the country. Somewhere nobody sensible can see you because there are only other nutters around.

As for me, it's beyond me how anyone can like that miserable cold stuff. I walk on my paws. I keep them clean, I keep them neat. Snow? Half a dozen steps and all my efforts are for nothing. What it does to fur has to be seen to be believed. It really shouldn't be allowed.

Well, the other day, after a tough night's mousing (mostly tough for the mice) I was a bit tired and slept later than usual. I didn't immediately notice the snow.

So, when I saw domestic number 2 by the door, I trotted over quite optimistically. I've got him trained to spot when I want to go out, though it did take some time and a lot of effort to get him to cut out the sarky comments. You know, quips like:

"What, too lazy to use the cat flap and climb the fence?"

It's not as though he doesn't open the door when he makes that kind of silly remark. He does, but it wouldn't do any harm to keep his unhelpful comments to himself. Life would certainly be more comfortable. All round, really, because I don't think he finds it all that comfortable when I let my teeth teach him to control his tongue.

Anyway, the other day was a terrible let-down. Sure, he opened the door. But what did I see? Bloody white stuff all over the place. Cold white snuff. Wet white stuff.

No joke.

I shot back inside before he could push me out. Not that he usually dares – that's a domestic number 1 trick – but you never know when he might try it on and risk the consequences.

Of course, he laughed. "Ah, not so keen now, then, are we? A bit cold on the delicate little paws?"

Like he goes out barefoot in the snow…

Though, if I'm honest, when it comes to going out, the funny thing about him is how often he does. I don't mean that he goes out on lots of occasions. I mean that often he seems incapable of going out just once, on one occasion, but has to go out two or even three times. It's a habit of his. Probably not intentional.

It happens most when he takes the rubbish out. It always

seems to require multiple trips. You know, he'll go out with a couple of cardboard boxes, walking straight past the empty plastic bottle by the sink. Then he comes back in again, sees the plastic bottle, swears a bit and takes it out too. And next time he remembers the yoghurt carton he'd forgotten after carefully leaving it near the door so as not to forget it.

You have to wonder whether he just enjoys his little visits to the bins.

Still, I'm not complaining. Each time he opens the front door, I get a chance to slip through. And I treasure every such opportunity. So, as he approached the door for one of his usual supplementary outings, I followed him again hoping I could get outside, even though I'd already taken a look out and rejected the idea the previous time he'd opened the door.

"What, really, you think the snow will have gone?" he asked. "In ten minutes?"

He *will* keep living down to my expectations, you see.

Well, the snow might have gone, mightn't it? I readily admit that it had never happened in the past, but it might happen someday. Everything's unprecedented until it happens for the first time.

Though, in the event, on this occasion, it hadn't. The world was still white and cold and wet outside.

He enjoyed having a good snigger at my expense. Smug git.

Not that he had anything to be smug about. After all, it didn't suit him particularly to have the stuff lying about on the pavements, what with domestic number 1 insisting on skiing, which she's bound to do as soon as there's enough snow to cover the cobblestones. We don't actually have any cobblestones, but you know what I mean. Just a sprinkling and out they'll have to go. It's got to be hard work pushing yourself around on skis in the streets. I'm sure he'd far rather just stay on the couch with me.

Normally, I'd prefer that too, but he'd been so thoroughly obnoxious that I just laughed to myself when she forced him outside. I'd have sniggered except that's what he does, and I refuse to sink so low.

In any case – here's a thought. Why does he put up with the stuff in the first place? I can't see why he doesn't just get rid of the snow. Don't tell me it's beyond his power. He's the man who conjures meat out of a tin. Without even hunting. Pulling off a trick like that must make getting rid of snow kitten's play. Which is why I really *did* think, that time when I followed him to the door again, that he'd maybe sorted something out in the ten minutes since the previous visit to the bins. If he had, it would have been a bit less cold and wet. Easier for him as well as for me. I admit that I *was* just a tad hopeful when I followed him to the door. He might have cleared up the painful white stuff, mightn't he?

Seems not. Magicking food out of the fridge? No problem, apparently. But getting rid of snow? Not something he's prepared to do. It's like the mess he made of putting in a cat flap.

Ah, well. I just have to learn. I've got to expect him to let me down. That way I'll avoid disappointment. It does me no good to expect him to amaze me. Or rather, to amaze me in a good way.

The other way he's really good at.

Misty has a shock

He thinks he's so clever, that domestic number 2. But he *so* isn't.

Domestic number 1 cleared off again this morning, on another of her incomprehensible trips away from home. I was left to cope with the inferior service of number 2.

He decided it was time to share some information with me. He had the smug self-satisfied air of someone who has news to break that doesn't bother them but will be a real pain to you. You know that attitude? Infuriating, isn't it?

"You'd better get ready for a shock, Misty my boy," he announced. "A big shock."

He seemed to think he was getting something over me. Not that he ever does, though he likes to act like he can. That really winds me up, that condescension. It makes my claws tingle. It's stronger than me. Just like they, the claws, are stronger than him.

Well, I didn't say anything. Partly because I can't see any point in again letting him know I can speak, something he persists in pretending he hasn't noticed. But in any case, I didn't want to say the only thing that would make any sense, which would have been:

"You can't prepare for a shock, you poor fool, can you? If you could, it wouldn't be a shock, would it? It's like checking with a friend whether he's free on Thursday night for his surprise party. The whole point about shocks is that they happen when you *don't* expect them. There's no preparing for them, except by just being generally alert, and I'm alert all the time."

Misty Baleful
By Senada Borcilo

Instead, I just gave him my look. You know, the baleful one. Should leave him withering on the floor, but it never does. You can't imagine how short of sensitivity he is.

But then, when number 1 got in at last, I realised what he'd been on about. A shock? This was nothing short of majorly infuriating.

She's foisted on me… this… this smelly, runny-aroundy, bundle of fluff. A… a… well, I can't think of any nicer way of putting it. An animal. Yappy. Bouncy. Whiny.

Sound familiar? Yep. A specimen of the canine persuasion.

A bloody dog.

Now, I can imagine people might say to me, "well, you liked Janka, didn't you?"

First of all, I didn't *like* Janka. I just got used to having her around. I thought it would make her feel better if from time to time I walked around her, rubbing myself against her, and purring. Even if her response when I did that was to stand rooted to the spot looking, poor clumsy oaf that she was, a smidgeon uncomfortable. I knew that at heart it mattered to her that she should feel appreciated by the boss, so I'd give her a little appreciation from time to time.

And I'll admit it left a bit of a Janka-shaped hole in all my lives when she suddenly switched off and never came back. There one moment, gone the next. Not seen since.

If domestic number 1 had brought Janka home, I'd not complain. I was used to her. I'd be happy to see her in the family again.

But, and I can't stress this too much, she wasn't a *dog*. She might have smelled like a dog, and barked like a dog, and behaved a bit goofily like a dog, but that didn't mean she *was* a dog.

It meant she was Janka.

This new arrival? This thing that's just been dumped on me? They call her Lucy to make it sound like she has a personality. They even misspell it 'Luci', to make her seem original. But she's just a dog, through and through. A small variety. They called her a toy poodle, but I prefer my toys not to bark at me. She's young too, a puppy I think they call that. Though, honestly, I can't tell one dog from another.

What's for sure is that her being here means I have a chore ahead. One I wasn't planning for. I've got to start out on a new training programme. Breaking her spirit. Cowing her pride. Cutting the crap, basically, sorry for the language.

Hard work, and not something I wanted to take on at my time of life.

What an imposition. They really have no idea. I think I'll pop out. You never know, if I stay out long enough, things may be back to normal when I get back in.

And if they're not, well, I don't know exactly *what* I'll do. Though I think it might involve the expression of displeasure. And *that* will involve claws.

Luci settles in

Well, I seem to have fallen on my four feet. Or at least my new humans' four feet. Which is just as good.

There are two of them. It was the female one who came to fetch me from the family where I was before. Human number 1, but not just because she was the one who met me first, but because there's no mistaking a pack leader. So the other one's human number 2.

They both have grey tops. I've learned that this means they're incredibly ancient. That has its plusses and its minuses. Not so good for playing, like the puppy humans in my last family, but a lot easier to get your own way with. In fact, I've been told I shouldn't call them humans. I should think of them as domestics. But they like to boss me around and, hey, since they feed me, and don't expect me to feed them, I go along with it, doing what they say.

Most of the time.

One of the first things they did when we got here was take me into the garden. Outside, would you believe. It was terrifying. There was just big open sky overhead. Which anything could come out of. We didn't do any of that frightening outside stuff in my last place. Going out in it without any kind of protection over me, that took some getting used to.

Still, the outside place where they take me has got fences round it, at least. I suppose that makes it reasonably safe. It took a while, all the same, to get comfortable with it. By yesterday, though, when the sun came out, and it was quite warm, it felt good to lie in it. Nice warm earth which felt good on my belly. Till Human number 1 came out and told me to get off the vegetables. No idea what she meant – it was just a patch of brown earth, but she seemed to think it was important. It was no skin off my snout though, so I got out like she asked.

Human number 2 keeps giving me orders too, but he's got the concentration of a goldfish (well, that's what I've been told, though to be honest, I don't really know what a goldfish is). He tells me to do something, or stop doing something, and then gets buried in one of his books or what he calls his laptop. So, I just get on with whatever I was doing before.

Silly thing that laptop, by the way. After all, it takes up his lap. The woman keeps saying I'm a lapdog, which is fine with me, but that means the lap's mine. No place for some silly machine. I find that walking on his keyboard is generally a good way of getting his attention. He can be a bit shirty, but he usually makes me some space.

So, yes, I'm settling in. Though there was a bit of an odd thing during the first few days. I had this growing sense that it wasn't just the three of us here. There were odd noises from time to time, and a passing scent that certainly wasn't either of them. They'd say strange things too.

"He must be out in the garden, sulking."

"Yes, and coming in at night when there's no chance of meeting Luci, having a bite to eat, sleeping in the front room and getting out again in the morning."

Imagine my horror when I was confronted one day, inside the house, by this enormous animal. A gigantic beast. I gave him the bark, of course, and then – I really don't know what came over me – I dashed at him, instead of hiding behind the sofa like I wanted to: he must have outweighed me three or four times over.

To my amazement, he made a beeline for the garden door. And ran straight through it! I've no idea how he did that. There was a great clattering sound as he went, and he was gone. I couldn't understand it at all.

Oddly enough, human number 1 later pushed me through the door as well. She said I'd soon learn how to do it. I'm glad she's confident, because I'm not. It completely beats me. I mean, I've actually done it (when she pushed me) but I still don't know how. Getting through a solid door? How's that possible? I don't mind learning, but she's going to have to show me again.

Later I met the same beast in the garden. My natural caution abandoned me again, and I tried to get close to him, doing some of my best barking. He disappeared over the fence.

But a few hours later he was back in the house. I heard one of the humans saying, "I've shut the cat flap". This time the beast didn't decamp when I showed up. He ran at the door like before but stopped dead. He made a funny grumbly sort of noise. Then he turned around and came back. He jumped on a chair under the big table we have here and, do you know, I think he did it to hide from me. Which was a bit funny, seeing how much bigger he is. And seeing how I could see him anyway.

I was dancing around the chair, jumping up at him, until he reached out one of his paws and gave me such a biff on the nose! It suddenly occurred to me that the rumbling sound he'd been making wasn't to do with playing, it was him growling.

Weird. No kind of growl I'd have recognised.

And then an even stranger notion began to grow on me. This wasn't an intruder – he belonged here. The humans were talking to him, trying to stroke him on the chair he seemed rooted to.

"Now, come on Misty, Luci's nice. You just need to get to know her. She's not going anywhere, you know."

"Look, Luci," human number 1 told me, "this is Misty. Our cat. You're going to like each other a lot."

Misty. It's a good name, isn't it? For a cat. And he's *our* cat. Isn't that great?

Eventually, he came off the chair, and I decided to treat him with a bit more respect. Especially if he's here to stay. Especially since he packs quite a wallop in that paw of his.

Bit by bit, I think we're getting to know each other. There are moments when I think we could be friends. Sometimes he doesn't mind playing, and that's fun. But sometimes he's had enough, and boy, does he let me know it. He makes a funny sort of low howling sound and comes after me, both front paws flailing. I find the best thing to do then is lie on my back and look unthreatening. That usually makes him stop.

He can be quite nice, if he feels I'm submitting to him. It was Misty who explained that the humans weren't in charge, they were our domestics. He told me about the goldfish and human number 2's concentration too, which sounded like really useful information, but I didn't dare ask him to explain what a goldfish was. Later. Maybe. He did explain that it's easier to get that human – domestic number 2, as he calls him – to do what we want than the other one.

That's proved useful. Usually, the woman gets up in the middle of the night and lets me out for a pee. But if she doesn't, all I have to do is find the man's elbow and gnaw on it a bit. That wakes him up quite quickly. And instead of batting me with a paw, like Misty would, he takes me downstairs to let me out.

A good arrangement.

It was Misty who told me about keeping a diary too. He's had one for ages. Long before I was around.

I think I'll do the same. This is an interesting place where lots of things happen. More than enough to fill a diary.

Though, quite honestly, you can quickly have too much in the way of interesting things. I'm not keen on mystery. I don't need any other strange inhabitants showing up in the house. It was OK with Misty: he's turned out fine. When he's in a good mood. But that's enough, thanks.

On the other hand, the humans do keep letting more of their kind in, which is a pain – they're *so* big. It makes you wonder what the point is of having walls around the place, and fences around the garden, if you don't stop strangers wandering inside them.

Still, none of them has stayed long. Most of the time we only have my two humans and – lots of fun! – Misty. If that's how things remain, I'll have nothing to complain about.

And this diary will be a happy place.

Meeting Luci. And not too sure about it

By Dana Mallon

Luci learning the ropes

Wow, Misty, our cat, is just great! Isn't he? I'm getting on *so*, so well with him these days. We're proper friends. Really. Even if he still beats me up a bit. Well, a lot, actually. But only when I've really stepped out of line and he needs to correct me. As he always makes clear.

"This is for your own good, little girl. Life will be much easier for both of us if you just learn certain lessons. And I'm the one to teach them to you."

And he's just *so* exciting.

He goes outdoors and comes back indoors without a care in the world, as far as I can see. All that sky, and it doesn't seem to bother him. I mean, I seem to be getting used to it. I go for walks now, as long as a human's with me, and most of the time I'm hardly scared at all. It's only bad if there's a big noise or something terrifying like that. Another dog, say.

Inside the house, all the comfortable places to sleep on are Misty's by right. It took me a while to get my mind round that, but he's very good at making that kind of thing really, really clear.

The other thing he's just so good at is jumping. I thought I was good at it, but he's *so* much better: his food is kept way up in the air, far out of my reach, but he just leaps up there to eat away.

Of course, my food is in a bowl on the floor. That means he can get at it too, and does, but it's odd because the only time he doesn't beat me up is when I push him away from my bowl while he's trying to empty it. It's almost like he doesn't feel comfortable about eating my food. I mean, I understand why *I* don't think it's fair, but does he secretly think that too? I'd like to ask, but I'm a bit worried I'd get more of an answer than I want.

There's one thing I've worked out about him, though, where he's not being quite as clever as I thought. There was a time I believed he could just walk straight through a solid, closed door. In from the garden. Silly me. It's not like that at all. There's a sort of flap in the door. You push it with your head from outside, and it opens inwards so you can slip through.

I was really pleased when I worked that one out. Now I can get in from the garden if it gets a bit cold or wet, and they leave me outside on my own. Actually, even if it isn't cold and wet. I don't like being out of doors too long anyway. Especially on my own.

But there's still a trick I haven't mastered. He seems to be able to get *out* through the door too. Smart operator. I haven't sussed out how he does that. I can't see another flap. You know, the out flap. Could it be magic after all? I wouldn't put anything past our Misty.

The humans are fun too. She is, particularly. Tough, but you know, loving. Looks after me. Takes me for walks without letting me get too frightened. And food! She's the one for food.

I spend more time with him, though. She clears off somewhere or other during the day, but he's mostly home. So I can lie next to him. Get a lot of rest, actually. Mainly because he gets terribly shirty if I walk on his keyboard, and he seems to have a keyboard on his knees practically the whole time. Hits it with his fingers – you'd think it would hurt and he might stop after a while. Why doesn't it annoy him? It annoys me. But, like I said, it's no good trying to distract him – he just gets irritated.

Still, he takes me for walks too. And I'm getting him reasonably trained: he takes me by car to the places we're going to walk, instead of forcing me to get there along those nasty, smelly streets. Drives me to the park gates, you know, just like any sensible dog would want. If he can just learn to give me food, he'll be basically all right.

All right. Yes. For now that's all he is – just all right and no better. I mean, apart from anything else, a couple of times he's taken me to a different, *dismal* place. The house of lamentation. Full of unpleasant smells, lots of strange people, wailing dogs, even the odd cat I don't know. There's a weird woman there who takes me into a back room and does nasty things to me, prodding me and pushing me and even sometimes sticking needles in me.

Well, he took me there for the second time, just a few days ago. It was horrible. And then, you know what he did? Instead of taking me home, he drove me away to somewhere else. A long, long way away.

"We're going to see my mother," he explained, "she'll like you. Which means you'll like her."

Of course she'd like me. I'm a right-sized dog with a winning personality. What's not to like about a lapdog that fits on a lap? A lapdog who wants nothing better than a lap to fit on?

But all that time to get there! It made me a bit indelicate at the end. You know, I don't know how to put this, I coughed up a bit of my breakfast. Most of it, actually. I wasn't happy about it, and nor was he when he found out. It really makes the whole exercise pointless, doesn't it? It only put us both in a bad mood.

Still, I did get a couple of nice walks out of being wherever it was he took me. Not that they were any better than the walks near home. Certainly not *so* much better that they were worth driving ages and *ages* for.

When we got back, human number 1 joined us again – joy! – and we all went for another walk – double joy! – but then he started throwing a pine cone for me to chase.

After that day. Can you believe it? I was exhausted! The pummelling in the house of lamentation. And then all that driving. I had no energy left.

Still, I didn't want to hurt his feelings. He was doing his best. So I fetched him his pine cone three times. But that, I decided, was enough. After the third time, I wandered off and pretended to be interested in some grass. He stopped throwing the cone.

He's nice enough, but he needs a bit more training. In empathy. And understanding.

It looks like I've got a bit more work to do…

Misty on toys

Imagine a *really ugly* plastic toy. Some misshapen representation of a character from a nightmare, perhaps. It's painted a nauseous blue, with some clashing red and yellow. Somehow all the more off-putting for, rather than despite, being faded.

Basically, it has no redeeming features. I think it's supposed to represent some kind of bird but, frankly, I've seen birds that looked more attractive, more cheerful even, while caught in my claws.

OK. Got the picture?

Seems to me bad enough to have one in your living room at all. But if you could bear its presence, would you care *where* in the room it was? Well, actually, I suppose out of sight might be a preference. But if you had to see it at all, would it matter whether it was at the kitchen end of the sitting room or the front door end? You'd think not, right?

Well, now try to comprehend a mentality that makes its owner – perhaps I should say victim – feel that fetching this wretched toy from one end to the other is a matter of overwhelming urgency. Justifying the expenditure of frightening amounts of energy. I mean, we're not talking about fetching it in calm and dignity, but at top speed, claws scraping and slipping on the floor, with two or three little leaps thrown in for sheer exuberance.

All this despite the fact that the toy is doing absolutely nothing. Lying on the ground. Motionless. Soundless.

Having caught it, thanks, you seem to believe, to your

prompt and swift action, you pounce on it, growling with a level of menace that would be barely frightening if it were twice as fierce. The growling, no doubt, is intended to overcome the last traces of the toy's resistance. Which it isn't offering.

That all seem senseless? You've not heard the half of it.

Because, having wrestled to the ground a foe who may be dastardly but, if you're honest enough to admit it, also lifeless, and already on the ground, you seize it in your mouth. And dash back to the other end of the living room with it firmly clutched in your jaws. No doubt this is to prevent its effecting the escape which it isn't attempting. Not that mere good taste wouldn't welcome any escape the ghastly thing could make – vanishing into the remote distance would be the kindest thing it could do for its own sake as much as ours.

Having courageously got it back to the sofa end of the sitting room, what do you do with your hapless adversary?

You hand it back to the very domestic who flung it to the other end in the first place. And promptly does so again.

At which point the whole process starts over from the beginning.

Honestly, who invented dogs? Or, more to the point, why?

That being said, I've got to admit I'm getting used to having Luci around. To be absolutely honest, she livens things up a bit. Dull she ain't. Whether she's chasing an ugly toy, or just trying to work out how to use the cat flap – *my* cat flap – she's hilarious to watch. She's just about learned how to use it to get *in* from the garden but hasn't quite grasped that it works the other way too. So when she wants to go out, she just sits there looking forlorn until a domestic opens the kitchen door for her (that would be domestic number 2) or pushes her through the flap (number 1). Pathetic.

More important than the cat flap, however, is that I've got her trained, so she understands who's due respect and who isn't.

For the record, I want it clearly understood that the respect never, but never, flowed the other way around. Domestic number 2 may have come up with some deluded and, may I say, rather offensive notions about some alleged fear I may have harboured towards Luci, that minute mockery of a hunting animal, in the early days.

He really thought I was scared of that diminutive bundle of fluff?

If I didn't push past her in the doorway, it was because at the time she was new to the place and I thought she was a guest. Don't confuse courtesy with fearfulness.

If I stayed out in the garden, it wasn't because I was afraid of confronting her by coming in. I was making a point to the domestic staff, so they registered my extreme displeasure and didn't repeat this inexplicable act of inflicting an alien animal on me, without so much as consulting me beforehand. Don't confuse an expression of dissatisfaction with anxiety.

If I didn't come through the cat flap while she was on the other side, that wasn't because her guarding it inspired any concern in me. I just didn't want to knock her over. Don't confuse responsible behaviour with trepidation.

Scared! Me? Wash your mouth out.

Anyway, there's no doubt who's scared now. I've been on her back a couple of times, let me tell you, all in the spirit of training her to a proper standard of behaviour. And I've sunk my teeth into her neck.

Well, perhaps not her neck exactly. There's so much fur there. But I sank my teeth anyway. It was quite satisfying. Especially when she ran away squealing.

That upset domestic number 2. Would you believe he pushed me away? I don't know if he thinks that'll stop me training her. She needs the training, so she's going to get it. And pushing me around only makes me feel that I may need to provide a little more training for *him* too. He seems to need rather a lot, as any progress in his behaviour is slow and provisional, liable to be forgotten within a dismayingly short time. But I don't care. Delivering correction to him is almost as much fun to me as it's salutary to him.

Meanwhile, at least I've got domestic number 1. Who's got me my own toy. A rather superior one, I'm happy to point out. A toy one can enjoy in a dignified and intelligent way. You know, batting it around the floor with my paws in a civilised manner.

"Wonderful," says domestic number 2, "now they both have ugly toys."

I control my anger. I certainly don't show it. But sometimes he takes his irritating comments just a tad too far. He's definitely going to need another bout of education, I fear.

Luci's toy's ugly. Mine's a triumph of design, worthy of a discriminating cat. Not the repellent plaything of a dotty dog.

Luci, Misty, stray food and training a human

Got it! I've worked it out! That Misty, who thinks he's such a smart cat and knows so much more than me, won't be fooling *me* about the flap in the kitchen door anymore.

"You mean the cat's out of the bag?" he asks me.

What on earth does that mean? He was never in a bag. I wasn't talking about bags.

"It's called a pun," he explains. "Some people think they're funny."

"Do they? I bet lots of others don't."

What I was talking about was the flap that lets me get back in from the garden into the kitchen. I spent a long time looking for another one to get out by. But it turns out that I can use the *same* flap. It works both ways. I can get out that way too.

What a breakthrough that is! I can get out whenever I like. And then back in. Magic!

And it's really nice out there. They've left some *fantastic* patches of earth, with interesting little plants in them, where I can just dig and dig. Even the humans have noticed.

"Do you know what the dog has done?" human number 1 said today, just as soon as number 2 got home.

"Oh, Lord," he said.

"She's been digging huge holes in my vegetable patches."

"I suppose dogs just do that, don't they?"

"Well, she's really good at it."

See? See? Human number 1 was really impressed.

I wonder what a gate is? Because human number 1 said she thought it would be a good idea to put one up. I can't wait to see what it is. I bet it'll be something else I can have fun playing with.

Because, you know, they're good at getting me things to play with. The other day they brought me this *wonderful* new toy.

"I found this dog toy in the park today," human number 2 said when he came home. "It think it's supposed to be some kind of bird. A bit of a deformed bird from a horror movie but – well, it's a plastic toy – do you think Luci might like it?"

Like it? It's just *amazing*. Human number 2 throws it across the room for me. And I go running after it, which is wonderful fun, because I can slip and slide across the floor towards it, like it was trying to get away from me, so I can catch it, and leap on it and absolutely shake it to death. And then bring it back to the human and let the *whole thing start all over again*!

It's brilliant!

The only one who doesn't seem to agree is Misty. He stalks off. Like he disapproves of the whole thing. I get the feeling that he thinks the toy itself is nasty. He's a bit snooty about it, to be honest. But, hey, why should I care? No one's asking him to play with it.

As it happens, Misty's still as cranky as ever, always pretending to be cross with me. Underneath it all, I *know* he likes me. He used to try to bite me, but he doesn't do that anymore. Or not so often. And when I run at him, he just chases me back and we play, until he scoots away to hide, but not *really* hide, because he looks out at me like he's daring me to run at him again. Which I do. Hey, why wouldn't I?

He obviously enjoys it as much as I do. He *must* like me. Mustn't he?

The latest thing I've discovered about the humans is that they're quite messy. They drop things from time to time. Sometimes it's nice things to eat. And the good thing is, I'm *quick*. I get to any good morsels fast. I've had bits of orange, pear, apple, before they can even *think* of bending down to pick them up. It amazes them, because they think I should only like the kibble they put in my bowl. Which is odd, when you think about it, because I reckon that if they're eating it, it's got to be a lot more interesting than some monotonous little bits that always taste the same.

Not that I don't like kibble. Keep giving it to me, I say! But it's just ordinary. What the humans drop is *special*.

And another really fun thing! Yesterday the humans took me to a training class, and I really enjoyed it. Well, I was quite worried at first, because I thought I'd be training the main human (Misty calls her domestic number 1, but I know a boss when I see one, and I know better than to cheek her. Or at least only to cheek her when she's unlikely to notice. Or at any rate, only when I can be irresistibly endearing afterwards.)

Fortunately, when we all got there, she just sat down and sent the number 2 human out to be trained instead. He didn't want to go, but she told him like a good boss should. Firmly but calmly.

"No, I think it should be you. It would be really good for you to get a close relationship with Luci too."

"But... but... I thought you were going to do this bit..."

She just looked at him. The kind of look that has me rolling over waving my legs in the air and cranking up the endearment setting to max level. He grumbled but he knew he was beaten. He put himself on the lead so I could take him out onto the main floor where the training happens. Among all the other dogs with their humans on leads. You could tell he was terribly uncomfortable.

To be honest, I wasn't that comfortable either. "Other dogs". Easier to write those words than to live with the reality. I don't like other dogs. They bark. They're bigger than me (well, practically all of them are). They have teeth and big paws. They smell *doggy*. I like some of the dogs we meet in the park, the ones that are a sensible size, and I can race around with having lots of fun. But I don't like many others. And there were more than I could count in the room.

Still, I got used to them in time. By the end of the evening, I was quite relaxed. Even went up and smelled one or two of them. I reckon it was all down to the training bit. It isn't easy to train a human, and the work took all my attention. Which meant I didn't think too much about the frightening sights around me.

It worked well, anyway. Within minutes, I'd got him, to use a human expression, eating out of my hand. Which really meant that I could eat out of his. Eating wonderful little treats. It was quite funny. I'd sit down, and he'd give me a treat. I'd stand up, and he'd give me another treat. I'd lie down, and he'd give me a treat. I'd look at him instead of at the treat, and he'd give me a treat.

A brilliant system! I love training. And he was really well trained in no time.

And the other thing that made me laugh: the training lady said "your dog doesn't speak English." I like that word "your". Always nice to underline the fact that I'm in my pack. But "doesn't speak English"? Of course, I don't actually speak it. But hey, I write it.

Maybe someday she should read my diary.

Luci contemplative
By Senada Borcilo

Misty, domestic number 2 and the Luci thing

It's funny, I've been getting on better with domestic number 2 lately. It's almost as though the arrival of Luci has changed our relationship. For instance, I lie on his knees a bit more often in the evenings, and he doesn't push me away so soon anymore.

Sometimes I think it may be our way of saying, "the other two are female, we need to look after each other." But then I think again. After all, this is number 2. The one who needs the simplest things carefully explained. He isn't the kind to catch a mood or seize a subliminal message or anything subtle like that.

Take breakfast, for instance. I like to have a change from the dry food in the dispenser from time to time. Well, who wouldn't? A bit of wet food. Chunks of meat and all that. Surely one's entitled to a bit of that every now and then? Perhaps once a day? Right? Right?

Not a complicated idea you'd think. But it seems a hard one to get into his head. Fortunately, there's a relatively straightforward way of making that happen.

It takes training. I'm glad to say that he's moderately trainable. With effort and patience, but trainable all the same. Consider what I like to think of as 'the bath tap business'.

I've got him well trained on that. He knows I like to drink water straight from the tap. The trick, I find, is to run between his legs when he's heading towards the bathroom. To start with, that nearly trips him up, which is fun in itself. But then it gets him thinking along the right lines. I know that because you can pretty much see his mind slowly whirring into action.

"Misty? Bathroom? Ah. He wants water from the tap."

So he goes in and turns the tap on, carefully adjusting it till it's dripping just right – not so fast that I get my paws wet, not so slow that I can't drink from it properly.

"There you go," he says, "the water's on for you."

It's good that he's mastered that. Even if it's quite funny that he persists in talking to me, though I'm sure he still thinks I don't know English.

In any case, I've now moved on to the advanced part of the course, which covers service to deliver to me over and beyond turning on a water tap. I make my request and wait to see his reaction, which is usually to provide water once more, since that's as far as he's got in understanding my needs.

"See?" he'll say, "the tap's on. You can jump in the bath and have a drink."

Now I have to try to get it across to him that water isn't the only requirement I have in life, and that we're moving on to a different kind of need. I've taken to the amusing tactic of just sitting there and looking at him. Or even turning my back.

"What is it?" A tone of worry starts to enter his voice. "What's the problem? You don't want water?"

The penny's beginning to drop...

"Not water, then? You want something else? You've got kibble. You've been out in the garden. What else could you need?"

I give him a long, level stare.

"Would you like some wet food, perhaps?"

Ah. There at last.

But boy, what a struggle. Who wants to go through that every day, before breakfast? You'd think after a couple of times he'd get his mind around it.

Ah, well. He may be slow, but you have to make allowances, don't you? If he gets there in the end, you can probably forgive the effort of pushing him along the way. And I still like sitting on him in the evenings. Even though he's such a sad case. Unimpressive intellectually. But he's friendly, he does feed me eventually if I ask clearly enough for long enough, and he can be persuaded, from time to time, to stroke me the way I like. So I'm open to showing him a little gender solidarity, against the frightening phalanx of females.

Bet you didn't know cats could do alliteration.

OK, OK, I know 'phalanx' doesn't actually start with an 'f'. But it does sound that way, doesn't it? Go on, admit it.

In any case, as it happens, the females are worth cultivating too. Domestic number 1 keeps buying things for the crazy Luci puppy thing. Beds, for instance. She's bought two of them for her. Two! Luci's tiny, but she gets two beds?

Strangely enough, I'm partial to a dog bed. Not sure why. It was the same with Janka: I liked to sleep on her rug sometimes.

Well, a lot of the time, actually. She hardly ever got to use it herself.

Domestic number 1 piled the two beds on top of each other last week. Which was wonderful. I could lie on both of them. At the same time. So Luci couldn't get at either. Boy, she was put out. Which only added to the fun. She hovered for a while, looking envious. And I stretched luxuriously and really enjoyed the warm fluffiness. Brilliant.

Though then she went rushing over to the sofa – she hardly does anything except at a rush – and leaped up between the domestics. *My* domestics.

Suddenly the beds, even though there were two of them, and even though I was depriving Luci of the enjoyment of either, didn't seem quite so satisfactory a way of spending the evening. It's a good thing to monopolise the pet beds, but not at the price of giving up my claim – my exclusive claim – on the domestics.

Time to wander over, I felt.

But what to do once I was there? Domestic number 1 seemed wholly preoccupied with the Luci bundle which was occupying her lap. So I stared at number 2 for a while. As usual, there was no response at first. After I'd stared at him for long enough, though, he started to wilt and paid attention.

"Oh, hello Misty," he said eventually. "Did you want to come up on the sofa too?"

He stretched out his legs to the coffee table, in the time-honoured manner of a domestic providing a proper lap, so I walked around to his end of the sofa and quietly, without urgency, hopped up.

"Misty!" he proclaimed with delight, as well he should, "you've chosen my lap for once!"

Pathetic, isn't it? Just because, if it were up to me, I'd sit on domestic number 1. He hadn't cottoned on that I was resorting to him as second choice since the Luci thing had slipped in and commandeered my preferred option. If it hadn't been for my generosity in letting Luci briefly enjoy her small win, I wouldn't have picked *his* lap at all. So his pride and happiness at being selected almost made me feel sorry for him.

With providing a lap comes the duty of stroking me. Which he did correctly, behind the ears. And I only had to scratch him occasionally, when he let himself get distracted by the TV and stopped stroking me or stroked me in that kind of unfocused way domestics sometimes adopt when they're really thinking of other things.

Boy, that annoys me.

Still, I limited the scratches to just those circumstances. It felt right to give him a chance to enjoy the moment we were sharing. Though I reserve the right to keep using the teeth and claws on him whenever circumstances warrant it. I just decided they could be sheathed for the time being. They'll be just as effective if I need them another day.

But that's not to be mistaken for a sign that I'm getting soft.

Luci carries on training the humans

Training humans is *so* rewarding.

It's mostly the number 2 human who keeps coming to me to be trained. I just love it. I've taught him to give me a treat each time I do one of four things: come to him, lie down, stand up, wait. Which is great because I have four paws, so I can count all of those things. They're not exactly hard to do, so mostly I just do them. But I have found out something a bit odd about him: he likes to explain things to me, even though I've long since understood them. Misty reckons it's because he likes to believe that *he's* training *me*. So sometimes I look at him as though I'm confused and it's terribly hard, until he explains it carefully to me and shows me how.

It doesn't matter, though. Because whether I do the thing right straight away or have him explain it to me first, I get a treat anyway. That makes me quite proud because it shows I've trained a human well.

Fantastic.

Basically, it's money for old rope. Not that I know what money is, of course, let alone having any use for it. Or old rope either, come to that, but hey, I didn't invent the expression.

I have to say that one of the things did take me a while to master: lying down. The word of command sounds like "plotz". God knows why. "Wait" – well it's pretty obvious, isn't it? "Stand" – yep, not a big problem either. "Come"? OK, I can get my mind around that too. But "plotz"?

It turns out it's all down to human number 1.

"She's from a place called Alsace," Misty the cat explained to me, "which is where I come from too. We're Alsatians, both of us."

"But… you're not dogs. Are you?"

"No," he said, and I think the word for the tone is "icy", "we're exiles, far from our own country. You didn't think we were from *here*, did you?"

He said "here" as though it was a sad and shameful place. You know, like that House of Pain they take me too from time to time where people stick needles in me. It makes me unhappy just to think of it and I could see that Misty, too, was looking noble and long-suffering.

"And they talk funny there, do they?" I couldn't help asking. Which must have been the wrong question: he stalked away.

Anyway, how on Earth was I supposed to know she came from somewhere else? And why would they use silly words, in any case? If they want someone to lie down, why don't they just say, "lie down"?

Besides, what's all that about being Alsatians? I've met Alsatians. My humans are nothing like Alsatians. Why, they're not even canine enough. And if they're going to talk to me like an Alsatian, does that mean they think I'm going to be one too? Let me tell you, the Alsatians I know are a bit different from me. Mostly in scale.

Misty's not too happy about this training business. He says I ought to have more pride. Stand aloof from the whole palaver. Refuse to be pushed around.

"We animals need to lay down some ground rules to the domestics."

That's what he calls the humans. He reckons that I'm letting them train me. Which is odd, since I'm pretty certain it's me that's training them. And, in any case, even if he was right – *there are treats at stake.*

Treats are quite funny. The effect they have on me. The other day, human number 2 got the treats out and I automatically went and did the plotz thing, before he could even ask. It was just stronger than me. I thought he'd see through me and realise I was a jump ahead of him, just doing it for the treats, but he didn't. He was pathetically pleased about it. Told number 1 when she got home. Got her giggling.

So no harm done.

The other thing I like is the nightly garden run. It's a little ritual we have now, number 2 and I. He doesn't like it, but she always makes him.

"Does Luci need to be taken out?" he asks every night.

"Yes," she always replies.

You'd think he'd learn, wouldn't you? If he doesn't want to hear that answer, why does he ask the question? How can anyone be that slow?

Perhaps he needs some treats of his own, to focus his mind a bit more on the things he needs to learn.

Anyway, the humans seem not to have grasped that I use the little dog flap. If I need to do my business, I pop out and do it. So this nightly outing's just a bit of fun. Some quality time number 2 and I can spend together before going to bed. I sniff around the flower beds and the vegetables, which is good, and he stands around looking pained and saying, "go on, Luci, have a pee."

He tries to make it sound quite affectionate, even though I can hear the exasperation in his voice.

Sometimes I force one pee out just to make him feel better. At other times I just keep wandering around to see how long he can stand it, before he finally gives up and starts to go back in, calling me to come with him. I follow him but the fun's not over yet. Once we're indoors, I go and whine by the door again, like I've suddenly realised I desperately need to go out and don't know how to use the flap. Well-trained as he's becoming, he takes me back outside.

"Oh, Lord," he says, "this time just have your pee, will you?"

It's always amusing, and a good way to wrap up the evening. A ritual that sets me up nicely to go jumping around the bed when they're trying to get to sleep. The humans seem to think it's adorable, which is a joy. Personally, if someone behaved that way when I was trying to sleep, I'd be pretty fed up. And I reckon Misty would just bite me But, you see, I've been putting in the time to train them. I'm getting them well under control.

Even Misty thinks it's funny that they put up with it.

What? Human number 2 resting? We could be playing.
By Dana Mallon

Luci, puppies, cars and water

It's got *so* hot! A while ago, things weren't like this. All the humans around me were whinging about how cold it was, but I couldn't see anything to complain about. They just needed a fine fur coat like mine.

In any case, it's quite funny that they were grumbling about the cold back then, and the heat now. Humans, eh? Always whinging about something.

Still. It's true it's terribly hot. Not like when I was a puppy.

"Not like when I was a puppy"! It feels odd writing those words. I'm not used to them yet. But it's true. I'm not a puppy anymore. I'm a *big girl* now. The humans took me to the house of pain the other day, the place with the needles, but for once no one stuck anything in me. What did happen, though, is that they told me how much I weighed. 4.1 kilos!

If you think that point-one isn't important, think again: it puts me in the big dog category for my flea treatment product, and that *matters*.

And I don't care about the silly human we met in the park with one of those oversized dogs – a Rottweiler or something. He pointed out, with a silly laugh, like it was funny or something, that I was just the size of one of his dog's meals. All I can say is that there was much too much of the dog that was taking him out for a walk.

I didn't really react to that unpleasant remark. I was too busy panting, what with it just getting hotter and hotter. Even though human number 1 has got my fur clipped really short, going out for walks is a lot less easy than it was. That's a pity, because walking is one of my best things. After food and belly rubs, anyway.

Oh, and playing with Misty. That's another favourite thing. One of those things that are good enough to take my mind off the heat. Though, to be honest, playing with Misty isn't quite what it used to be. He's got funny about our games. These days, he often has a moan while we're playing. A kind of plaintive mew, and it gets a reaction from the humans.

"Luci," they say, "stop tormenting the cat."

Yeah, right. Can you imagine me "tormenting" him? He's twice my size! Well, a bit less than twice, now I'm such a *big* girl. But still. There's no way I can "torment" him. Maybe he just complains because he doesn't always get on top of me these days and pin me down. Maybe with a big girl like me he finds the rough and tumble just a bit too rough and tumbly sometimes and has to get the humans to help him out.

Not a problem, anyway. While he lets me play with him, I'll play. If he gets the humans to make me stop, I'll stop. There'll always be a next time.

It's not just Misty who's fun to play with. Puppies are great as well. And I've worked something out: humans have puppies too. They're the small ones, the kind that runs around and makes a lot of noise. They're puppies, and a lot of fun.

We met some in the park the other day. I don't know if everyone has this problem, but whenever we meet humans, they always seem to want to touch me. They come up saying silly things like "oh, isn't she cute?" (or irritatingly, "isn't he cute?") and then, inevitably, they follow it up with "can we stroke her?" (or "him").

The puppy humans in the park were just the same as the big ones. They all kept asking whether they could stroke me. It was human number 2 who'd joined me for that particular walk, so it was completely useless them asking. I mean, did they really think he had some kind of say over who gets to stroke me or not? Hah! I showed them. And him. When he said yes, and they moved in on me, I just shot off. Like I always do when someone I don't know gets too close.

But with the puppies, something different happened than with most humans. Because when I ran away, they ran after me. Joy! Suddenly instead of the horribleness of having a stranger trying to stroke me, I was in a *game*. They were *chasing* me like someone playing with me is supposed to. But the big humans never do. You have to be a puppy, human or doggy, to want to do that.

"Horribleness?" says Misty. "You used the word horribleness?"

"Oh. Should it have been horribility?" I ask.

"It shouldn't be either," he says, just a tad too superior for my taste, "they're both horrible."

Maybe he's right. But, who cares? He shouldn't have been reading over my shoulder anyway.

So, like I was saying, the human puppies in the park weren't horrible at all, they were brilliant. We had *such* a great time. Even in this terrible heat. In fact, I barely noticed the heat, while we were playing. Funny how much you can put up with when you're having a good time.

In any case, I've found out what's good in this heat. Water. Go right into it and it cools you down like magic. I don't think I mentioned before that I'd learned to swim. Well, I have, and it's just what you need when it's hot.

I found out about all of that when the humans took me travelling. And travel's just great!

Now, I didn't always like the car. I have to admit that. My humans even have to clean up a bit of – well, you know – regurgitated material on some trips. But I put up with it because generally we end up in nice places.

I think the humans find it a bit odd. They don't really understand why I'm so happy to jump in the car, either on the way to a walk or on the way back. But, hey, it makes sense. I like the places we go to walk, and I like home. So *obviously* I like going either way. And because the car always takes me walking or home, I *like* the car.

Except when the car doesn't take me to those places, of course. Sometimes they take me to that terrible place where people stick needles in me. But that doesn't happen often.

On the other hand, you *can* get too much of it. We had hour after hour the other day. By the end, I was getting a bit fed up. But then we turned up in this most fantastic place. The humans said it was in Yorkshire, which some people say is God's own county. I've decided that sounds good, even though I don't know just what a county is, let alone God. Still, there's nothing you can say about Yorkshire that I'd think was too nice.

I was really pleased to get there, and so were the humans, just as soon as they'd cleared up the regurgitation.

First of all, you can walk, and walk, and walk. We stayed in a place called Malham. There's grass all over the place. With loads of new things for me to get to know – sheep, for instance, and rabbits – and lots of crows to chase. Wonderful.

And there's lots of *water*.

Now, in my bowl water's useful but a bit dull. It just lies there, doing nothing, waiting to be drunk. Then you get it in other places where it isn't dull at all, but nasty and tricksy. Streams, for instance. The water never stops moving. It tugs at you. It swirls at you. You can't trust it at all.

Well, near Malham's there's this *great* place. It's a big patch of water. And it behaves itself like it should: it sits still even though there's *loads* more than in a bowl. So you can go in and jump about and have fun. And, boy, it *is* fun. What a blast.

It keeps you cool when you're hot. Which I think I already said is the way things are right now. Not like when I was little.

There are other great bits of that Malham place. Pubs, for instance. Where they actually want dogs to come in. Fantastic. There was a character in one of them who decided that what he really, really wanted to do was share his meal with me. He gave me half his hamburger. See what I mean? God's own county.

We had such a good time in Malham that I was really happy to get back into the car. That surprised the humans again – "if you like this place so much, how come you're happy to go somewhere else?" *Obviously* because I guessed we were going somewhere else nice.

They really are a bit slow sometimes.

I was right, too, about going somewhere nice. We went to a place called Scotland, and there was a puppy human in the place we stayed. Wow. I *really* like the puppy ones. And this one kept trying to train me. I learned ages ago that training is almost as good as playing, because it means doing things you're happy to do anyway, like sitting down or coming to her, and getting treats for doing it. So I could get *her* to do things *I* wanted her to do, by doing easy little things *she* wanted *me* to do. Fantastic. An amazing arrangement.

From what my humans were saying, she's our granddaughter. Which is great, except I don't understand why she doesn't live with us. If she's ours, shouldn't she be with us all the time? Then we could play together even more. And she could give me lots of treats all the time. I think we should take her home.

But there was more water. *Another* kind. So *big*. Salty too – no good to drink. And, wow, does it move. Worse than a stream. Sometimes it piles itself up into great heaps and throws itself at you. That can be scary. It even chases me up the sand next to the water, which is unfair, because I have to run really fast to get away from it, and that isn't easy. Besides, afterwards the sand's wet and cold, which isn't fun at all.

Still, we enjoyed ourselves. It was a good trip. I liked the humans. I liked the food. I liked the places. Why, to be honest, I even enjoyed the heaps of water, though they were a bit frightening.

And then: joy! We got back into the car. And we went home! Magical. Wonderful.

The car's fantastic. Even if it does make me feel funny sometimes. And even if I regurgitate a bit.

Luci and the chase

It's still fearfully hot. Walks are a bit slow. I really can't go as quickly as I'd like. Unless I find someone to play with.

Fortunately, there's plenty of them. My latest find is squirrels.

They're small and grey and furry and they rush around. Basically, toys I can play with without even having a human to throw them for me. They're wonderful. I discovered them this week. The humans say they've been around for ever, and they think it's quite funny I didn't see them before. But, hey, who cares? I've seen them now. And I'm making up for lost time.

The trick is to try to catch them in the open. They always seem to have a tree they can run towards. And then they do something *really* clever. They disappear. I've never worked out how they do that. I mean, one minute they're between me and the tree. Racing towards it. Then they get there and vanish. I'm right behind them but I can search and search, all around, among the roots, everywhere, and I can't find a trace of them anywhere. It's weird.

Still, the fun bit's chasing them. So, I don't mind. In fact, to be perfectly honest, though I get close to catching them, I'm not that sure what I'd do if I actually did. I mean, I can smell that they're made of meat and all that, but – you know – all that *fur*. What are you supposed to do with it?

Besides, they might have teeth. They've never turned on me, but one might. Especially if I managed to get close enough to catch it before it vanished inside the tree. And then where would I be? I think it's better just to chase them around a bit.

Like birds. I knew about them even before I'd discovered the squirrels. Specially crows. They like to stand around in the park just waiting for me to chase them. That's such fun! They let me get even closer than the squirrels do – maybe they think I'm going to change my mind and stop or something – and then they go flapping off making that strange creaky noise of theirs.

I'm really quick these days, now that I'm a big dog, so I can keep up with them for a while even when they're in the air. That's fun too. After all, they don't come back down, which would be worrying. They seem to have understood that it's my game they're playing with me.

Actually, that's a point. Maybe that's what happens with the squirrels. Maybe they don't go inside the trees. Maybe they fly off like the crows do.

"Don't be silly," says Misty, "hasn't it ever occurred to you that they just go up the tree?"

"Up the tree? How can they do that? They don't have wings."

"So, if they don't have wings, what makes you think they can fly?"

"Exactly! You're right. Silly of me. They can't fly. So, they really *must* be going inside the trees."

There's another park near *our* park, with a lake in it, and on the lake there are ducks. I nearly caught one the other day. It was on the wrong side of the railings round the lake. When it took off towards the water, it couldn't get high enough fast enough, and just crashed into the fence. That brought it back to earth. If it hadn't been able to slip through the bars, I'd have had it.

Though, a bit like with the squirrels, I'm not sure what I'd have done then. First of all, I have nice-sized jaws. Not some great cavernous maw like those nasty giant dogs. Like your Alsatians or Labradors. I'm not sure if I could have got my jaws to close round a whole duck. That could have been really embarrassing. Besides, fur over meat is bad enough, but *feathers*? I can't imagine anything worse. Why, they'd catch in my throat. I like my meat in nice lumps, with gravy round them. And failing that, I like kibble. Meat with fur or feathers? No thanks. Others may like that but I'm much too dainty.

"You're crazy," says Misty, "dainty? Forget dainty. It's grace that matters. And we cats have it in spades. *And* it doesn't stop us getting to meat even if it has got fur or feathers round it."

Oh, well. I suppose other people have other tastes. And I'm not arguing with Misty about his: he's still too big for me.

As well as birds, there's other dogs. Not the big ones. With the big ones, I find the most sensible thing is to keep behind the legs of whichever human I've taken out with me for the walk.

But with the right-size ones like me, it's just play, play, play. Which I enjoy all the more now that I'm so quick. There's not many of them that can get away from me or, when we turn around and chase the other way, catch me. In fact, the only annoying thing about them is that sometimes they just stop and lie down panting. I have to keep running up to them to get them back on their feet.

Not like the human puppies. They can keep going for ages. I know I've said it before, but it's true. They're the best. Even better than squirrels and crows. Like the ones I played with in the park. Or the one in Scotland who thought *she* was training *me* when *I* was getting *her* to give me treats. Little girl human puppies? You can never have too many of them, I reckon.

What a great world. Full of strangers you have to approach warily, or back away from. But every now and then, one of them turns out to be a friend who was just waiting to meet you. And a friend's someone you can play with.

Human puppies. Right-sized dogs. Crows. Ducks. And now squirrels. All just there to give me a wonderful time.

That makes even the terrible heat less of a pain.

Luci winsome
By Senada Borcilo

Misty still a jump ahead

Well, life's certainly become less dull since Luci moved in.

Not always in a good way. She likes to say hello to me almost every time she sees me. That's fine, except that when she says hello, she likes to jump up on my shoulders with her forepaws like she was trying to pin me down or something. That's silly because it's as though she were trying to establish authority over me, even though I could throw her off with a shake of my shoulders.

Not that it's as easy as it once was. With the amount of food the domestics keep giving her, it's no surprise that she's starting to put on a bit of weight. Disciplining her has become just a tad harder. But only a tad: she's done no more than move from the featherweight to the lightweight category. Still not much of a challenge for a fine figure of a cat like me.

Take the other day. There was rather too much of that running around and yapping at me. Fun for a few minutes, but then it palls. After a while, serious action needs be taken. I brought the teeth into play. That's not something I often do with her – it's a bit of an extreme measure. But this was becoming an extreme situation justifying such measures. I got her on the nose. It can't have hurt much – I didn't bite down properly and she has so much hair, even around her nose, that it's hard to get at anything I could hurt if I tried. Still, she yelped, which was quite satisfactory. Though, to be honest, she yelps for pretty much anything anyway.

And then she came back for more. Which is her through and through. Crazy animal. What does she think's going to happen if she keeps bugging me? Fortunately, I've got the domestics reasonably well trained: when number 2 saw what was going on, he shouted at Luci, "leave him in peace, Luci, stop tormenting him." And, when she'd gone trotting over to him, like the dutiful little creature she is, "you know you could end up getting hurt if you push him too hard."

He's got that right.

On the other hand, I can't believe how he talks to her. And she takes it all to heart. She was going on about it the other day.

"Did you hear him? Did you hear him? He said, 'who's a lovely little dog, then?' Isn't that good? Isn't that good? Isn't it, isn't it?"

"Err... yes, it's great, if that's the kind of thing you like..."

"What's not to like? I mean, think about it, just think about it, Misty. There aren't any other dogs. He must mean me, mustn't he? It's got to be me who's lovely. Isn't that good?"

"Yeah, right, it's fantastic. But... err... like you said... there aren't any other dogs around, are there? He's not really got a lot to compare you with, has he?"

"No, no, but so what? It's still good."

"And didn't you also hear him say, 'who's a crazy dog, then?'"

"A crazy dog? Do you think that's me too? That can't be right. Crazy's not such a great thing to be, is it? Is it, Misty?"

"If the fur fits, wear it," I told her, "now let me get back to sleep."

But she wouldn't. So I jumped the back gate, which she can't, and went round to the front of the house and my bed of leaves there. It's one of the most comfortable places I know to lie on. And free of pesky dogs.

Jumping's quite a thing, incidentally. The domestics are training her to jump. They've got this hoop that they hold up for her. They keep it so low she could hardly crawl under it. Then they hold half a pathetic little dog treat on the other side, and – surprise, surprise – she jumps through the hoop to get it.

And this is a major achievement? You should hear them cooing about it. "Good girl! Well done! You're really getting it."

"Look at me, Misty, look at me," she likes to crow, "I'm jumping! And *so* high!"

So I jump up on the table and look down at her, vainly struggling to follow me.

"Very impressive," I say, "Now come and join me up here."

"I can't, I can't, Misty," she says, "but didn't I do a great jump?"

It's not as though I don't show her how jumping's really done. I do it quite often. I leap up to get at my food. Now that's three or four times her height. And the reward isn't half a treat. It's a bowlful of proper food. And, what's more, it's got this brilliant system which means whenever the bowl gets close to empty, more flows in from above.

Now that's what I call a sensible reason for a jump. Not like some miserable fraction of a treat. And it's proper jumping.

You should see her face. Down below at floor level. Looking up pathetically. *So* funny.

Luci and the Misty mystery

The humans don't like it much when I jump on Misty. I wonder why? It's such fun.

He lies on his own little bed at the bottom of the humans' bed. I sleep *on* the bed, of course. When we get up in the morning, I jump on him. It's wonderful. He wakes up and makes that funny growly noise of his, the one he comes up with most times we play. I think it's funny.

The humans don't see it that way, though.

"Leave him alone, Luci," they say to me, sounding irritated, "can't you hear him growling? Don't you see he doesn't like it?"

Well, no, I don't see that. They're not real growls. After all, what usually happens is that he goes running downstairs, which is exactly what I want, because that way we can play chase. Well, I play chase. He plays run-away. But it's fun, fun, fun.

It's true that sometimes he scratches me and bites me, which can be quite painful, but I think that must be because he just doesn't know his own strength.

"Now that's an amusing delusion of yours," says Misty, reading over my shoulder. Like he does. Which must mean he wants to be close by because he likes me so much.

"And there's another one."

I must find out what 'delusion' means.

Anyway, if he scratches me a bit too hard, it can't be because he means it. It can't be because he doesn't enjoy our chase games. After all, it's *playing* and everyone likes playing, don't they? Of course they do. How can you not like playing? No, obviously he likes it, he just gets a bit over-excited sometimes.

"Yep. You really need to find out what a delusion is."

Often, when he's playing run-away, he goes right into the garden which is even better. Then I can play chase out there too. At least, until he jumps up on top of the fence and vanishes over it. I wonder where he goes? He's so *brave*. I wouldn't want to go wandering out there. Beyond the fence? Wow. Not for me. I like it in the garden, but I like having a good, safe fence around me. I think he's a hero to go out there, the other side. You wouldn't catch me doing it.

It's odd, though. Recently he hasn't been going out into the garden anything like as much as he used to. He goes tearing down the stairs just like normal but when he gets to the small-dog flap...

"The *cat* flap, Luci, the cat flap," but then Misty always says that.

Anyway... when he gets to the small-dog flap in the kitchen door, he just stops. Stops dead. Why, the other day I ran right into him. I was so surprised, I didn't even think of licking him like I usually do, or jumping up on his back.

"OK, that's it, little one," he growled at me, and this time it didn't sound so much like fun, "I've changed my mind. I'm not going outside. But you're leaving me alone, got it? Unless you want another taste of my claws and teeth."

Well, he sounded like he really meant it this time, so I backed off till I was clear of his claws. And then backed off a bit more, so I was clear of a pounce. And then backed off a little further still, for safety.

"But... but... what is it, Misty? Don't you want to play anymore? Don't you, Misty? Don't you?"

"Not right now, I don't. No. Maybe later."

"But... but..."

"No buts. Later. Maybe. Not now."

"But you *like* outside. Why don't we go outside? It's always fun outside. Sometimes there's strawberries. I *like* strawberries."

"There won't be any strawberries. You've eaten them all."

"Ah," I told him, feeling much cleverer than him, "they come back. They always come back."

"Not all the time, you silly animal. The season's over. You've had the lot this year."

I didn't say anything. Year? I wasn't quite sure what one of those was.

"Don't you worry about years. You haven't had even one yet. I'll explain it all once you have. But, take it from me, it means you're not going to see any more strawberries for ages and ages now. Still, if you want to go out, be my guest. Strawberries or not."

"But... but... how can I be your guest if you're not there?"

He batted me round the head then – I'd drifted a bit closer while we were talking.

"Just go, if you want. I don't feel like it. I'm staying in."

So I went. Outside. On my own.

There didn't seem anything odd out there. In fact, it was great, because at the end of the garden there were two crows pecking around on the ground. Like the ones I have such fun chasing in the park. Here they were, in my own garden. I was *so* pleased that I went rushing up to them, until they took off like they always do. Oh, what fun it was!

Still. It's a mystery about Misty. A Misty mystery, in fact.

Wow! Wasn't that great? Did you see what I did there? I made a joke. Based on Misty's name. Mysterious Misty.

Funny, wasn't it?

Misty not tempted by the garden

Gardens. Their pleasures are overrated, aren't they? I suppose a cat must sometimes do what a cat must do, and the garden's as good a place to do it as any, but I can do that – what the domestics call "my business" – at night, can't I? Then I can stay indoors during the day. It's much more comfortable, as I move from my favourite bed, the one the old dog Janka used and which still smells slightly of her, to the domestics' bed, to the couch downstairs – basically anywhere I feel like lying and thinking great thoughts about the universe. With my eyes shut.

"Wake up! Wake up! Wake up, Misty!"

"What? What? What?" I respond to this brutal interruption of my deep reflections, as a great weight lands on my back.

"Come on, Misty, come on, come on." And I can feel that pointy muzzle prodding my head and that long tongue licking my ears. Dogs! Particularly playful poodle puppies. They're a pain in the neck, particularly when they dig their claws into it.

"Stop it, Luci! I wasn't asleep. I was thinking."

She seemed to freeze.

"Thinking? Really? With your eyes closed? I always think with my eyes open."

"Well, I've often seen you with your eyes open, but I don't believe I've ever seen you think."

"I'm thinking now. I'm thinking really, really hard."

"Well, while you're thinking, would you mind moving your

paw off my neck?"

"I'm thinking about you," she replied, making no move to get her weight off me, "how would I know when you're thinking instead of just asleep? They look the same."

"Well, just even if you assumed I was sleeping, which I wasn't, why would you feel obliged to jump on me anyway?"

"Oh, I don't feel obliged. It's a pleasure. So we can play."

That's the trouble with Luci. She always has an answer. A lousy answer, usually, but that doesn't make it any easier to demolish. So I just resorted to one of my big battle mews, with a couple of growls thrown in, till she let me go. I made a beeline for the kitchen door, and my cat flap.

But as I got to the flap, I heard a noise that turned my blood to ice.

There was a cawing in the garden.

I hauled on the brakes, stopping so suddenly that the little dog ran into me. If I hadn't been so shocked, I'd have been amused by her look of surprise. She never even thought of giving me a nip or a lick.

When she got her act together, she couldn't contain her surprise.

"Why, why, why? Why aren't we going out to play in the garden? What's wrong, what's wrong, what's wrong?"

Well, I was having none of it. I didn't care for the garden just now. It was cold and wet. The inside was much warmer and more comfortable. It made much more sense to stay indoors. Not that I was worried about anything out there, of course. Just that it struck me that there was nothing to do in the garden that I couldn't do just as well in here. Better, even. And at least in here I wouldn't be dealing with anything more monstrous than a bouncy puppy.

Whereas out there – the crows were back.

Luci amazed by Misty

What a strange sight!

Just for once, Misty went out in the garden on his own. He's not been doing that much the last few days. Today he took the plunge. I was having my belly rubbed by human number 2, when I heard his voice from out there in the back. Naturally, I went straight out of the small-dog flap and ran over to see him.

And then stopped.

Misty was up on the pointy part of the roof of one of the sheds. Amazing how he can balance there. I know I couldn't. But then I couldn't get up there in the first place.

That wasn't the amazing thing, though. What was weird was that Misty was spoiling for a fight – with a crow! For a moment I thought maybe he'd come around to my way of seeing things and wanted to play at chasing crows just like I do in the park.

But then I saw something strange. Misty was looking straight at the crow. And the crow was looking straight at Misty. Even though Misty had all his muscles tense, his back legs twitching, like he was ready to pounce.

Now I've never actually caught a crow. Not sure quite what I'd do with one if I did. The fun all seems to be in the chase. But I've seen Misty take a mouse or a small bird. I've found the feathers which is all that's left of the bird once he's finished with it, or the small bit of bitter meat that's all that's left of a mouse – I tried to eat one once and it was *horrible*.

So now I was about to see another bird getting turned into a little pile of feathers. And this time it would be a crow. Amazing – I thought they were too big. I was frozen to the spot, watching the master at work.

Suddenly Misty pounced. But – missed! The crow took off, just like they do when I chase them. Misty was left, his jaws working, his eyes staring up in the air, his paws empty.

When, just as suddenly, another crow appeared. Right behind him. On top of the roof, at the other end, strutting around like the first crow. Cool as my food from the freezer when the human hasn't let it thaw properly. A crow looking like he owned the place.

Misty spun round. And went straight into the prepare-to-pounce position again, muscles working away, eyes fixed on his prey, jaw open, all death and destruction ready for a miserable bird.

But then the same thing happened all over again. As he leaped – off the bird flew, just out of the grasp of his jaws, wings beating, flying out of his reach, leaving Misty with nothing to grab hold of.

At which point, the first bird reappeared. Would you believe it? I mean, I know I didn't at first, even though I was seeing the whole thing. It landed where it had been before, which was behind him now. And it started strutting around, claws clicking on the wood, so that Misty spun back around and concentrated on him again.

This happened two or three more times, as I sat watching amazed. I could hardly believe it. Two birds were having a go at Misty. Playing with him. Toying with him. *My* Misty. And I could see he wasn't enjoying it. Not like when I play with him.

Finally, I couldn't keep quiet any longer. I barked. And it was like I'd broken in on a complicated dance. The crow that was on the roof took off and joined the other one that was already in the air. Then they both circled above us a bit, cawing, before flying to the tree at the bottom of the garden. Misty just looked at me. A weird look. I'd never seen it before. Like he was a bit crazy. Or waking up from a dream.

Then he dashed past me and back into the house. Really. I've never seen him move so fast. I followed more slowly.

Inside, the humans were talking.

"Looks like the crows must be rearing some young," said number 1, "they've been warning Misty off."

"Warning him off?" asked number 2.

"Yes. I've been watching them from the bedroom for the last ten minutes. They've been teasing him. Tempting him to pounce and then flying away. Showing him he can't mess with them, or even catch them. I'm afraid it makes him look… well… a bit silly."

"Not the respect he feels is due to the proud incumbent of the top of the local food chain?"

"That's it. No good for his self-esteem." She looked out into the garden. "They must have a nest in the tree down there and you know how it is with crows: there's always at least one fledgling who falls out before learning to fly."

"Which is like serving up a tempting meal to Misty."

"Exactly. So now they're telling him to mind his step."

"No wonder he looked so upset when he came in."

"Oh," she said, "did he come back in?"

"Yes. And shot straight upstairs. He's probably trying to recover his dignity."

It was all very strange. I don't even really understand what they were talking about. I mean, what do they mean by 'young'? And what do they mean by 'warning off'?

And – what on earth is 'dignity'?

Misty wants to stone the crows

What *is* the point of crows? They fly around, land and strut about, make themselves look highly edible, but turn out to be uneatable. "Uneatable" not because they aren't made of good meat, but because they just won't stay still long enough to be eaten. Practically uncatchable, I find them, which is why I keep out of their way.

This morning, I checked the garden out carefully. A perfectly crowless view greeted me. So I took my chance and nipped out, did, well you know, my business, and decided to get up on a shed roof to enjoy the sun, which seemed to be getting a bit warmer, a rare joy in England at this time of year. And blow me down, I'd barely got up there when one of the loathsome creatures landed right in front of me.

"Aw," he cawed. I think it was the "he". "Hallaw, cawt. Whawt do you want, cawt? You like craw? You like to try craw meat?"

I know better than to be tempted. I know when I jump at him he'll fly away just before I reach him. So I don't even try. But then I did. Because I fall for the damn trick every time. Blast it.

As soon as I pounced and found nothing there but a faint scent of vanished crow, the female landed behind me. I think it was the "her".

"Aw, aw, you thawwt you'd catch a craw, did you? Maybe you think you catch our little ones when they come? You think we'll let them be cawt? We'll let you eat young craw?"

If I turn to catch her, it'll be just the same. As I leap, the taste of bird already in my mouth, feel of flesh and feathers already making my claws tingle, she'll be gone and I'll end up with a mouthful of fresh air. It happens every time. And every time I let it happen. It's stronger than me.

Terrible pesky things, crows.

Even worse than little dogs, come to think of it.

What *is* the point of dogs? They distract the domestics. They get uppity and try to jump on me. And they're always right there just when you least want them.

I was focused on the crows as they landed, each in turn, first one side of me and then the other, giving me the impression that if this just went on a little longer, one would make a mistake and get too close. Then they'd see, as I got my claws in and shut that insolent voice up for good. But suddenly we were interrupted. A great volley of barking.

Well, I say barking. It was Luci – of course – and she doesn't do barking. She just yaps. The boxer across the street barks. Big deep-throated threatening shouts of warning. It worried me at first, till I realised they kept him behind a locked gate, so now I just throw him a look and wander past. Still, the time they let him out I was over the back gate into our garden quicker than you could say "cat hunt". He's certainly inspiring when he's out and free.

But Luci – well, she comes up with little high-pitched excited cries, not proper barks at all. Even so, they worked. The birds and me, we all spun round, our concentration shot. For a moment, we all just looked at her, as we tried to adjust to a clownish distraction from serious intensity. A little joke of a ball of fluff yapping her heart out, what could be more ridiculous?

It was the crows who recovered first. They gave a great flurry of wings along with their "awk, awk" cries and flew off towards the tree where they live. It took me a few more seconds to readjust my mind to what was happening but, when I had, I made a dash for the cat flap and shot back into the house. And upstairs, out of sight, I hoped.

Eventually, though, Luci came looking for me. As always.

"What did they want, Misty? Those crows? What did they want? What were they doing?"

"Nothing to do with you, little girl. Don't get involved in what you know nothing about."

"But I want to know, I want to know. Why did they keep doing that to you, one taking off in front of you as the other one landed behind you?"

"You mean – you were watching the whole time?"

"Well, some of the time. It was – odd. What was it, Misty, what was it?"

"Just crow business. And cat business. Not silly little dog business. All you need to do is take my advice: keep well away from crows. They're bad news."

"But why? But why? It's fun to chase them. And they always fly away."

"Well, you'd better hope they always do. It's no fun if they don't."

"Why? Why? Why? What do they do?"

But I'd had enough of her questions. I reckoned the crows would be gone for a while so headed back out to the garden and over the gate, where she can't follow. And out to the pile of leaves at the front where I like to lie in the sun. That helped me soothe my feelings. Resettle my fur. Steady my breathing.

Well away from caws. Or yaps.

Luci and the crowstorm

Wow! *Now* I know what it is crows do when they don't fly away.

We were woken up really early this morning by the most terrible racket from the back of the house. I'd call it cawing except it was *much* louder than that.

It was a crowstorm.

Human number 1 was lying in bed, barely awake. And then she wasn't lying there anymore. Just like that. Here one moment. Gone the next.

She was standing by the window looking out. I hadn't seen her move. How does she do that?

"Oh no!" she cried, "Misty's got a baby crow! It's terrible. It's in his jaws."

Human number 2 was still getting up, rubbing his eyes and looking as though life was much too difficult for him just then. Usually, when he goes downstairs he makes himself a cup of a horrible-smelling concoction which makes him reasonably awake, and then another one, which makes him able to take sensible decisions, like refilling my bowl. But when he first gets up, it's just hopeless. He can't do anything.

"Go on," number 1 was saying, "get down there. See if you can help."

He was muttering about slippers.

"The parents are there!" she shouted, "They're attacking him! Go quickly! You may be in time."

That finally got him moving. He stumbled downstairs, and I went with him: I had to see what was happening.

The racket was coming from the path beyond the back

garden. The human fiddled with the gate to get it open and then we stepped out. And what a sight we saw.

Just like number 1 had said, Misty had a young crow in his mouth.

Which, by the way, explained that word, young. I see it now. The crows' young are their puppies, aren't they? Or whatever they call their babies.

But what was most amazing was that we couldn't see much of Misty. He was hidden by a black flurry of wings beating like crazy, in the middle of a storm of the fiercest crowing I've ever heard. Both crows were attacking him, pecking at his head, scrabbling at his back with their claws. And he couldn't do anything. He was keeping hold of the crow in his mouth. That meant he couldn't fight the crows off. He was trying to weave, moving his head from side to side, crouching and dodging to get out of reach of the talons and beaks.

He wasn't having the best of the fight.

But to me crows only mean one thing. Before the human could say or do anything, I did what I always do: I ran at them barking.

Just like the other day, everything stopped. Misty and the birds froze. They all looked at me. And then suddenly it was wild activity again.

Misty dropped the baby bird and ran for our garden fence.

The parent crows fluttered off the ground screeching and cawing. This time they didn't fly away, but just perched or hovered near the little bird. That was great, because no crow had ever stayed anywhere near when I wanted to play with them. So I went racing round and round, barking and jumping at them if they looked like coming down.

"Luci! Stop. Get over here."

I kept playing. They so obviously wanted to play with me. Just like Misty, even though he says he doesn't.

"Luci! *Now*. Come here."

Well, it was only number 2, and I reckon you can generally get away with ignoring him once – he sometimes forgets what he's told you to do and doesn't follow up. Now he'd said it twice, though. I reckon it's probably wiser not to ignore him twice. So I went over to where he was standing.

We went back into the garden. Before he closed the gate, I looked back. The little crow was on his feet. He didn't seem too much the worse for wear. And both parents were on the ground, inspecting him from each side.

I went looking for Misty. He was back upstairs, a bit fed up.

"What do *you* want, then, noisy girl?"

"I wanted to see how you were. Are you all right, Misty? I hope you're all right."

"No, I'm not all right. I've been pecked and clawed by two birds – two *birds*, for the love of mouse, and forced to abandon a prey I'd got fairly into my mouth. What's all right about that?"

"But are you injured at all? Hurt on your body?"

"Nothing that won't fix itself in an hour or two. But the wounds to my dignity will take longer."

"Dignity? Someone mentioned that before. What is it?"

He sighed.

"You really don't know anything, do you? Dignity's the most important thing. You can't survive without it. It's a kind of pride that comes from living in a way that measures up to your sense of what you're worth. That shows everyone you're worth that much."

"A kind of pride? And a wound to pride's as bad as one to your body?"

"Worse. Body wounds fix themselves quite quickly. Wounds to dignity can last a lifetime."

"But... but... you can't eat it, can you?"

"Dignity? Of course, you can't eat it. You can be made to swallow it, which is a terrible thing, but you can't eat it."

"And you can't play with it?"

"If anyone trifles with your dignity, that's terribly wounding."

"It doesn't stroke you?"

"No, it needs stroking for its wounds to heal."

"Well," I said, "I don't see any point in it."

"Luci!" It was human number 2 again. "Time for training."

I shot down the stairs. Training means treats. And those *do* have a point.

Luci after the crows

Well, the crow affair seems to be over, after all the excitement ten days ago. Misty's even going out to the back garden again these days. He didn't for a while, but he seems fine with it now.

I'd taken human number 1 for a walk the other day, when we caught sight of a little crow – well, not that little anymore, actually – sitting in the gutter a few doors down from our place.

"Oh, look, Luci! That's the little crow that Misty caught the other day," she said.

I wanted to run at him barking to see if he would play, but I had her on the lead.

"Stay here," she said, "the last thing he wants is a big lump of a dog charging down on him."

A big lump? *Me*? Delicate me?

Still, I could see her point. Even if he's bigger than he was, I'm a lot bigger still.

"Besides," number 1 was still saying, "you'd get into trouble."

She was pointing up into a tree from which some cawing was going on. There was another crow there, right above the little one. Keeping an eye on him. And, as I was watching, there was a lot more cawing and the other one showed up. And I realised they weren't so much keeping an eye on him as keeping an eye on us.

"Remember what they did to Misty?" she went on, "they'd do the same to you if you had a go at their young one."

Just then the small crow started taking a few steps further down the road. He even fluttered his wings a bit, but he didn't so much fly as hop, out of the gutter, onto the pavement.

"He'll be flying in a day or two. Just seems silly that he got out of the nest before he could fly at all. He should have stayed put, safely with his parents."

It's so nice of her to explain things to me. But I don't understand why she does: I know she thinks I don't understand English.

By then the young crow was close to the next tree along, and with more cawing, his parents flew across to it, landing in its lower branches. They were on guard again.

It was all very interesting. "Very instructive," as I'm sure Misty would have put it. Crows seem to be more than just things to run after in the park.

I went to see Misty soon after we got back.

"Misty! Misty! We saw that crow again."

"Which crow was that?" he said. Airily, I think.

"The young one you caught last week. It's grown a bit and will fly away quite soon."

"Good, good," he assured me, "nothing better with a crow than to know it's gone away. Nasty noisy things. I hope they'll stay well away from my back garden. They're very annoying company."

"Well, I drove them away, Misty, didn't I?"

"*You* drove them away?" He seemed to be getting more and more airy about things.

"Why, yes. I barked at them and ran at them and they flew away."

"Oh, you think *you* did that, do you? I had the situation completely under control the whole time. I was about to give them a lesson they'd never forget when you turned up and distracted them, with your infernal barking. They'd have been gone for a good long time once I'd finished with them, let me tell you."

"But..." I started, and then changed my mind. What was the point of trying to convince him? He's my *friend*. Why should I try to change his mind? He's happy with his explanation.

And I'm happy for him.

Luci and the pain of entering adulthood

Oh, the last few days have been difficult. I don't know what's been happening. I'm just *so* nervous all the time. And I've been *bleeding*. That I don't get at all. I mean, blood is what you get from meat if it hasn't been cooked. But you don't get blood from me. Do you?

It made me terribly anxious. And I may have whined a bit. That's what anxiety does to a sensitive dog.

"Whined a bit?" says Misty. "If that was a bit, I'd hate it if you whined a lot."

Eventually the humans took me to the house of pain, where people in white coats stick needles in you. Though, to be fair, this time they didn't. Instead, the human in the white coat just said something completely bizarre.

"Yes, she's in season," she said.

In season? I'm always in season. That's the thing about a good fur coat like mine. It's never out of fashion. *Or* out of season.

"She may be a bit clingy," White Coat added.

Later on, human number 2 said the same thing.

"The vet said she'd be clingy, but I had no idea it would be this bad. Now she's jumping up on her own into my lap, which she's never done before without being lifted. And if she doesn't jump she scrapes at me with her claws to get me to pick her up."

"Well, what are you complaining about?" Human number 1 told him, "don't you want her to be affectionate?"

Well, exactly. What's not to like about affection? And I've got loads. Anyway, once I'm on his lap he just strokes me in his slightly distracted way. It would be an improvement if he really focused, but still it's better than nothing. It makes me feel much nicer inside and not anxious at all anymore. Which, I reckon, must do him a lot of good too. I mean, if it leaves me feeling better to be stroked, it's got to make him feel better to do the stroking. Right?

Of course, a lot of the time I jump up on number 1's lap instead. She does focus a bit more. And she says nice things about me.

"It isn't easy to move into full womanhood, you know," she said the other day while rubbing my ears.

"Especially for a woman," he replied. A bit too casually, I reckon.

"Just as bad for a little dog," she said, and I didn't mind. I'm a right-sized dog, not a little one, but I know there are a lot of oversized dogs, and when she talks in that nice tone, and keeps stroking, I don't mind if she calls me little. Especially if that means not horribly gigantic like they are.

Still, human number 2 wasn't completely wrong. Before, I used to be quite happy just to lie next to the humans – better still, between them – on the sofa. That doesn't entirely do it for me anymore. At least, not when I'm anxious. And I'm anxious most of the time.

A lap's much better. Human number 2's is fine, but he has this way of covering it with a laptop. I try to teach him, but it's quite hard to get him to understand that laps are for lapdogs not laptops. So, when he puts the laptop on his lap, I just walk around on those black and white keys of his until I get his attention. Which doesn't usually take very long.

"Get off my keyboard, you pesky little dog!" he says. Or something like that.

"Now, now," says human number 1. "You know she's a bit upset at the moment".

Then he gets rid of his laptop and makes a fuss of me, which was the aim of the exercise, so, hey, I'm not complaining. Though he still grumbles.

"Why can't she go to your lap? You're not using your laptop."

Well, normally I would. She fidgets less. And she gets her legs out in front of her in just the right way to lie on them. With him, they're either too far apart so there's a gap, or they're too close together so the lap's too narrow. Then again, he sometimes just fidgets and fidgets which is hopeless when you're supposed to be supplying a lap to a lapdog. But even all that doesn't stop me sometimes wanting to sit on him instead, and not always on her. I don't want him to feel left out or anything.

It seems there's a problem with our garden. It has a fence all round it. Which is nice because it lets me feel much safer out there. And I go out there quite a lot, now that I've worked out how the small-dog flap works.

"Cat flap," says Misty.

"If you say so," I sigh.

"Don't you sigh at me."

"Cat flap. Cat flap. Of course, it's a cat flap."

"That's better," he says. "Try to get it right first time, next time."

Human number 1 wasn't happy with the fences, though.

"A male dog could get in," she said, "look, there's a gap at the bottom there. And there."

"That's not a gap," he said.

"It would be with a bit of digging."

"Well, there'd be a gap under the Great Wall of China if someone dug enough."

It's quite funny how she hits his arm sometimes. Judging by the sound he makes, it hurts him a bit, though he doesn't complain. But then, if human number 1 hit me (which she doesn't), I probably wouldn't complain either. I'd be too afraid she'd hit me again. Maybe he's worked that one out too.

"A dog who smells a female on heat goes mad. He'll dig under any fence he can. He could certainly dig under that one."

"So what do you suggest?" he asked.

"We're going to have to lock her in."

That evening when I tried to get out of the small dog flap, I just pushed and pushed but nothing happened. It wouldn't move. It was terrible.

"Do you want to go into the garden, Luci?" I heard human number 1 ask.

She opened the door and let me out. But she stayed with me until I was ready to go back in. Which was fine, actually. I prefer to have company.

But later I saw Misty. He was staring at human number 2. Who was sitting on the couch and tapping away at his laptop, like he always does if we don't take steps to stop him. Which Misty's stare eventually did. He looked up, saw the eyes, and went all guilty. Why, I could smell the guilt coming off him from where I was sitting.

"I know, I know, I understand. You're saying you're unhappy about the cat flap. You want to get out into the garden and you can't. Here, I'll come and let you out."

Which he did.

By the time he got back I was lying with my head on his keyboard. And instead of getting annoyed and chucking me off, he just sat down and stroked me.

"Poor Luci. It's not easy, is it, this passage into womanhood?" Then he sighed. "Worst for you, of course. But boy, it's not that easy for anyone else around you either."

Luci observing the world
By Senada Borcilo

Luci contemplates
her birthday

Today's my birthday!

I have no idea what that means. Except that it's *mine*, and I know what *that* means.

Misty tried to explain.

"OK. Things go round in years," he said.

I looked around the room. Everything seemed to be standing still.

"Nothing's going round," I carefully explained to him.

"No. OK. Not like that."

I think he sighed. He does that sometimes when he's explaining things to me. Poor fellow.

"Do you remember how hot it was a while ago?"

I'd forgotten. But he was right. It was coming back to me. It was really uncomfortable for a time, and I even wrote about it in my super-interesting diary.

"Right now," he went on, "it isn't hot anymore. In fact, it's cold and the leaves are red. In a while there won't be any leaves and it'll be even colder. And then the leaves will come back again, all bright green. And after that it'll be hot again. Well, since we live in England, it'll just be quite hot, and then only when it isn't cold and raining. So, OK, let's say it'll be quite hot, quite often. More often than now, at any rate."

"Yes, I remember," I said, "when things were like that."

"Well, that's it. Those things come, and then they go, and then they come back again. So when the leaves are red, that's autumn, and that's how they were when you were born. They're red again now – autumn's come back – and it's your birthday: a year since you were born. When you first became a little dog."

Born? Little? When I first became something? What was he getting at? I've always been here. I can't remember a time when I wasn't here. And except when I was really little, I've always been a right-sized dog.

But Misty was still explaining.

"It's your birthday. Your birthday's here because autumn's back. You're an autumn dog. Each time things come back like that, a year goes by. You've had one year, you're starting another one now, and that means you'll have all those things happen again."

How can things happen again? I mean, I met Misty for the first time, ages and *ages* ago. Am I going to meet him for the first time – again? I mean, Misty always talks sense, so maybe it's just me, but that just makes no sense at all.

Oh well, I'll just have to see how things work out. I often find that's the best thing to do, because lots of things seem weird to me when Misty explains them. But then, when they actually happen, they turn out to be not that hard after all.

Though not always.

Take the other day. Human number 1 was all dressed to go out. So I was jumping around waiting for her to put my lead on. And then she said to human number 2:

"I'll just pop out then. I'll be back shortly to take Luci out."

Where's the sense in that? Coming back *in* to take me *out*? Why not just take me out straight away? Honestly. Humans do talk a lot of rubbish sometimes.

Even worse, and even harder to understand, was finding Misty eating my food last weekend. His food is kept up high because he can jump all the way up there, and I can't. But my food is kept down at ground level. Basically for the same reason: because I can't jump up like he can.

Now there's a problem with that arrangement.

"A flaw," says Misty.

Well, yes, I know there's a floor. That's where they put my food bowl.

The problem with the arrangement – pay attention because it's quite complicated – is that while it's sensible to keep my food low, because I can't jump up like Misty can to get it, it means that Misty can get at it too. Even without jumping for it. He can get at my food but I can't get at his. Now that's not a sensible arrangement at all. In fact, it's a very *bad* arrangement.

It would have been all right if Misty didn't like my food, which I thought he didn't. In fact, the humans said he didn't like it. Even he said he didn't like it.

"You shouldn't believe everything I say," he tells me.

"You mean… you mean… you sometimes lie to me?"

"All is fair in food and war," he says, with that superior air he adopts when he's stalking off. Which he did, looking well fed. On *my* food.

Him eating my food isn't right. Especially as the food I get in the evening is this super good "eat me, eat me, eat me" mix of rice and bits of turkey my humans make for me. One of the great joys of the day is when they put out my portion. And it lasts me right through to just before we go to bed.

Or it would if Misty didn't decide to help himself to part of it. *My* best meal. That wasn't supposed to happen. I couldn't believe my eyes at first.

It didn't make sense, so I decided to clarify things a bit. And, since actions often clarify things better than words, I acted rather than talking. I jumped on top of him. I'm getting quite good at it. He puts up with it even if he complains a bit, and it does stop him doing what he's doing. Which is good when what he's doing is eating my food.

"OK, OK," he said, "you can get off me. I'll stop eating your stuff. I don't like it anyway."

He doesn't like it? The stuff he was just gobbling down? You think I believed him? Did I heck. You can fool me with a lie once. The same lie twice? Not a chance.

It may have helped that number 1 was having a go too.

"Misty! Eat your own food. Leave Luci's alone!"

Which he did, and things got back to how they should be. But from now on, I won't be leaving any of my rice and meat in the bowl once I've started. I've learned my lesson, and Misty will find an empty bowl in future.

You see what happened? When I first saw him eating my food, I couldn't understand what was going on. Now I understood. Which meant I'd been able to do something about it.

But the key thing is that I'd gone from not understanding to understanding completely. Which proves it can be done. Maybe the same will happen with this "year" thing Misty was talking about. It won't seem so confusing after a while. I'll get used to it.

Meanwhile, it's my birthday! Whatever that is. I'm going to enjoy it.

"There'll be extra rice and turkey mince for you," Human number 2 told me.

Yay!

Luci goes bananas. And suffers shampoo

The other day, number 1 wasn't feeling too well, so she went to bed. It's true that normally I lie next to number 2 on the couch as he taps away annoyingly on his computer. Sometimes I bite his hands to get his attention, which it generally does. But it also gets him irritated which means he has to have a moan.

"Stop that, Luci," he says in a pathetic voice, "lie down."

But he always strokes me while he's saying it, so what does he expect me to do? If he rewards me, I'm not going to stop. If he punishes me, I might.

Well, I assume I would, but he's never actually got around to punishing me, so I'm not sure what I *would* do, really.

Then again, maybe he thinks raising his voice is punishment enough? I just bark at him. And I make a lot more noise than he does, so I tend to get the better of those exchanges too.

Anyway. Like I was saying. Normally I lie on the couch next to him while he gets on with what he calls work, though I don't understand how anything you do sitting down can really be called work. But the one who'd gone upstairs was *number 1*. The important one. And she was *in bed*. Much more comfortable than a couch.

Of course, I went upstairs instead.

Maybe he was upset. You know. Felt neglected and all that.

What he did was sneak into the kitchen. With a banana. A *banana*. My absolutely best food ever. Maybe he thought I wouldn't notice. But you know the noise a banana makes when the peel gets broken? It's *so* distinctive. Of *course* I heard it, and I dashed downstairs immediately.

I knew I had to be specially endearing. He might have been upset by my deserting him, after all. So I did the whole act. I made sure I went tappy-tappy-tappy with my claws on the floor, because he likes that. And I got the tail going so hard it made my whole behind wag. And the eyes thing: very pathetic so they just cry out, "please, please be nice. Feed me, feed me."

It worked, too. He'd eaten quite a lot of the banana but there must have been a third of it left, I reckon. And, instead of chopping it up into silly little bits, he just fed me the whole thing. Much better than the choppy-uppy way. I got lots more.

It turns out he was amazed that I'd heard him.

"How did you know?" he kept saying. "All the way upstairs, with doors in between and everything, and you still knew I was having a banana."

Well, yeah. Duh. Of course I knew. Or I wouldn't have come tearing downstairs, would I? I mean, if there hadn't been a banana going spare – or at least ready to be eaten by a banana-loving dog – why would I have given up on a perfectly good rest in the bed with number 1?

That same day, the humans went out for the whole evening. On their own. Leaving me behind.

The worst of it was that, when they got back, number 2 smelled of dog. Another dog! All over his hands. Like he'd been stroking the ghastly thing. I had to lick his fingers for ages just to get the smell off them. Though, in a funny kind of way, that was actually quite fun. You know – just licking the hands was like a game. And, by the end of the process, his hands smelled of me. They smelled right again.

Talking about smelling right, the humans decide every now and then that I need to smell of something else. So they wash me.

"What gets into them?" I asked Misty last time they did, "why do they say I smell? I don't smell."

"You *do* smell," he said, "you smell of dog."

"Well, what's wrong with that?" I asked, "what's a dog supposed to smell of? You wouldn't want me to smell of cat, would you?"

"I don't know. Cats smell good. I wouldn't mind if the whole world smelled of cat. Except for the bits I want to eat."

"That's just silly. You *like* my smell. That's why you always want to lie on my blanket."

He looked a bit embarrassed then, like I'd caught him out in something he didn't want to admit. He just sort of mumbled back at me.

"I just like the feel of the blanket. It's a good blanket. Nothing to do with you."

"Anyway," I went on, bringing us back to the subject in hand, mainly because I've found in the past that it's not a good idea – not a *healthy* idea – to pursue one which makes Misty embarrassed. "I'm a dog who maybe smells a little bit of dog. That seems exactly right. It's no reason to wash me, is it?"

"I keep telling you. They're domestics. That's what they do. Wash things. Clean things. Clear things away. If you let them. They'd do the same to me if I let them, but I don't. Food service I'm keen on, but washing is something I do for myself. But then, unlike you, I've shown them who's boss. You just let them push you around, so you get washed. Serves you right."

It wasn't very nice. Hot water and nasty shampoo. They say it's dog shampoo. Hah! Anti-dog shampoo, more like.

The process lasted for ever. And left me all wet. So wet that I had to run around and roll everywhere just to get a bit drier. That left the couch quite wet which made it less comfortable to lie on. I wasn't pleased and nor was human number 2. He doesn't like it when he can't sit at his end of the couch and play with his dratted computer. It makes him quite irritable. Usually I try the sad little doggy act – you know, the eyes and everything – but this time I was fed up myself, what with being all bedraggled and all that.

"Don't blame me," I told him, "it was number 1 who put me in the bath. Why don't you get her to stop?"

But it didn't do any good. He never understands when I talk to him. It's sad, isn't it? Humans. Such limited intelligence.

Misty, dumb domestics and a tedious injury

It was strangely warm the other day, and the domestics had lunch together in the garden. Luci came out with them and lay down on the ground under the table. They think that's terribly touching. They're sure it's all about affection. Yeah, right. it's because they're even more casual about dropping things on the ground in the garden than they are indoors. The little dog isn't as stupid as she looks. She can make quite a good meal for herself from what they scatter about, if they eat out there.

I stayed a while but, without a lap to climb on, I got a bit bored. So I climbed on to a shed roof and started playing with a flower.

"Look at the cat," said Domestic number 1 in a disapproving tone, "he's worrying the honeysuckle."

Well, I was batting the top flowers with my paw. Perhaps the domestics thought that unfair: it's true the flowers hadn't done anything to me. And they weren't fighting back.

"I shouldn't think they'll mind," said number 2, who's very good at pointing out the downright bleeding obvious. I mean, I don't expect they even noticed. They're pretty dumb, flowers.

"Yes," she said, "but I don't see the point. Why can't he leave them alone?"

There's something about domestic number 1. When she said that, I felt I just had to stop. I hadn't thought about what I was doing being pointless, but when she mentioned it like that, I couldn't ignore it anymore.

So I got up and wandered off into the neighbour's garden, where I could worry flowers without a domestic whinging about it.

"I thought you didn't want the humans to know you understood English?" Luci asked me later. "They'll work it out eventually if you always react to what they say like that."

I was surprised she'd even noticed, what with her nose being glued to the ground as she hunted for crumbs. But her question had an easy answer, so I gave it.

"I don't care either way, to be honest. In any case, if they haven't spotted it after all the time I've been with them, I can assure you they won't notice now. Trust me on this one."

She nodded. Sagely. As though she has anything to be sage about.

"Terribly nice, but not that bright, are they?"

She sometimes surprises me. She's beginning to understand some of the fundamental truths about living with domestics.

Recently, I've been carrying a bit of an injury. It's so tedious. Interloper cats really get on my nerves. I mean, sure, yes, I sometimes stray outside my own territory. But when I meet another cat, I just greet them politely, make my excuses, and get the hell out.

So here's my question: why does that ghastly black and white cat from two doors down behave as though he owns our garden? *My* garden? More to the point, when he invades it and I courteously tell him he's in my territory, why doesn't he just get out like I would, instead going for me with tooth and claw?

He reckons he's better than me because he's from around here, and I'm an outsider who's moved in. So what? The place doesn't *belong* to him, does it? And I've been here four years. Practically half my life. I reckon that gives me the same rights as any local.

Sadly, that's not how he sees it.

The ghastly animal got me in the face the other day. Took me completely by surprise. When I was younger, I'd have given him as good as I got but, these days, I'm not the aggressive scrapper I used to be. Put on a bit of weight, perhaps. Nothing excessive, of course, but you know how it is, I'm not quite as quick as I once was.

Still, I'm quick enough to leg it back into the house pretty fast. Had to nurse the injury. It certainly needed nursing: the wound blew right up, a nasty red and black colour, and it hurt like hell. The domestics were full of sympathy but, hey, what's the use of sympathy? I needed help.

Luci tried, of course. But, you know – a toy poodle? About as skilful as a poodle toy.

I had to sort it myself. Got my claws into the nasty mess on my face, and *that* hurt badly too. But it did some good. Some vile liquid came out and the whole thing shrank to a sensible size which hurt a lot less.

Next day, once they'd had a decent night's sleep themselves, the domestics actually got around to helping me.

"It looks less bad," said number 1, "it's like he's managed to lance it himself."

I'll say. You weren't going to do it, were you? Had to do it myself.

"Still, we'd better get him to the vet," she went on.

There was a time when those words would have filled me with horror. But, you know, though you get poked and pricked there, at least you end up feeling better, eventually, than you did before you visited the vet. Sometimes, it's quite a surprise how much good it does. Not that it makes me like the actual process of getting there any better. It means being stuck into that ghastly sort of brown cage thing they use to carry me around. It's made of cloth but, believe me, it's as much a cage as if it were all iron bars. Got Luci all upset too – she went bounding around yapping and sniffing and saying useless things.

"Don't stay in there, Misty, come out and play. Come on. It can't be nice in there. Just come out."

She had plenty to say, but did absolutely nothing useful. No way she could unzip the bit to let me out. Useful as a wet rag, that dog. I've said it before and will doubtless say again.

Anyway, I put up with it. We were off to the vet and I guessed it would do me good. So I did my best to be nice. I mean, when he jabbed me with a needle – and he did it twice – I didn't give him a HOWL, more of a half-power protest. Quarter-power. Sort of Mrrrr. Just to mark the fact that I knew they'd stuck me with steel and they shouldn't start to think that just because I'd put up with it, I was going to go on putting up with it forever.

He's good that vet. Did the trick. When I got home, I was feeling a *lot* better. Comfortable, basically. Practically normal.

Domestic number 2 opened the door to the nasty cage thing – when I saw it was him trying to open it, instead of letting number 1 do the job, I half suspected he'd be defeated by the difficulty of the process, but it turns out he can work a zip – and I emerged. In a dignified way, though I did lower myself to nuzzling his hand and letting him stroke me. I mean, I didn't want him to think I wasn't appreciative.

And of course, little Luci came dancing round.

"You're out of that nasty carrier thing!"

"Cage," I corrected her.

"Who cares? So long as you're out of it."

She was dancing around so much she didn't notice she'd left her blanket empty, so I curled up on it. I left her a little space near the edge and she joined me. Which was fine. It was quite nice having her silly wet nose pushing against my back. Companionable.

I was feeling good about things again. There's nothing like getting rid of pain. Why, I could even think of the nasty black and white cat from two doors down and, you know, I didn't even feel bitter about him anymore. Revenge? What good would it do? Would it even be worth the effort of a fight?

Though if he gets too close to my claws, with his back turned, I might just change my mind about that.

Luci on the right size for dogs

There's a comfortable size for dogs, right? And then there's uncomfortable.

The right size for a dog is about the right size for a cat. Well, a large cat anyway. Like, say, our cat Misty. But *lighter*. He's just a bit on the heavy size, is our Misty.

"On the heavy side?" growls Misty.

I hate his habit of reading my diary over my shoulder. Just because it takes me a little while to get it written.

"Only heavy relative to me," I quickly assure him. "Not really heavy. Not for a well-built cat like you."

He grunts and goes away, which is just as well. The alternative would have been him doing what he calls 'discipline'. And that's never fun.

The thing about his weight, right, is that when he lies on you, well, you really know he's lying on you. If he's at your kibble bowl, pushing him away isn't an option. Barking helps, but only because it wakes up human number 2 who'll come out and tell him to leave my food alone. And that only works if I make enough noise. And quickly enough. In time to save some food.

Still, Misty's weight isn't really the point. It's his *size* that's about right. We can look each other in the eye, we two, him and me, without having to look up or down. That's what I call about right. Size-wise.

Smaller's OK too. Smaller runs around and yaps a bit but

generally you can see it off. Or if you can't, you can certainly outrun it.

See what I mean? Comfortable. I can cope with that.

Then there's uncomfortable. I never thought you could have too much dog. But the truth is you can't have too much *right-size* dog. But then there's the other kind. The kind where there's too much dog in just one dog, if you see what I mean.

Ruddy great galumphing beasts. Paws the size of food bowls. Silly slobbering mouths full of massive teeth.

"Hello, little dog," they say to me, and before I can even say back, "little? I'm the right size," they say, "let's play, little dog, let's run around and jump up and down and look silly."

And they go ahead and do it, as though your peaceful enjoyment of a pleasant walk simply didn't matter. They bound up and down. I don't mind the *up* so much, but the *down*'s a bit of a pain in the backside. Literally. That's exactly where one of those far-bigger-than-necessary dogs came down on me the other day.

See, some of those lumpy outsize dogs aren't just big, they're surprisingly nippy. I'm pretty fast on my paws myself, but when you've got legs that long, you can cover as much ground in one step as I can in two. Maybe three. That's why he was able to come down on my backside like that before I could get away.

A puppy, his human said.

He felt like about fifty puppies to me. A right-size puppy's a feather-like creature, you barely notice it jumping on you. I know when I jump on human number 1, she says silly things like "oww – that hurts!" but that's just her way, she's just playing. Anyway, human number 2 laughs, so it can't really be hurting number 1, can it?

Though I notice he doesn't laugh half so hard when I land on him. Odd.

Still, all that's beside the point. The real point is that proper-size dogs are just right. They play nicely and they're fun. So why is the park – *my* park – so full of big-lump dogs? What is the point of that?

And what I don't understand is why human number 2 lets them get away with it. I mean, after the silly human said that about the giant dog being just a puppy, he just laughed one of his irritating laughs.

"Yes," he said, "I can see he's a puppy. Just wants to play. I don't know why she's so shy of other dogs."

You don't know why? How would you feel if a human ten times bigger than you came down on your backside with his ruddy great paws? Would you still be laughing?

Then you might understand what the difference is between the right size and *too big for comfort.*

Toffee coming home
By Senada Borcilo

Luci deals with a new arrival

Strange things are happening. I don't get what's going on at all. But I know I don't like it.

Human number 1 went out at lunchtime and came back with some wonderful bags. A big one of food and a small one of treats. Oh, the scent was just fantastic. I made a beeline for them and sniffed in a meaningful way. So meaningful that I don't think anyone could have misunderstood. But instead of opening the bags and giving me a taste, she said something that left me completely confused.

"No, Luci, sorry, it's not for you. This if for your new little friend."

New little friend? What friend? My friend is Misty, and no one could call him little. I mean, he's twice my size. And he isn't new.

In fact, it was Misty who got me really frightened.

"What's this puppy business?" he asked me.

"Puppy?" I said, "Well, I'm the puppy. But I don't know about any particular business."

"You? A *puppy*? Good Lord, woman, you're getting on for *two*. When I was two I was dominating a neighbourhood. I hadn't been a kitten for a year and a half."

"I'm not a puppy anymore?"

It was a chilling thought. I've been the puppy for *ages*. I'm not sure I'm ready to stop.

"Well, you're not. So let me say it again: what's all this puppy business?"

"I don't know. I thought I was the puppy around here. Now you tell me I'm not a puppy at all. So I have no idea what you're talking about."

"Take a look at those bags that domestic number 1 came back with. They say 'puppy'. Why?"

"The bags? They say 'puppy'? How can a bag say anything?"

"It's *written* on them."

That's the thing about Misty. He's *terribly* clever. He can tell what bags and cans and packets and things are saying. It's all this *writing* stuff. I have trouble enough writing my own stuff, let alone understanding anyone else's. Misty's just wonderful. Magical, really. An intellectual. I'm not cut out for that role myself, but it's got to be good to have one intellectual in the family. Hasn't it?

"Mark my words," he said, "they're up to no good. They're plotting something. And I'm not happy about it."

Oh, I'm so worried. What are they up to? And what's plotting? I don't know what I'm supposed to do.

Maybe I'll just have a sleep. I find that always helps when things turn tense. It stops me worrying.

Oh wow, oh wow, oh wow! This is so exciting! There's this huge *dog living in my new home! She's black and she's called Luci and she's so big she can get up on the sofa on her own. I can't do that. I can get down, if the humans aren't watching – they don't like it when I do – and I don't so much get down as splat, but at least at the end I'm on the floor. Luci just jumps on and jumps off when she wants.*

I mean, she's as big as a cat. I know that because I've seen a cat now. That's something else we have in this house. A whole cat. All of our own. Well, at least we used to. He seems to have vanished. But Luci says he'll come back. She says he's sulking, but I don't know what that is. And she says he's sulking because of me, but I don't understand how he can be doing anything because of me. Specially when I don't even know what he's supposed to be doing in the first place. And, in any case, he's ginormous. As big as Luci. Probably bigger.

Anyway, it's all terribly exciting. And I'm having a great time. And everybody thinks it's great I'm here.

Well, you'll have guessed that wasn't me, Luci, talking. That was Toffee.

"What's a Toffee?" you'll be saying.

I imagine that you'll have guessed it isn't a kind of sticky sweet. And you'd be right. That would have been much nicer. Instead, in our house, it's turned out to be a new puppy. She saw me doing my diary and said, "What's that? What's that? What's that?" and when I'd told her, of course she wanted one too. But she can't write – she's only a little puppy – so I had to write it for her.

She's only a puppy. Yes. You read that right. It seems Misty was right when he got me worried about some strange 'puppy business'. Turns out what it meant was a new puppy showing up in the house. In *our* house. Which a new puppy was about to waltz into. And now she has. She has, she has, and she's Toffee. And it looks like she's here to stay.

She's a menace. I mean, making me write her diary wasn't even the most infuriating thing she's done. She may be smaller than a squirrel, but she gets everywhere. And once she's got there, she does just what she wants.

For instance, she pushes me away from my food bowl. She goes burrowing in headfirst with never so much as a nod or a 'OK if I have a bite?' and helps herself. It got so bad that I left her my bowl and went and ate the food from hers. I thought that was quite smart but later I heard the humans saying they'd put my portion in her bowl and her portion in mine That made me feel a bit silly. I was terribly proud that I'd finished emptying her bowl before she finished emptying mine, but if her bowl had a smaller portion to start with, maybe that wasn't so clever.

Still, she has to sleep in a cage downstairs and I get to sleep on the bed with the humans. So I'm definitely the top dog. As I tell her when she pushes me away from my food bowl.

The sad thing is that Misty's gone away. I mean, not really completely away. I saw him last night in the garden and we compared notes.

"They do this, the domestics," he told me, "they bring some ghastly yapping little dog into the house without even consulting me. You're living perfectly comfortably and then suddenly you're being crowded out by puppies."

"Well, to be fair, there's only one."

"Believe you me, one puppy can be a crowd. I know. I've been through this before."

"Really? When?"

"Do you think they asked me whether you could join us?"

"But that's different! What? With me? But we get on all right, don't we?"

"Well, yes, maybe. I've got you part trained. But this one – I could tell at once – she's untrainable. She's going to be unbearable and stay unbearable. I'm making myself scarce."

"But... but... Misty, you're not really going away, I mean completely away?"

"Yep. This is it. They can't keep doing this to me. I've had it. I'm off."

"But... you're here now, aren't you?"

"Now? Well, of course. I haven't had my dinner yet."

"So... you're only going to disappear between meals, then?"

He looked at me like he couldn't expect me to understand.

"Naturally. What do you think? We've all got to eat. But I'm not hanging around with that ghastly little nuisance in there."

Funny thing is, I'm not sure he's right. I think maybe Toffee won't turn out to be unbearable. Which may not be a good thing.

See, a couple of times she's got me to come down off the sofa and chase around with her. She comes racing across the room towards me, those silly little paws making little clicky noises on the floor, and when I jump over her and head for the kitchen, she comes after me, and when I head back for the sofa, she comes racing back. And then when I jump off next to her, she leaps up and down and tries to lick my nose.

And you know what's odd? It's quite fun.

Wouldn't that be the worst thing of all? That ghastly little ball of fur moves in and starts pushing me around and eating my food. And I end up *liking* her.

Oh, no. That can't happen. It would be too awful for words.

Toffee making sure she gets her rest
By Senada Borcilo

Misty deals with the same arrival

Well, I told them. And when they didn't listen, I showed them. I hope they've learned their lesson.

The domestic staff have introduced a new dog – or rather, far worse, a new puppy – to the household. I made it clear to them how badly I felt about that last time, when they turned up with that little tyke Luci. I know I've got used to her and we basically get on OK now, but that's no excuse for going out and doing it all again. They can't be in any doubt what a dim view I take of that kind of behaviour.

The new thing's about the size of a medium rat but with less meat on it. Apparently, it goes by the name of 'Toffee'. I'd warned them how I'd feel about this kind of behaviour, so when they went blithely ahead anyway, I did what I'd told them. I vanished. I was gone. Vamoosed. Into the garden, over the fence and far away.

It's true that the little Luci saw things differently.

"But you're still coming back for your food, aren't you?"

Well, *of course* I was coming back for food. Eating's important, isn't it? I mean, what does she think? How naïve can she be?

Still, mustn't be too hard on her. She's young and doesn't get it. What I was doing by disappearing was taking a stand on *principle*. What I was doing by coming back for my food was taking appropriate action in *practice*. Principle is great but practice means you don't starve.

Or you can think of it like this. A principled stand makes you feel good about yourself, and boy do you need *that* when there's a new puppy in your life. But not eating can leave you strangely *thin*, which isn't a good feeling at all (at least, I don't reckon it can be, though I can't pretend I've ever really tried it). So bad that it would rather wipe out the good effect of taking a stand on principle in the first place.

Anyway, I'd made my point. And you do have to show tolerance towards the benighted. So, after a while I came back and hung around the house a bit, just to show them I didn't hold grudges, and could be magnanimous towards the afflicted. Of course, I got a bit afflicted myself, by that Toffee-thing – it kept running at me and trying to nip my ears or my legs, worse than Luci when she was small – not that Luci can ever have been *that* small, I reckon. Eventually I had to resort to stern measures that I'd rather hoped I was done with, after I'd finished training Luci. Things like hopping up on a dining chair under the tablecloth, and laughing at her, until she jumps feebly towards me and I catch her on the nose with a paw.

Still, she seems less sensitive to that kind of behaviour than Luci was. Like she's not that bothered about getting the occasional clout. She keeps coming back for more. Toughy-toffee, as domestic number 2 calls her. Still, if there are things a good cuff around the ear with velveted paw don't cure, there's always a gentle reminder administered with the very ends of my teeth. Delicate they are, my teeth but, if I say so myself, pleasingly sharp too.

I'm gratified to say that she seems to be a quick learner. The smallest of delicate bites produces a little squeal and then a welcome cessation of annoying attention. Welcome peace.

Trouble is, she learns quickly but forgets as fast. Cessations of annoyingness don't last long. In no time, I'm having to start all over again.

What I don't know is why it's always me that has to train these new arrivals. I did a good job with Luci, but you know how it is: a good job well done only leads to being given an even bigger job. The domestics seem to have abdicated responsibility with Toffee as they did with Luci. They're leaving things entirely to me. Which is all very well for them, but no joke for me. Toughy-Toffee's certainly going to be a challenge.

The worst thing with her is food. I've never seen anyone like her. Once she's got her head buried in a bowl of the stuff there's no getting it out anymore. I watched the domestics literally struggle to get a bowl away from her. She's like a silent version of one of those ghastly vacuum cleaners they use on the carpets, though with her it only works with food bowls. Hers, Luci's, anyone's she can get her nose into.

I'm just glad my food's up high, where I can reach it but the dogs can't. Long may that be the case.

Because if she ever got to it, I'd end up as hungry as if I'd disappeared in practice as well as in principle.

The things Toffee likes

Luci says she won't write my diary entries anymore. Spoilsport. She thinks she's *so* superior. But I'm getting my own back. I'm going to write my own.

So there. Nya. I may be a puppy but I'm mature now.

Things are working out pretty well here. There seems to be lots of food, which is my best thing. The humans say I'm like a magnet, whatever that is. It seems to mean that when I get my nose into a bowl they can't get it out any more. But why should they get it out? Once I've started eating, what would be the point in stopping?

There's another thing I don't really understand. The humans seem to get terribly upset when I carefully use the carpet as my toilet. I don't get it. I mean, they always go in afterwards and clean it up, so where's the problem? They leave it nice and clean-smelling, ready for my next time.

The best thing of all, though, is the cat. He's called Misty. He's HUGE! Lots of times bigger than me. But he's just *so* interesting. He keeps running away from me, but I chase him, I chase him. After all, he's a strange grey thing with an interesting smell – I've just *got* to get close to him to find out what he's all about. I like to curl up to him, which he seems OK with, but I have to admit that when I'm really close, I have to start chewing bits of him. His tail. His ears. His neck. It's stronger than me. Which is bad, because when I give in to things that are stronger than me, he sometimes does things that show he's a *lot* stronger.

I mean, I'm friendly. Warm-hearted. Affectionate. But he

doesn't see things that way. He has a go at me with his claws, and he's got *lots* of claws. Well, probably no more than I have, but it *feels* like lots. And they're sharp. Besides, when *he* bites *my* neck, it isn't affectionate at all, I can tell you. His mouth looks all delicate, but when it closes on you, boy do you know about it. I yelp and he stops but it still hurts.

I'm not giving up, though. I know some day he'll learn how loveable I am. So I keep going back and being loveable to him. Even if that does involve me using my teeth just the *tiniest* bit and him using his teeth back on me a lot more. *Some*day he'll see I'm fun to have around.

And then there's walks. They're fun. We go with Luci. Poor thing, she has to walk the whole way, but I get carried to the park and sometimes part of the way even in the park.

"What's the point of being carried?" she says. "If you're out for a walk, you ought to be walking."

Well, yes, sure. Maybe. But when you can sit nice and warm inside a jacket instead, why would you give that up?

Still, I don't tell her so. She's trying to put a brave face on her bad luck, and I don't want to rub it in or anything.

We chase each other around a bit in the park and that's a good game. It's just like when we're back at home in the sitting room, but bigger. And we don't get humans complaining about paw marks on the sofa and things like that.

There's lots of other people in the park, including some humans. It's exciting to follow them around. I like pretending I'm going off with them, because it's fun to see my humans running really, really fast to catch up and tell me not to.

We usually get food, too, after a walk, which makes it really special. They try to get me out in the garden afterwards, because when you've eaten, well, there are certain things you just have to do, aren't there? Still, if I'm quick enough, I can usually get to the carpet before they grab me.

Oh... oh... oh... I may have to stop writing... Oh, yes, I must go, I must go, I must go... It's the cat, it's the cat, it's the cat. I've got to run after him and try to chew his ears. It's *so* exciting.

Misty teaching Toffee discipline
By Senada Borcilo

Luci enjoying Christmas and Toffee.

The last few weeks have been just great.

Two of the young humans came to see us, and that always means we have a good time.

They're very good at playing with dogs. And it means there were four humans in the house. Oh, the laps to sit on, everywhere I looked! Our young puppy Toffee and I had a wonderful time. They call this season Christmas and a lot of humans make a fuss about it – not just my humans but others too – so I'm all in favour. Let's have lots of Christmas. It's good.

One thing that's happened, what with having Toffee around, is that I've learned to eat a lot faster. There was a time I could take my time over meals, have a bit now, leave it for a while, go back and have some more. The worst that could happen was that Misty tried to eat some of it, but a run at him with a few barks was generally enough to drive him off. And if that didn't, it would attract a human to rescue my food for me.

Doesn't work with Toffee. She thinks any food around is hers. And once she's started eating it, there's nothing anyone can do to stop her. Not Misty. Not me. Why, even the humans find it difficult. She's not much bigger than a bag of treats, but she has determination like other dogs have fleas. And nothing makes her more determined than food.

The trick is to eat fast. As soon as it's served, home in on it and suck it up quick. Eat it now, or it'll be gone. And when I say 'gone', I mean into Toffee. Leaving some of it for later? Forget it.

That's a thing of the past.

Still, I mustn't complain. It's not all bad having her around. It makes walks more interesting. It's good to have the company.

We do a lot of playing. She likes to chase me. That's fine. I'm happy to be chased when it's by something as small as that. Besides, there's no way she's going to catch me. When I take off, I leave her way behind, I can tell you. She doesn't stop – she keeps trying, I'll give her that – but she doesn't get close.

That's all fun. Besides, it spares me having anything to do with other dogs – those big, noisy, smelly ones in the park, full of strange scents and threatening motions. When Toffee and me chase each other, we can ignore them. Not that they bother her: she just runs up to them, jumping up and trying to lick their faces, saying "like me, like me, like me." Some of them seem to, though I must say I'd find that kind of thing infuriating if some strange dog did it to me.

Anyway, I just hang back a bit, well clear of any other dog, and wait for Toffee to finish. Then she can play with me again. Which gives me another chance to show her how much better I am at it than she is. As I streak away from her.

There's a bit of an argument between the humans about that.

"She's barely growing," says number 1, "she's going to be a teacup poodle."

"Nonsense," says number 2, "she's doing just fine. She's put on *hundreds* of grams since we've had her. I think she's developing a bit of an Eiffel Tower syndrome."

I don't know what an Eiffel Tower is, but apparently he thinks she's going to be enormous. Now number 1 knows more about dogs than number 2 – a *lot more* – but what if he's right? Is Toffee going to be bigger than me? Will she start catching me when she chases me in the park?

It doesn't bear thinking about. What *would* I do?

Toffee on when people go away

Something odd happened just recently. I can't work out why, or what it meant.

We were all just fine. That's Luci, my sidekick poodle, Misty, our mighty cat, our two humans, and me. That's – two humans. And then suddenly there was just one. Our number 2 just vanished. Gone. No sign of him.

No one said anything. It was like they didn't want to mention it. Weird. After a while, I even started to forget about him. After all, we still had the number 1 human and she's the one who understands about dogs and looks after us properly. But it was a bit sad not to see number 2 anymore, because he's, well, he's…

"He's a wimp."

That was Misty, who has this way of stalking me when I don't know he's there. He was reading my diary over my shoulder, which is pretty sneaky really, and he shouldn't do it.

"Try and stop me."

Well, of course I won't.

Anyway, "wimp" sounds a bit nasty. Our number 2 isn't bad. I'd say he's a softy, which may sound a bit pathetic, though it's pretty good for us. I mean, there's no one better for treats. He gives Luci and me treats for having our leads put on, and for having our leads taken off, for reaching the park, for setting out to go back home, sometimes just for being us. If we want an extra treat, we just give him our sad look. It always works.

"That," says Misty, "is what I meant by wimp."

Besides, he's the only human who lets us lick his face or bite his fingers. Got to be good to have a human that lets you do that, hasn't it? I was sorry he was gone. I was just thinking about that the other day, about how sorry I was.

And then suddenly he wasn't gone any more at all! He'd come back! It was great. Luci and me were jumping all over him and even Misty came out to say hello (he doesn't do much jumping at people, our Misty).

I decided it was silly not to talk about things, so this time I asked.

"What was all that about? He was gone and all that? And we didn't say anything about it?"

"Not mentioning the human in the room? Or the human not in the room?" said Misty with the tone of voice he uses when he's being what he calls witty, but I have no idea how that was supposed to be funny about that.

"Sometimes," he went on, "people go away. And don't come back. A long time before you were here, before Luci was even here…"

He seemed quite sad. I was trying to understand: Luci's always been here.

"Before Luci was here we had a nice dog in the house called Janka. She was fun. Not a noisy little runt like you. Or even Luci. She knew how to behave properly to a cat. But then she went away. She's never come back. That's why I don't talk about it when people go away. You don't know if they're coming home."

"So… what happened?"

"For a while there was just me and the domestics, and I thought that was terribly sad. Until Luci turned up and then you, when I realised I should have been happy when things were quiet. Be careful what you wish for, that's the lesson I learned."

"You mean you didn't wish for us?"

"If I'd known what it was going to be like, I surely wouldn't have."

"Oh, Misty, you don't mean that."

"Huh," he said, and stalked off. He's good at stalking, our Misty. Or, in this case, stalking off. Stalking off *and* stalking. But stalking off is for all of us and stalking's just for mice and birds. Or me when he's going to read my diary over my shoulder.

Still, he must have been happy to see number 2 back because he went and lay in the suitcase with all the human clothes in.

"That'll stop him leaving," he explained.

"That's good of Misty," I told Luci.

"Yeees," she said, in that tone of voice that doesn't really mean yes, "it's kind of him to think of keeping number 2 at home for us all. But I think he may have other reasons for doing it."

"Other reasons? What do you mean?"

"Well, he's always running the humans down, calling them domestics and everything, but he's a lot more attached to them than he makes out, and there's nothing he likes better than resting surrounded by their smells. That's why he likes to climb into their wardrobe."

It's true. I'd noticed he did that.

"So... the suitcase... it's like the wardrobe?"

"I think there's a bit of that.'

"But that's not what he says."

"You can't always trust what people say."

"What?" I asked, thinking I was being clever, "not even you? Not even now?"

"You'll have to make up your own mind about that."

Anyway. It's fun having number 2 back. He's taken us for a couple of walks and there were lots of treats. But there was one boring thing too: he made me put on a coat to go outside.

He calls me "Toughy-Toffee" which is right. So why does he think I need a coat? Luci doesn't wear one. He thinks I can't cope with a little cold? I'm tough. Cold means nothing to me.

He's a softy, but not soft enough, I think. Luci explained to me that the humans need training. I reckon, with him, it'll take plenty. He says he's going to a training class with me soon. I'll start knocking him into line there.

He may be nice, but he needs to learn what being Toughy-Toffee means. And I'm ready to teach him.

Luci finds Toffee weird.
Like Human number 2

I'm not sure I get that little dog Toffee. She's fun to play with and all that, but she's *weird*. She has all these strange habits I just can't get my head around.

Like she never stops eating. And she'll eat anything. I mean, even bits of wood or the buttons off coats. Or at least, even if she doesn't eat them, she gives them a thorough chewing.

But then really good things she just doesn't like. Popcorn, say.

Human number 2 has this thing about being fair. So he always gives a bit to me, a bit to her. She jumps up and down to make sure she gets her bit. Terribly enthusiastic. "Gimme, gimme, gimme," she seems to be saying. But then she just sort of rolls her piece around her mouth and quietly drops it out on the ground.

Fortunately, human number 2 has another thing, about "waste not, want not". So he picks up the bits that Toffee drops and gives them to me. They're still perfectly good popcorn bits, after all, so why wouldn't I be happy with that?

This means I get twice as much as I was going to. I just don't understand why she has to pretend she likes the stuff when she obviously doesn't. Or why he feels the need to try to give it to her before passing it to me. After all, in the end it's always me that eats the stuff. Why not cut out the middle-Toffee?

It was the same with the best thing to eat of all. Banana. It's just so awesome. It doesn't matter where I am or what I'm doing, if I hear a banana being peeled, I'm there like a shot. I don't even need to think about it. It's like something driving me from inside.

But Toffee does the same trick as with the popcorn. Wants her share and then spits it out. What a waste. Or it would be if I didn't get it in the end. Which, again, means I get a double share. Joy!

Or, rather, scratch that, that's how it used to be. Until just today, just now. She's been gobbling all the banana human number 1 has been giving her. And not spitting any of it out anymore. I know it means I'm still getting my share, but since I thought I'd get hers too, it feels like I'm getting only half a share.

Why does she do that? Change her mind like that, I mean. I liked the way she felt about banana before, for Kibble's sake.

She changes her mind quite a lot, actually. Take being gutsy, for instance. She used to be scared of nothing. She'd go up to strange humans and say hello to them. To strange dogs too. Hey, big dogs even. It used to terrify me, though it made me feel a bit guilty. It made me feel I had to go up to a few humans myself, even if I only knew them a bit. Not the ones I didn't know at all, of course. Wouldn't catch me going up to them. But maybe humans I'm barely familiar with. Maybe. If I'm feeling brave.

As for big dogs, not a chance. You've got to be joking. Get close to them? I always stay far enough away to make sure I have a good start if I need to make a dash for it.

Toffee didn't care though. She'd try to make friends with anybody. Which made me feel just a tad guilty because I wasn't looking after her. I mean, I'm bigger than her and everything. I think the humans expect me to protect her. But – with complete stranger humans? Or big dogs? *Really*? Would I have to do that too?

Well, it's obvious, isn't it? I'm a right-sized dog. With a proper sense of caution. There's no way I could protect Toffee against those giants. But I don't feel entirely comfortable about hanging back while she's wandering right up to a set of huge fangs.

But then suddenly, just a couple of weeks ago, Toffee suddenly went right over to the other extreme. Got completely terrified. Well, I understood it a bit. She got playing with a couple of big dogs and they jumped all over her. Of course. That's what big dogs do. Big, clumsy oafs. She got trampled.

Served her right, really. Taught her a lesson, I reckoned. But it did more than that. She got nervous about everything. A dog barks anywhere near the park (not even in the park) and she high-tails it for home. She terrified human number 2 once: Toffee went running up the road towards home and nearly got squished by a car.

Anything sets her off. A noisy car. A man dropping a plank. A flock of birds taking off (well, that scares me too, but she's much worse than me). She gets her ears back, head down, and makes a break for somewhere she thinks is safer.

And now I feel guilty again. Because I suppose I really ought to stick with her when she clears off. Keep her company. Look after her. But... that would mean leaving my humans... and that's just as bad as walking up to a big dog.

Anyway, the humans have gone back to keeping her on a lead when they walk us. Which is quite funny. Because she hasn't worked out that, if you're on a lead, you've got to walk the same side of a lamp post as the human. It's so hilarious when they end up on opposite sides.

One time it happened with human number 2 and a big tree. He went one side, Toffee went the other. The human started chasing after her, following the lead, and calling her. So of course she went chasing him, the other way. Both of them kept running around the tree, always on the opposite side of each other, with the lead between them.

"Stay, Toffee, stay," he kept calling.

"I'm coming, I'm coming," Toffee yipped back.

I just sat and watched. It was "enthralling", as Misty would say. But I kept quiet and didn't laugh, because "you mustn't mock the afflicted", like he also says, though he's always mocking everyone.

In any case, who are these afflicted he's talking about?

Perhaps it's human number 2. He does seem to be afflicted by Toffee. And just being Toffee is what afflicts her.

Toffee fitting into the family
By Senada Borcilo

Misty and bed privileges

Oh, we had such a storm in a teacup here the other day.

The little dog was in a state. That's the funny ginger one we're calling "Toffee" though there's nothing sweet about her when she catches your tail, let me tell you.

"They're taking my home away!" she was moaning, "where am I supposed to sleep tonight?"

The domestics were taking her pen apart. It was where she'd slept ever since she turned up and became such a pain in the backquarters for us all.

Sorry. Luci tells me I shouldn't talk that way about her. I'll rephrase. Ever since she turned up and added her special brand of charm and spice to our lives.

That means the same thing, by the way.

Anyway, she seemed worried when the domestics took her pen away. Though nothing like as worried as I felt she ought to be.

I decided to reassure her. "Who knows. Maybe they've worked out what a great idea it would be to send you somewhere else. Now that they've noticed what a nuisance you are. It took them long enough, after all."

She gave me a look she probably thought was withering, but with those puppy dog eyes, she just can't do it.

"Don't be silly. They wouldn't do that," she said, but she didn't sound sure. So Luci decided to get her pennyworth in.

"Now, don't be silly, Misty. You ought to be ashamed of yourself, trying to worry her, poor thing. Of course, they'd never do that. Don't worry, Toffee, you know how fond they are of you. After all, they even let you drive me off their laps. I'm sure they've got plans for you."

"Just what I was saying," I reassured Toffee, "they've got plans for you."

It was great to see how much consternation I could create with just a few words. Well-chosen words, I like to think.

"Good plans," said Luci, and she *can* do a withering look.

Of course, I knew what their plans were. There was a time, back in the dim and distant past, so remote I can barely remember it, when things were properly ordered in our family. The dog of the time, Janka, used to sleep on the floor in the bedroom, and I slept on the bed. Well, the domestics did kick me out occasionally. I *do* like to sleep *on* things, and legs are great if you can't get bellies. But the domestics would sometimes get shirty about my sleeping on them and boot me out.

Otherwise, I slept on the bed even if I wasn't actually on top of them, and a very fine place it was too, for a cat who knows what's due to him.

But then Luci showed up. She took my place! Imagine. A smelly, snivelling dog got my place of honour on the bed.

I could see what was going to happen with Toffee. They were taking her pen apart so she could join them on the bed too. Making it even less likely I'd get my rightful place back any time soon.

I'd been usurped. And now I was going to be doubly usurped.

And that's *exactly* what's happened. The ghastly little orange thing has joined Luci in depriving me of my spot on top of the duvet.

I still had to laugh, though. That little Luci has competition now. And Toffee, she's a tough competitor. It'll be interesting to see who gets the best position in the bed, up near the domestics' heads, once things have settled down a bit.

Meanwhile, at least downstairs life is peaceful these days. No Toffee jumping up and down in her pen at the crack of dawn, clamouring to be let out. Now she can just jump up and down on the domestics and show them how wrong they were to chuck me out in favour of dogs. Kicking a cat out to let dogs in! What *were* they thinking of?

The first morning after she got to sleep with the domestics, she was dancing all over the place.

"See? See? See?" she kept bubbling, "they had me on the bed with them! They want me on the bed with them! I'm the special dog!"

"You are?" asked Luci.

"We both are! We both are! Me and Luci. We're the special dogs."

"There aren't any other dogs," I gently reminded her.

"That's right! That's right! I told you we were special. And I'm specially special."

When she'd calmed down a bit she came over to make a point.

"See?" she said, "they didn't send me away."

"No," I agreed. "I never thought they would, more's the pity. But all I said was that they had plans for you, didn't I? And they did, didn't they?"

I've never seen her at a loss for words before. It was fun to walk away while she was trying to work out an answer.

And failing.

Luci, victim of injustice

They locked me up! In the bedroom! On my own!

Me! The good one! The well-behaved one!

Even my humans admit it. I do what I'm told. I come when I'm called, even if there's a bit of mouldy bread to eat in the park. I stop eating Toffee's food when they tell me too, even if there's some left. I don't persecute Misty, even though he's a cat.

But today they put me in the bedroom and closed the door. And went downstairs. To chat with their friends. And Toffee was with them. They left me there even though I was whining for all I was worth, with a few barks thrown in for good measure.

It was all because their friends had brought their puppy-human with them. He's terribly, terribly small. Well, for a human that is. Ruddy great hulking thing he is, compared to proper-sized creatures like us. But he's always going after Toffee, trying to play with her. They say he likes her, but I have to say he has a very odd way of showing it. He squeals and waves his hands around.

Now I don't mind squealing. Not as such. Not in itself. We squeal a good bit too, Toffee and me. But when we do it, I know what it means. Mostly it's when we're playing. Sometimes it's when we're hurt. Specially if it's me, squealing. If it's me, it means I'm *badly* hurt, because I'm a brave dog and only squeal when it's serious. It's only nastiness that makes human number 2 says "oh, there's nothing the matter with her, you know what she's like, squealing at nothing."

What does *he* know about how badly I hurt?

Anyway, that little human keeps squealing and I don't know what it means. So when he goes rushing over at Toffee with his arms flailing like some offensive weapon and *squealing*, well, I get worried. So I get between them. And *of course* I growl.

I mean, who wouldn't?

But human number 1 didn't like that. She grabbed me and pulled me off the couch.

"She was going to bite him!" she said.

Bite him? I didn't bite him. I never touched him. I just growled a bit.

"Yes," Misty told me later, "but you were going to bite him, weren't you?"

"Well, not exactly *bite*. Nip a little maybe. Just a warning."

"What, sort of, 'keep away from Toffee, she's mine and I'm the only one allowed to beat her up'? That sort of thing?"

"Oh, you make it sound so nasty. It isn't like that. I just get worried when people get noisy and wavy with their arms. They feel dangerous to me. And I don't like dangerous. And as for Toffee, I never hurt her. Or only a little bit."

Misty shook his head.

"They don't like it, the domestics. You're not supposed to hurt their puppies. They get very upset if you do."

He didn't actually say "puppies", he said "kittens", but you know how it is with cats, they get confused with their words and sometimes you have to help out by translating. So normal people can understand what they mean.

"But how could she have known I was going to nip him, anyway? I mean, I didn't, did I?"

"Oh, she knows. She knows. That number 1, she knows everything. She knows what we're planning to do before we've made the plan to do it."

Thinking about it, he may well be right. Maybe she was a jump ahead of me. She's really smart that way. Perhaps I might have been just a teensy bit aggressive towards the little human if she'd let me. And if he'd continued.

Still, shutting me in the bedroom, alone. For something I never actually got around to doing, and probably wouldn't have. I reckon. That's just going far too far.

So unfair.

Toffee and her house

The humans went away! Both of them. For ages and ages. It got light and dark again lots of times while they were gone. More than my number of paws, and I've got lots of paws.

Not that it was all bad. When they went away, we got the one Luci calls human number 3 staying with us instead. She's brilliant. She has all these things that she likes to do stuff with. And which I can do stuff with too. Pencils – beautifully crunchy. Bits of knitting – beautifully chewy. Even purses – beautifully portable.

Playing with them is fun. So I take them to my little house where I can keep them safe and come back to play with them a bit more later.

"That's not your house," says Misty, "it's mine. You've just nicked it from me."

Nicked it? It's obviously mine. It's a nice house. Made of something all squashy, so if I jump on it from outside, it squishes down, but then jumps up again when I go. Which is quite fun. Inside, it has a nice furry floor I can scratch as much as I like, and plenty of space for me to lie down when I've finished scratching. Everything about it says it was obviously made for me. I don't know *what* Misty means by saying it's his. I mean, it even *smells* of me.

"Well, of course it does, with all the time you spend in it. But before you started making it smell of you, it really, really didn't. It was mine and smelled good. Properly feline. Clean."

Oh, well. He's a bit like that, sometimes, Misty. A bit sore about things. But I don't care because it doesn't make any difference to the house. It's still mine.

Once things are in my house, no one can see them. But I don't know what it is about human number 3, because she finds them each time anyway. Maybe she can smell them, which is odd, because generally humans don't seem to have any sense of smell at all. Or barely any.

Actually, she wasn't that good the first time she went looking for something. That was the time of the missing purse.

It was all a bit odd. First, she did all the things she does when she's going out. Putting on a coat. Fetching a bag. Looking for one of those portable roof things they use when it's raining, instead of just growing proper hair. But then she started saying odd things.

"Oh, no, Where did I put it? What's happened to the darned thing? I can't have lost it."

That kind of thing.

At one point, she went and stood by the couch. Then she bent down and felt around it a while, even behind the cushions and down the cracks. As she kept looking, I could feel all these waves of disappointment coming from her. And then something else, something more like anxiety.

So I went over and stood by her. She seemed to need a bit of comfort, and I know I'm good at that. I wagged my tail and tried to look helpful.

"Oh, hello, Toffee," she said, bending down to pat me absent-mindedly. "Do *you* know where I left my purse? I thought it was on the couch, but I can't see it."

I wagged my tail because *of course* I knew that she'd left it on the couch. That's where it was when I found it. Just before I took it to my little house. Not that she looked there. Instead, she wandered over to the dining table.

"No, not here. Did I leave it in the kitchen?"

It wasn't there any more than it was in the bathroom, on either of the mantelpieces, on the bookshelves, or anywhere upstairs either. In fact, it wasn't anywhere that wasn't my house, but she didn't look there, even though she looked in all the other places.

I was trailing around after her to see if I could help at all, and in the hope that she'd hand out some more stroking, but all I got was an occasional tap on the head and some running commentary.

"Oh, dear, what have I done? Where on earth could I have left it? Sometimes I can be so absent-minded."

I'd say. Sometimes she just gives me a tap behind the ears. She calls that stroking? Distracted hardly covers it.

Luci had joined us by then and was following us looking as bemused as the human.

"What's she doing?" Luci asked.

"Looking for her purse. She thinks she left in on the couch and when she went back, it wasn't there anymore."

"Ah," said Luci, giving me an odd look, "but it was once, wasn't it?"

The way she said that made me feel a tad uneasy. I mean, I've been in trouble before, and the way Luci sounded made me feel I might be again. Still, it wasn't worth trying to deny it.

"Yes," I said in a small voice.

"And has she looked in your little house yet?"

"No," I said in an even smaller voice.

"Oh, I don't know," said the human, "I don't understand it. Where can my purse be?"

She turned towards me, a bit distraught.

"Do you know, Toffee? Do you know where my purse is?"

And then she went all quiet for a bit, giving me one of those serious looks that last too long. I could see how an idea was beginning to form in her mind.

"Perhaps you *do* know," she said eventually and shot downstairs to look in my house.

She stood up holding the purse and sounding strained.

"Oh, Toffee. You can be *so* naughty sometimes."

"So bloody silly, if you ask me," said Luci. "I mean, human number 3's nice to us. Why would you do that to her?"

"Silly?" I said, "it seems a good place to keep things if you want to play with them later. Sensible, actually, not silly at all. It seems the obvious place for her purse. I don't know why she didn't look there straight away."

Ah, well. It would have been fun playing with that purse a bit more. But I mustn't begrudge human number 3 her little pleasures, and she did seem happy to find the purse.

Oddly, it's since that time that she seems to have shown a much keener sense of smell. Like I said before. Now she keeps finding things I've put for safe keeping in the house. She just goes straight there and finds them at once. Like she had some kind of sense telling her to look there. It's a bit irritating, to tell the truth. Still, like Luci says, she *is* very nice to us, so I try not to get too annoyed.

We had a good time with her while she was here. And now the other humans are back from wherever they went, so life's all good and normal again.

"Yes," says Luci, "and you're as silly and naughty as ever."

Well, I don't mind if Luci says I'm silly and naughty. She can't really believe it. After all, she's my *friend.*

She wouldn't be my friend if she really thought I was that bad. Would she?

Misty on a champion in the weirdity stakes

Right. That's it. Official.

The new little dog – well, she's not that new after six months, but you know what I mean – is absolutely the weirdest thing the humans have inflicted on me.

So far, I hasten to add. I don't want to tempt providence by ruling anything out in the future. I'm not sure there's any weirdity that's beyond my pair of domestics. You won't catch me saying, "they'll never introduce that into our household" because they'd probably go out and get one the next day.

"A poisonous snake?" they'd say, "wonderful! I bet Misty would like one of those."

Anyway, that puppy Toffee – I suppose she is still a puppy, judging by her behaviour, whatever her age in months – really is bizarre.

Every morning the domestics give her and Luci the best kibble I know. A bowl for Luci in the kitchen where she does the sensible thing, and just gobbles it down.

"I don't gobble," says Luci, "I'm ladylike."

OK. There's some kibble in her bowl one moment. There's none the next. Somehow it's got from the bowl into her stomach (I assume ladies have stomachs, though they probably don't like to admit it). Is the process that gets the kibble from one place to another something one can call gobbling? I wouldn't like to say in the presence of one with pretensions to being ladylike. Let's just say that it's fast. And effective.

What about Toffee?

Well, she used to be just as impressive as Luci. A real canine vacuum cleaner. Once she had her nose in a food bowl, there was no way to get it back out until the bowl was empty.

But she's gone all strange just recently.

She gets the domestics to put her bowl on a little rug she likes, so she can think about it. Breakfast in bed. And, just for the record, like the little house she's taken over, that particular rug used to be mine before she muscled in on it.

Thinking about the kibble is exactly what she does next. She sniffs at it from one side. Walks around behind the rug to sniff at it from the other side. Climbs back on the rug and pushes the bits of kibble around with her nose a while.

It's maddening. I'd like nothing better than to get at it myself. It's so much nicer than what my inadequate domestics give me.

"It isn't any nicer, you know," domestic number 2 tries to tell me, "it's just because it's somebody else's that you want it. I know you better than you do."

He knows me better than I do? I don't think so. I think I'll be the judge of what kind of kibble I like or don't like. He's never even tasted any of the stuff – far too high and mighty to enjoy the food he gives us – so how can he possibly tell?

What amazes me with Toffee's way of nosing around her food for ages and *ages* is that there are other things she just goes for straight away. Toys, for instance. She gnaws and pulls at them until they fall apart. Domestic number 1 has even bought a new mechanical device, a kind of manual vacuum cleaner she pushes around, to pick up the little bits of toy from the carpet where Toffee leaves them. The dog we used to have here, Janka, the one who went away and never came back, used to rip up toys too but she was a proper size and at least the toy would be dismembered in no time. This one takes forever, like she wants to make their suffering last.

And bits of wood! Toffee just loves them. Brings them in

from the garden. If she sees the domestics around she hurries into her little house – what used to be *my* little house – and gnaws and gnaws and gnaws. If she can get away with it, she jumps up on the couch and gnaws and gnaws and gnaws. Then she gets bits everywhere and domestic number 1 has to get into action with the funny little push-around-thing to pick up the bits.

"Oh, Toffee, what have you done?" she says.

I hope the question's rhetorical. Because it's bleeding obvious what she's done: exactly the same thing as she did yesterday.

"Oh, you really are the naughtiest dog we've ever had," she goes on, which is about right, except that in my opinion the word "weird" needs to appear in there somewhere along with "naughty". What on earth is the point of gnawing wood? Especially with such enthusiasm? Especially when all you do with really good kibble is push it around with your nose for ages and ages?

The worst of it is that Toffee sometimes stops nosing the kibble around and walks away. So of course I move in. After all, the bowl needs to be emptied. If she's not going to do it, I'm more than happy to help out. But the moment I start on the job, in my helpful way, she comes rushing back to push me away. It's as though she just can't bear the idea of my eating her kibble even if she isn't. So she barks at me and pushes me away with her nose. Which, for reasons I can't explain even to myself, I somehow can't prevent. So generally she gets her bowl back. And if she doesn't, domestic number 2 will have a go instead.

Still, sometimes they both get distracted. I'm a pretty determined plunderer of unguarded riches so sometimes, just sometimes, I get away with grabbing her food when she's decided not to absorb it herself. And number 2 isn't around. Oh, the satisfaction. The delight. The sheer joy of emptying Toffee's bowl unobserved.

Doesn't happen often but, boy, is it good when it does.

Anyway, she's weird, that Toffee. I try to keep her a bit sane by beating her up from time to time. But nothing seems to work, not even that.

I live among strange creatures. I thought the domestics were bad enough. And then there was Luci to take things to a whole new level.

But now we have Toffee. A true champion of weirdity.

Luci on seasons and years

Wow! It's getting nice and cold again.

I've noticed this is something that keeps happening. It gets horribly hot so that even stepping out of doors for a walk gets you panting. But then it starts cooling off bit by bit, until it's a proper temperature again. Which is the best way for things to be.

Odd, though. Because then it starts getting hotter again. Why does it do that when it's just *obvious* things are better cold? What *is* the point?

"It's the seasons," says Misty. "First it gets warmer. Then it gets properly warm so it's fun just to lie on the woodshed roof. But then it cools off until you get to the winter when it's only nice to lie by a radiator."

"And those are the seasons, are they?"

"Yes. Warming – hot – cooling – cold. Four of them. In a year."

He's never explained what a year is. I really need it made a bit clearer.

"You're three years old now," he went on, with a sigh. "With three of them to look back on you really ought to understand what a year is."

Well, maybe I *am* beginning to understand. A bit. How these things seem to go round and round, again and again. But I didn't want to admit that so I asked a different thing. A much more *important* thing.

"What's the point?"

"What's the point of what?"

"Well, things going round and round and turning into years."

"Who said it had to have a point?"

"Well – it would be *pointless* otherwise."

"I tell you what pointless is: talking to you."

He often says things like that. But he always comes back to talk to me again, so I don't mind. It's just his way.

Anyway, I'm obviously starting to get the hang of this "year" thing Misty keeps talking about. Cold then warmer then uncomfortable then cooler then properly cold again. I get it. It may be pointless but at least you can make sense of the system. Except I could do without the hot bit.

When it gets nice and cold like this it's fun to go out and race about a bit. Toffee always wants to play, and that's not too bad when it isn't unbearably hot.

Though there is a problem playing with her these days. Another one of those year things, I think. She's got quick. Before she could never come anywhere near catching me, but now she can. Still, I can catch her too when it's my turn to do the chasing. I'm pretty quick too. It's just a bit worrying that we're both quick now, when before I was always way out in front of her.

Trouble is some of the chasing happens in the dark. That's part of the year business too, Misty tells me. When it gets cold enough for the walk to be just right, it also gets dark. Well, if the humans don't get their act together quickly enough. Number 2's the worst. The way he hangs around for ages and *ages* just banging away on his keyboard thingy. While it gets darker and darker outside.

I'm not so keen on dark walks. I can still smell things, of course I can, but it's nice to see things too, especially when it's another dog. Well, not nice to see another dog, but better to see it than have it sneak up on you. And there's other things too. Things I don't know. I reckon it's safer with things that smell like I don't know them, and which don't seem likely to be good to eat, if I can see them too.

So though it's good weather for Toffee-chasing because it's cold, it's bad weather to get too far from the family, because it's *night time.* You never know what might come out of the dark. Smell it and it's on you before you can see it and suss it out. And it might be big.

Not nice.

Luci on enjoying a smaller dog

Funny creature, the little one.

That's Toffee, I mean. Who *is* quite small. In size, that is. And even smaller in behaviour. Like a puppy. Though I don't think she can really be one anymore. Not seeing how long she's been here. I mean, it's pretty much as long as I can remember. In fact, I can only just remember a time when she wasn't here.

Anyway, once you've been around that long, you can't pretend to be a puppy still. Can you? Well, I suppose you *can* pretend, but it fools no one. Not me at least. Though I have to say the humans do seem to fall for the act a bit.

"Oh, look what the little one's doing," they say from time to time, all soft and dreamy like, as though she was doing something really endearing, when really she's just tearing one of my toys to pieces. Or eating my food. Or pinching my place on a rug. Or some such.

Now me, I've put all that puppy-dog stuff behind me. Long since. But then I'm already three. The humans have come to think a bit better of me these days. I don't go tearing around all over the place like I used to. Or like Toffee still does.

Not that I don't miss it. Just a bit. It was fun. Human number 2's always good at throwing things for a dog. You know, a ball or a soft toy or whatever. But human number 1 always likes to sit at the end of the sofa, near the end of the room, you know, where the sitting room blends into the dining room. When he throws the ball or toy or whatever it goes into the dining room.

Which means that I have to go past her to fetch it.

Not a problem, of course. I could just jump over her. Or even bounce off her, because when you're a right-sized dog like me (not like one of those giants we keep seeing in the park), you need places to bounce off in the middle of a really big leap.

The thing about number 1 is that she has a really nice, comfortable front to land on and take off from again. So in the days when I did that kind of thing, I'd land on her before jumping to the floor and skittering and skidding over to the toy, or ball, or whatever number 2 had thrown.

She didn't always appreciate that. She'd make a kind of "oof" noise as I landed, and then, once I'd done it a few times, she'd say to number 2, "oh, I think that's enough now. You don't need to throw that for her anymore. Do you?"

Well, if she'd been asking me, I'd have wanted to say, "of course he needs to keep throwing it". But when number 1 says something in that tone of voice, it's better not to answer the question, but just obey the tone.

"Of course, of course," says number 2 and he stops throwing the toy, pretending to concentrate on the telly instead.

Well, these days it's Toffee that does the jumping. The "oof" is a little less intense because Toffee is, after all, so much littler than I am. As for me, as becomes a three-year old, I just sit on the back of the couch and watch. With a small trace of envy, I admit. Oh, for the carefree times, before Toffee showed up, when that kind of behaviour didn't seem unbecoming and I could indulge in it myself.

Still, I think I've found a solution. Now it's Toffee that bounces on human number 1 and goes sliding over the slippery floor, her claws scrabbling away, to grab the toy (she particularly favours a little stuffed lion whose nose she's chewed off). All I do is watch and wait. And when she's getting close to the sofa, toy in mouth, panting and expectant, thinking only about how she's going to drop it in front of number 2 and beg him to throw it again, I go into action. Off the sofa I come and dart across the floor like a flash, on an intervention course. And Toffee fails to spot her impending doom every time. Seconds it takes me, sometime barely a second, to grab the toy from her nerveless jaws. Then I jump back up on the sofa and refuse to hand the toy over to number 2 to throw again.

And I growl. How I growl. Toffee knows I don't mean it but there's just a little bit of her that isn't quite sure. So she stays down on the floor looking a bit piteous, and yapping uncertainly from time to time.

"Grr, grr, grr," I growl at her, with the toy firmly gripped in my mouth, and she lunges briefly forward before backing away again nervously. It's as enjoyable as chasing the toy used to be when I was a puppy.

Eventually, human number 2 takes pity on her and takes the toy off me so he can throw it again. But I don't mind. Because it's just a chance to start all over again.

Clever, isn't it? I can get as much fun as ever, but without making anything like the effort. And without looking like a silly puppy anymore. Brilliant.

Having a smaller dog around can be useful. Sometimes.

Toffee on trains and puppy-making

Trains. Terrible things. Do you know them? I didn't. But I found out a week ago.

They go chunka-chunka-chunka for *ages* and *ages*. And sometimes woosh-woosh-woosh. Worst of all, when another one goes by, they go woosh-woosh-roar-roar-roar-clackety-clackety-clack.

It's horrible. *Especially* because it goes on and on and on.

Still, it was wonderful when we got to the end. That was in somewhere called Scotland. There's lots of great places. A river we can wander along. A field with lots of other dogs that Luci runs away from and I play with. And there was even a sea thing which was fun.

"Yes," says Luci, "where I went in and *you* ran away."

Not really. I didn't run away. I went in too. But I only went in just a bit. Paws, you know. That was far enough. The rest of the water just kept *moving*. I don't know why water has to do that. It's so much nicer when it sits still.

Luci may have liked it but I thought it made more sense to stay near the sand. Sand! That's great stuff. You can dig in it, you can run across it and when you get indoors, you can get it everywhere.

What's more, there were some really nice humans in Scotland. There was a woman who was like our human number 1, but she was even better at picking me up. Rocking me, you know, and stroking me and telling me how nice I was.

"She doesn't know you like our number 1 does," says Luci.

And a man too, who's terribly big. Bigger than human number 2. Amazing. And the third one's a puppy. I knew that because she was, well, puppy-like. She was taller than my humans and almost as big as the man, but still a puppy's a puppy, big or small, and you just *know* when you see one.

The human puppy knows how to keep dogs happy
By Senada Borcilo

Talking about puppies, something really odd happened to me this week. The humans told me I wasn't one anymore. Not a puppy. No idea why.

"She's in season," the humans kept saying.

In season? What on earth did that mean?

"It's summer," said Luci, "that's the season. Not that you'd know it with the rain. And it won't be summer for long, anyway. Trust me, I know. I've seen seasons come and go."

Seasons come and go? So what does *that* mean? That I'll stop being an adult and be a puppy all over again? I think I'd like that.

"Don't be silly," says Misty, "it's about when you can make puppies or not."

That was the worst of it. It made no sense. Making puppies? I like being one but I've no idea how to make one. I don't make things, except sometimes a bit of a mess or a lot of noise, but I know how to make *those* things. How can anyone make something when they don't know how?

Oh, why don't they just let me go on as a puppy myself instead of trying to turn me into some kind of puppy-making adult?

"The humans will sort it all out," says Luci.

It's all very well for her to say that. Misty says they've made sure Luci can't make puppies, and I don't know how they did that, any more than I know why they think I can but I think I can't.

"You'll find out," says Luci.

Oh, well. It was fun in Scotland anyway. But then we were off again. Chunka-chunka-chunka. Woosh-woosh-woosh. But it didn't feel so bad this time. Maybe I'm getting more used to it. And, after all, putting up with it worked out pretty well last time. Scotland was good.

Even if it was a bit of a pain getting there.

Luci finds walks a fitbit tiring

Humans can be *really* strange.

Mine have both started getting really weird about exercise every day. How many steps they've taken. How fast they've taken them.

It's unbelievably tiring.

I mean, apart from anything else, there's all that *counting*. You take a step and that's one. Then another and that's two. One more and that's three. It could go on and on. I just get confused. After four, I run out of paws anyway, and can't cope. As far as I'm concerned, beyond four you've just got "lots". Like "lots of kibble in my bowl". I don't see how you tell the difference between "quite a lot" and "a huge lot". I don't see why you'd bother, just as long as you've got a big enough bowl. And it's full.

Human number 1, who's really quite sensible, isn't being too silly about all this step business. But human number 2, much though I like him, can be just a bit dotty at times. In the old days, he was the one who preferred walking slowly. With him, we always got nice quiet strolls, with plenty of time to go and smell good things, or at least interesting things, and in Toffee's case, roll in them. We'd still be able to catch up with him afterwards. He'd never get that far ahead, wandering along as he did, lost in his own world where he couldn't see what we were doing (or rolling in).

With number 1, it was different. She always seemed

determined to get where she was going, even if it was only back to the start of the walk where she'd left the car. It was tough, determined walking. But still, the pace wasn't killing. And we could have fun on the way. It's just that with her, we never quite forgot that walks were for *exercise*, not just for enjoyment. I liked walks with her – after all, she behaved like she remembered we were with her – but they were still just a tad grimmer, a smidgeon tougher than with number 2.

Now he's got this thing he wears on his wrist to count his steps and tell him how fast he's going. He calls it his *fitbit*. And it's horrible. Since he's been wearing it, all that step counting has started, and he's been completely different. Suddenly walks have become a kind of race. We tear around the places where we would normally stop and sniff. There's no time to explore anywhere we're going past. In the mad rush to get to the end of the walk, we have no chance to enjoy what we're actually doing. And the end, when we finally get there, it still turns out to be the same place as the beginning, where he left the car. Just like with number 1.

So what was the rush for?

I wouldn't mind if we were racing *against* someone. You know, to get away from some mutt of a great dog that's decided that what he really, really needs is to get to know us better. From close up. But this is a race against *no one*. It's just a stupid drive to get 15,000 steps or something (what is 15,000? Lots and lots and lots?)

All very well for *him*. He only has two legs. We have four. *And* they're much shorter. If he takes lots of steps, we take lots and lots and lots and lots.

It's got so bad that number 1 finally noticed.

"What's the matter with the dogs?" she asked after she took us out for the last walk one day.

"What do you mean?" he said, but I could smell that he had an uneasy conscience.

"They were exhausted. Toffee just lay down on the grass. And Luci tried to go back to the car."

"Oh. I was walking a bit faster than usual."

"And a bit longer, perhaps?"

"Well, a *bit*. Maybe."

"A bit? Or a fitbit?"

A new word for me, that. Fitbit. And I can confirm, it's all been a fitbit too much. I hope he quietens down soon.

Misty and the wrecking of his home

What on earth has got into the heads of the domestic staff?

They've gone away. Again. And they've haven't just gone away this time, they've *got people in to wreck my house.*

What weird perverse logic can have got into their minds?

We used to live in an excellent house. It had a couch that we all liked. That's all of us: not just me but the domestics and the capering canines too. The domestics would sit on it first, then the dogs would jump around on it with them. Then, once a space had been made for me among the dogs, I'd settle on a domestic's lap. Usually, number 1 because number 2's so fidgety – there's no way of getting him to settle down and make a proper lap of his knees, so a tired cat can have the rest he deserves.

Anyway, by the end of the process, we'd all be comfortable.

That struck me as a great arrangement. Which is why I just can't believe why they've disrupted it. The couch has simply *gone*. You might think I could lie on the floor but you'd have to think again. The *floor* has gone. Well, most of it. There's just dusty *hard* concrete now. Even the bath, where I liked to go to get a drink from the tap, has gone. *Gone*. Nothing there at all.

No wonder the family's left. Why would anyone want to stay in this place? Would you? No? Well, nor would I.

But they've *left me behind*. They've even put a bed for me in the shed. The shed! Can you imagine? My bowls are in there too. Both my board *and* my lodging. In the garden shed.

The *indignity* of it.

It's enough to make me despair. Or, more to the point, to want to exact the harshest revenge at the earliest opportunity. Which takes me to the worst bit of the whole ghastly business.

The domestics come over every day. The ideal opportunity, you might think, for me to avenge the awful assault on my pride as a representative of catkind, the summit of creation. For this unforgivable desertion. And yet, somehow, when they show up revenge seems to be beyond me. When they get to what's left of the house, with or without the painful poodles, instead of greeting them with fangs and claws, ready to inflict on them an injury as severe as their cruel mistreatment of me, I go trotting over mewing miserably. Like I'm pathetically pleased to see them again.

Which I am. Damn it.

"Oh, isn't he vocal?" says domestic number 1.

Really? She noticed? I'm mewing at the top of my voice and she spots that I'm vocal? Wow. So observant, right? You can't hide anything from her.

Besides, why wouldn't I be vocal? They've walked off and left me to my own devices. OK, OK, they top up my bowls, with wet and dry food and water, so I'm not just dependent on my own devices. But, hey, that barely mitigates the original offence. The abandonment. The disloyalty. Treason, actually – that's not too harsh a term for walking off and leaving me behind. Punishment is what they deserve. What I should be inflicting on them. Ruthlessly.

Instead, when they get here, I rub up against them. Getting them to stroke me. If they've brought the tiresome toy poodles, I even rub myself up against those pests. Including the noisy one, Toffee, though she pushes me to one side to run past me to get to the shed – *my* shed – to eat the food – *my* food. She's still living with the domestics, she tells me, in some other place, and probably being positively *drowned* in food, unlike me, forced to fawn on them and beg just to get my daily dose. And still she wants to steal mine.

But instead of beating her up, I rub myself up against her. Luci too. Sleek, well-fed Luci, who no doubt has a couch to lie on to this day. And *I'm* being affectionate towards *her*.

Oh, how low I've sunk. How low I've been forced to sink. How dismal my state.

Domestic number 2 tries to comfort me.

"It won't be long," he says, "We'll be back before you even really notice."

Like I haven't noticed? He thinks I'm an idiot? And what does he mean, they'll be back, anyway? There's no floor in the place, for pity's sake. What would they come back to?

"You'll see. The builders will finish. It's a mess now but they'll put everything back the way it should be, and then we'll come back. Even the pesky pets."

I don't think he really thinks of them as pesky. I think he's just discovered that I do. So he's humouring me.

"We'll have the couch back and we'll be able to sit on it again and watch TV together. You'll see. It'll be just like before and we'll all have fun."

All sitting on the couch again? Yeah, right. It's a wilderness where the couch used to be. And he thinks they can just turn it back into a home again? No way.

Or is there? Is that what he's trying to say to me? You *can* wreak so much destruction and come back to how things were before? If that's true, it's wonderful. But it does leave one question. One big question. And I asked it straight out – I'm not one for beating round the bush.

"So, if it's all going to be like it was, why on earth did you let any of this mess happen in the first place?"

Not that he answered me. He never does. Probably just wrote it off as me being vocal.

It's all part of his pretence that I can't speak English. It's a pretence that suits him. It means he doesn't have to answer awkward questions.

Like that one.

Misty's sense of desertion deepens

Things just get worse and worse in the house. There's dust everywhere now and, as well as the floor being wrecked, in the bit where the bath – my bath – used to be, there are great holes between the roof and the top of the walls. Awful. The wind howls in. And the rain follows.

They're still coming around to see me most days. The domestics. One or other of them. Sometimes with the dotty dogs. They're as noisy and bouncy as ever.

The dogs, that is. Not the domestics.

I still rub myself against them though. That's the dogs *and* the domestics.

I still can't work out what makes me do it. It's so bad for the self-esteem. Have I sunk so low that I'll abase myself just for food? Because they *are* still bringing me food.

That's the domestics, not the dogs. The dogs bring nothing. They just try to nick my food when the domestics aren't looking. Which is all part of the way they darken my existence. But even that doesn't stop me rubbing myself against them. Damn it.

As for the house, well, though I probably wouldn't want to go in there anyway, I now find I couldn't if I wanted to. They've added insult to injury: they've taken away my cat flap! Would you credit it? And they wanted to take it away so badly that they've taken away the whole door too... Unbelievable: there's just a brick wall where the door *and* my cat flap used to be.

And let's be absolutely clear: it *was* mine. That irritating Luci said it was a small dog flap, but it wasn't, it was *my* cat flap. I just let the annoying small dogs use it too.

Still, things changed a bit today. There's been a bit of a development.

"Look, look!" Luci said when the family was visiting me, "there's a new small dog flap."

"Cat flap, cat flap," I corrected her automatically, before I'd really taken in what she was saying.

Anyway, when I took a look, I saw there *was* indeed something there. A hole. In the wall of what used to be the bathroom before they wrecked it. Where they've put in a new bit of wall, right next to the new door they've put in it.

It's just an odd sort of hole. With no flap. Badly lined with messy wood. But it's true that looking at it more carefully, I can see that there's a vague sort of cat-flappiness about it, with a new cat-flap-shaped tunnel behind the hole, through the new wall, into the sad, floor-less, gappy-roofed house.

Could it really be a new cat flap? Well, I suppose it could be. In time, when it actually has a flap. But, you know, this just beats me. I mean, we have a new bit of wall. A new door. And now perhaps a new cat flap.

So what was the point of doing away with the perfectly good wall, door and cat flap we had before? Why on earth would anyone in their right mind brick them up, just to make a new wall, cat flap and door? What *is* the point?

Besides, why put a new cat flap in if there's no house to speak of behind it? I mean, there's a bit of a house. A shell of one. But can you call something a house if it doesn't even have a decent floor?

I blame myself. I just haven't domesticated the domestics properly.

I suppose the fact that they've gone away rather proves the point. It's all very well that they come back most days – well, pretty well every day – but that's hardly the behaviour I'd expect if they'd been satisfactorily trained. They wouldn't dare wander off like that in the first place.

Clearly, that's a long-term issue I need to work on.

Anyway, the last few days I've found a great short-term solution. There's a funny domestic lady up the street who really needs a cat to take charge of things but, amazingly, has no one. Though she thinks she does now. She has great food and she likes to keep the house nice and warm, so I've adopted her. It's nice because I get proper service from her and plenty of food, so when my real domestics show up at the old place and call for me I can just ignore them.

That's lots of fun, because I can hear them going "Misty, Misty, psst, psst, psst" and clicking a spoon against one of my bowls, over and over again, sounding more and more desperate as they keep calling. I just stretch out on the carpet by the electric fire – my adopted domestic is one of those grey-top ones and they like to keep the heat high – while I reflect on whether to go and see the other domestics or not. You see, if I don't go, I know they'll come back later sounding increasingly sorry for themselves and guilty about the way they're treating me.

As they should. There's no excuse for it and it's only right I should teach them to mend their ways. Besides, if they feed me too, I get a second meal out of the arrangement.

Luci coping with two homes

What on Earth's going on? We seem to have moved to a new home. And it's not too bad because we have our couch there, and our bowls (which keep being filled perfectly satisfactorily) and we still have a bed we can share with the humans. Those are the things that turn a house into a home. So it's home, isn't it?

There's even a great thing about this place. Downstairs there are two other humans who are really, really nice and they have this dog called Lina we can really play with. Well, Toffee plays with her lots, but I play with her a bit too, even though I don't generally like playing with dogs who I don't know really, really well. Which means Toffee, basically, as I don't know any other dogs *that* well.

We all go for walks together too. Three or four humans. All three dogs. We even go to the same places we used to go to before. Our park. The big open place they call the common. The other place with the human puppies on bikes and the big dogs I have to avoid, but which is nice anyway.

I reckon this place could be home, really. Except for one thing. Which is that we keep going back to the other home. So I can't get used to this one.

Still, if there's one thing I don't like about the new place, it's that Misty isn't here. I can't forget that because the one really good thing about going back to the old house is that he's staying there. On his own. I don't know why. I wish he'd just come back to be with us, but he doesn't. Which is really odd, because the old place doesn't feel right anymore.

Some of the smells are the same, like I remember them. But most of them are completely wrong: lots of dust, and funny wood, and the walls have changed colour and smell different too.

Seeing Misty surrounded by all that makes me all sad. I know it's the same place we all lived in before, but it feels like somewhere completely different. Not that he admits it.

"What do you mean, do I feel bad about being here? This is home, you know. It's you that have had to go away from your home to somewhere else. I feel sorry for *you*."

Sorry for me? We've got the humans. And Toffee and I have got each other. Poor old Misty's just got the old place smelling funny and brief visits from the rest of us. I can't see how that can be right. Or how he can be happy about it.

I'm not. I miss the chats. Even though he's sometimes rude.

That rather spoils my pleasure with the niceness of the new place. Not having Misty. Not being able to share the new humans and even funny Lina with him.

Things were pretty good when we were all together. So why did we have to change them at all? After all, no one can seriously tell me anything's better now.

Toffee's birthday

"Happy birthday," Luci said to me.

"Oh, good," I said.

"No, no, happy birthday to *you*," she said.

"Even better," I said.

"Just eat your breakfast," she said.

"Best of all," I told her.

Later on, we went to the old house and saw Misty. We moved out some weeks ago, which was a bit sad, but at least we had the important things with us: the couch and the food. But we left poor old Misty behind, which was a pity, but let's not forget the important things: the food and the couch.

Anyway, it was good to see him again.

"Luci said happy birthday to me today," I said to him.

"Yes," he replied, "happy birthday."

Somehow, he didn't seem half as keen about it as Luci was. It must be hard to stay cheerful when you're living all alone. And we've taken the food and the couch.

"What *is* a birthday?" I asked him.

"It's when you get a year older," he explained.

"A year?"

He sighed. "I've been through all this with your pal Luci. Get her to tell you."

"Oh, go on, Misty. Tell me, tell me."

He sighed.

"A year is when you go through all the cold times and wet times and warm times and hot times and start all over again."

I thought I'd drop the subject. It's always getting hot or wet or cold or warm, so how do you know when there's a year? Still, he clearly thought it mean something special for me. I decided to concentrate on just that aspect.

"So I'm a year older?" I asked

"Yes, you are," he said, with what sounded like patience. Or someone trying to sound patient. I couldn't tell.

"A year older than what?"

"A year older than you were."

"When?" I asked.

"A year ago," he said. He sighed again and walked off.

Oh, well. I still don't know what it means to be a year older. Or what a birthday is. But everyone seems to want me to have a happy one, so why would I complain? Human number 2 even went out of his way to make sure it was.

"Look," he said, "for your special day: a nice green dentastix. Enjoy it!"

A *green* dentastix? Who likes them? I mean, Luci eats them, but she'll eat anything. In fact, I was quite worried she'd take mine, so I hid it. I mean, I might not like it, but that didn't mean she could have it. Tssk.

"She didn't eat her dentastix," said number 2.

"She doesn't like the green ones," said number 1, who's really wise sometimes. She *understands* things. Important things.

"Oh," said number 2. "I'd better nip out and get some brown ones then."

"Don't be silly. You went out to get those ones."

She's wise most of the time, number 1, but sometimes she just isn't.

"Well, it *is* her birthday," he replied, as he was putting his coat on. Sometimes *he's* the one that talks sense.

So I got my brown Dentastix. And, to be fair, I did nibble a bit of the green one later too, which means that if it was my birthday, it really was a happy one.

Except I didn't finish off the green one and forgot to hide what was left. When I went looking for it, it was gone. But Luci seemed terribly pleased with herself. Tssk again.

Still, you can't have everything. And overall, I really quite liked this birthday thing. I think I should have another one soon.

"Next year," Misty explained next time I saw him.

That wasn't terribly helpful. All right for anyone who knows what a year is. Not so good for me.

"When's that?" I asked.

"Twelve months' time," he replied and stalked off again.

Ah, well. It'll show up some time, I suppose. And I'm sure it'll be fun when it does.

Luci keeping an eye out for Toffee
By Senada Borcilo

Misty's domestics
come home

I can't believe it! I don't know whether to leap for joy or spit for fury! They've come back! At last. The domestics are back. After leaving me on my own for days and days and *days*.

I don't know how many because there comes a point when even a brain like mine runs out of numbers. Not at a stupid level like four, which is all the yappers can handle, because that's the number of paws they have. I can count perfectly adequately to five, because that's the number of weapons I have. Not like them. It amazes me that they somehow put up with a mouthful of inadequate teeth and that's their lot. I have a fine collection of teeth that I keep convincingly sharp, plus four fine sets of claws, ditto.

That makes five.

And the family was away for not just five days, but for five days five times over, and then some more. Beyond my counting.

That's appalling. Unforgivable.

During the day, the old place – it may not have been much but I called it home – was a disaster area. There were lots of undomesticated domestics, noisy, clumsy, funny smelling, with great unfriendly boots. Clumping around. Doing things with wood and bricks and doors and windows. They made a complete mess, with dust everywhere. What was worse was that my favourite places had gone: couch, beds, chairs, carpets.

I spent most of the time outside, except when I went around

to the house of that other domestic who liked to give me food, some good stroking and a warm place to lay a tired head. Which, when your domestics have cleared off without so much as a proper discussion of where they're going, is welcome. More than welcome. Bloody necessary, if you ask me.

It wasn't right. Sometimes, I'd go out into the night again afterwards, and I'd keep catching myself thinking things like "hey! I'll just pop in for a bite of kibble and maybe a bit of a lie-down on the sofa," and then remember that, damn it, I couldn't. There was no kibble indoors. No couch indoors. No indoors.

It was a pain in the hindquarters, I don't mind saying.

Anyway, they've come back at last. And they brought the sofa. And the chairs. And a brand-new carpet, too. Which is particularly satisfying, the carpet is, because they wouldn't have brought it if there hadn't been a floor to lay it on, and the clumpy domestics eventually put one back in, where they'd taken it out before. Which rather begs the question, why did they take it out in the first place? I'm still no closer to getting an answer to that question than I ever was before.

Fortunately, they also closed the gaps they'd made between the walls and the ceiling. And put proper flaps on the new cat flap. Which is a better one than the old one, so there's been at least one improvement.

When that was all done, the domestics turned up again – not for them the place without a floor. Unfortunately, they didn't come alone but brought the yappers with them. I thought at first it would be fun to have them there, but that ghastly Toffee's been up to her tricks again. She mastered the new cat flap pretty quickly (that's the one she likes to call a small dog flap, though it was obviously made for me, and I mastered it long before she did). But no sooner had she learned to use it, with my kind – over-kind – indulgence, than she decided it would be fun to occupy it and keep me out. Just by lying inside the bit of a tunnel behind the flap. And sticking her head out to give me a self-satisfied look.

Imagine! As though I hadn't been kept out of the place *quite* long enough. Tiresome if you ask me.

Still, I suppose it's the price you pay for getting the whole household back together again. I don't like to admit it even to myself, and I certainly wouldn't admit it to the dogs or the domestics, but it *is* more comfortable having them around. Except when they block my cat flap, of course. But generally, yes, it feels better.

I mean, don't get me wrong, that doesn't make up for all that time away, and I won't be forgiving them any time soon, you mark my words. My vengeance will be terrible. I'm just waiting for a good opportunity to inflict it.

In fact, it's a bit odd that no opportunity seems to have presented itself yet, which is hard to understand. Somehow, I've never quite got into the mood for sinking my teeth or claws into them since their return. It's pathetic. Sometimes I could kick myself, except I *can't* actually kick myself.

That's not to say that I'm getting soft or anything. Oh, no. I'm just having trouble picking the time for revenge. But it *will* come. Just wait and see.

In the meantime, while I wait for the chance to avenge my damaged dignity, I'm enjoying getting back into old routines and having a little mild fun. As a sort of prelude to revenge. Like with domestic number 2. He's still such fun to tease. Take the other day when he was having breakfast.

He left the table, poor sap. So I hopped up and took his seat. You should have seen him when he came back, one hand holding a plate, the other a cup of that foul-smelling, hot black concoction he seems to enjoy early in the day. He stopped dead to look at me. Astonished, I'd say, to find his place occupied.

Well, who said it was *his* anyway?

"Ah," he said, "I can see I'm really home."

Damn right, I thought. You are. Back home. And it's *my* home.

Don't you forget it.

Toffee coming to terms with the new bed

One of the things about the new old house, or old new house – the house we moved out of for some reason and then came back to, though it wasn't the same anymore – is that our room is now a lot further upstairs. Up some new stairs where there weren't any before we moved out.

So now we have to go up two floors instead of one. Which is all very odd. Especially as the second floor didn't even exist before.

Not that it's a problem, really. What's a flight of stairs when you've got four legs? Must be tougher if you've got only two like the poor humans. But to the rest of us, it's just another set of more-than-four steps. Quite a lot more than four, but not so many as to be difficult. We just shoot up them, Luci and me, particularly as when we get to the top, our new bed is really comfortable with plenty of space. So big the humans can sleep in it too.

The only problem is that the bed's so *high*. Why, even Luci runs around it with her claws clicking on the wooden floor, upset about not getting up. So you can imagine what it's like for me. I mean, I don't just do the paw clicking bit, I positively *whimper*.

The odd thing is that the humans don't always react. It's not as though that clicking on the wood is exactly inaudible or anything. To say nothing of the whimpering. You'd think they'd lift us up just to have a bit of quiet. To stop the clicking.

To stop the whimpering. I've become a pretty good whimperer. I can make it *terribly* pitiful. I don't know how the humans put up with it because I find the noise *so* pitiful it even irritates me, though I know it's me making it.

Generally, one of them gives in eventually and lifts us up. Though each time, human number 1 has a go about it.

"I don't know why we spoil them like this," she says, "they can get up here themselves. They just want to be lifted, they don't really need it."

"I know. It's ridiculous," says number 2, "when they don't think about it, they just jump straight up. But I'd rather lift them than put up with the whimpering."

See? See? It works.

It *is* odd, though. There are times when we come dashing up the stairs and, suddenly, we're on the bed. High though it is. One moment we're not on the bed, next moment we are. No one helps us.

I don't know how that happens. Is there sometimes some kind of ramp between the door and the bed or something? A ramp that just isn't there most of the time? I mean it would make sense because it would make getting up on the bed *so* much easier. And that would explain how sometimes we get there without having to clatter on the floor or whimper.

But here's something else I don't understand. Why does the ramp go away so quickly after we've used it? I've never even managed to see it. And why don't the humans put it out for us every night?

"It's a mystery," says Misty.

"A mystery?"

"Life's full of mysteries. Things we can't explain Though I think I know how you get onto the bed without being lifted."

"Really? Really? Tell me, tell me."

"Oh, no. That would spoil the mystery."

Oh, he's so mysterious that Misty. Not that it matters. The bed is great and somehow or other we get onto it every night.

Which is all that *really* matters, isn't it?

Toffee and the
making of friends

Wow! It's amazing how many friends there are out there! I keep meeting them whenever I go for walks. It's like they're just out there waiting for me to meet them.

Well, some of them aren't that friendly. I have to be a bit cautious. Some of them are terribly *big*. I take some care about going up to them. I take it slowly, hanging back a little. If I get a whiff of hostile smell from them, I quickly run back to the humans, but if instead I get the friendly smell, then I go running across, and we have *so much* fun.

Best of all, though, are the friends that are the *right* size. Or, even better, *small*. Like the neighbour, Lina.

Well, she isn't really a neighbour. Anymore. We used to live in a place where she wasn't a neighbour, and now we're back in that place but with some new smells. In between we lived in a *different* place where she *was* a neighbour. I know that sounds complicated and believe me, I find it terribly confusing but, hey, that's what happened.

In that different place, where Lina was our neighbour, I decided that she was terribly nice. We used to jump around and play together whenever we met.

What's best of all is that her humans brought her round to see us at the new place. Which is the same as the old place. But different.

I *told* you it was confusing.

The important thing is that she's visited us here. *Twice*. It was *great*. We ran around the living room a bit, jumping on to the couch and off it, and rolling around a bit. You know, all the things you do when you're having fun.

And then her humans and mine took us for a *walk*. That meant we could race around in the grass and chase each other. *Just amazing.*

Luci was there too, of course, but being a bit prim and ladylike. I don't know what prim or ladylike mean, but Misty told me they're the right words. It seems to mean being quiet and sticking by the humans, which is fine, because it meant I got all the playing with Lina.

We went to my favourite place, where there's lots and lots of grass, and some extra *big* dogs. I wanted to play with them after Lina got tired of chasing around. She's such a *small* dog. There are times when I feel much, much bigger. But these ones were positively huge.

"They're not dogs," Luci told me, and I have to admit, they didn't really smell like dogs. "They're horses. They look placid but they can kill a dog with a single kick."

"How do you know? How do you know?" I asked her as I tried to find a way through the fence to play with them. After all, they're big and quiet and friendly. Actually, they smell of *meat*. More food than I can imagine, all walking around on four feet. What wouldn't I like about that?

"I just *know*."

"How? How? You haven't been kicked, have you? You haven't been killed. Have you ever seen them kill anyone?"

Luci sighed.

"Human number 1 told me."

"Ah."

That did quieten me down a bit. Human number 1 gets things right. In fact, if she thinks something's dangerous, I'm not sure that I'd want to take my chances with it.

It's true that she reacted pretty fiercely when she noticed I'd found a way through the fence into the bit where the horses – or big dogs - were. I'd barely started dancing around the nice friendly legs of the nice friendly dogs – or horses – when she bent over the fence and grabbed me.

"Don't ever do that again!" she said. Well, nearly shouted. "*Never* go up to a horse like that. You could get kicked."

I was struggling in her arms and trying to look at the big quiet animal. It looked just fine to me. If not very playful. But maybe, just maybe, I needed to be a bit more careful.

In any case, it all stopped mattering just then. Because that's when Ollie turned up. And what a meeting that was!

"He's like a small Doberman," one of Lina's humans said.

A small Doberman? Sounded good. I like the word "small", and I don't know what "Doberman" means so that was just fine with me. And he turned out to be *really* friendly. We went running round and round the bushes, and through them, until I got a brambly bit of stick, you know with thorns on, caught in my coat and human number 2 had to work with Ollie's human to get it off me. So Ollie tried to play with Luci instead, but that didn't work terribly well, because she'd only run in little circles round human number 1, and only ever *away*, never after Ollie, and he couldn't chase Lina because she was in her other human's arms – terribly tired, poor thing – and though he jumped up at her again and again, he couldn't convince them to put her down.

It was a really good thing when the brambly bit was gone and Ollie and I could start playing again so he could have a proper run.

It was magic. Though when we got home I was just a bit exhausted myself. A bit like Lina, if I'm completely honest. Luci and I lay down on the couch and slept on top of each other.

Well, me on top of her, really.

Ah, neighbourliness. And all the friends out there just waiting for me to meet them. Those are the things that make my kind of day.

Some stand guard while others rest

By Senada Borcilo

Luci's snow time

The little one was quite wild this morning.

"There's… there's… there's…" she gasped, "all this white stuff out there in the garden… white stuff… everywhere…"

"It's snow," I told her, quite proud that I remembered what it was.

"Oh, goody," she said, "I love snow."

"How do you know? You've never seen any before."

"I've seen it now and I know I love it."

She rushed downstairs and straight out of the small dog flap. I came through more slowly, waiting to see how she reacted when she *really* saw the snow.

"Oh, it's all cold!" she said, "and all wet!"

Aha, I thought. Now you've found out.

"I love it, I love it, I love it," she went on, jumping about like a bouncing ball and dancing on her hind legs like she does.

"You love it?" I was astonished. "Cold and wet? And you love it?"

"Cold and wet and white and soft and it covers everything. What's not to love?"

Completely crazy, that Toffee.

Misty was much more…

"Circumspect," he told me, "I was much more circumspect."

"Yes," I said, "and much more careful too. Wary, I'd say," I added, proud that I knew the word.

"Yes," he said, but he looked at me in the way he sometimes does when he's trying to tell me I look like something the cat brought in. A different cat. So I went to lie down on the couch:

he's no fun when he's like that.

Anyway, he really *was* wary. I saw him. He was at the back door looking out in the garden.

"Oh, look," said human number 2, "he wants me to let him out. I bet he doesn't go, though."

The human opened the door for him and Misty peeked out. He took one step outside and immediately pulled his paw back in. Then he turned round and made a beeline for the sitting room.

Human number 2 laughed. "He just shot away from the snow."

"He'll probably ask you to let him out of the front now," said human number 1, "in the hope that there's less snow that side."

"I'm sure he will," answered human number 2, following Misty into the sitting room, "look, he's heading for the front door now."

"Well, make sure you kick him out," she told him, "it's time he went outside and that's the only way you'll make sure he goes."

But he didn't have to kick him. Misty went out of his own accord. If a bit slowly and hesitatingly.

"He went anyway," said number 2.

"Of course," replied number 1, "he heard me tell you to kick him out."

Interesting. It seems number 1 has finally worked out that we understand what they're saying.

"Oh no, she hasn't," Misty told me, "She's just pretending to think we understand, she hasn't realised we really do."

That's too complicated for me, but Misty knows a lot about humans, so maybe he's right.

"Of course I'm right."

Anyway, he went out but I reckon he must have just shot into the back garden and inside again through the small dog flap.

"Cat flap. And I was gone long enough to do what needed to be done."

I wish he'd stop reading my diary over my shoulder.

"Then you shouldn't write it somewhere I can see you."

Well, he can keep reading if he wants, but he might not like what he reads. After all, so much fuss about a little snow! We all get cold paws out there, but that's no reason to go all nervous and shy, is it?

What's with a little snow, for Kibble's sake?

"Oh, you're *so* blasé," said Misty.

I like to think that 'blasé' means mature and sensible, but his tone suggested something else. Particularly when he added, "you've seen snow twice in your life and now you're all superior about it?"

Yes. Definitely not complimentary.

I ought to find out what blasé means. I'd look it up in a dictionary if I knew what a dictionary was. And I could look things up. In the meantime, I'm just going to go out in the snow again. Human number 2 is in the back garden and crazy little Toffee's gone out there too. I didn't realise wet, cold stuff like snow could be fun, but now I know it can be, I don't see why Toffee should get all the fun on her own…

Toffee having trouble with the bed again

I really, really like the new bed the humans have got for me!

I say "for me", but of course I let them use it too. What would be the point of getting me a bed if they went somewhere else? But this one's better than the other one. It's much bigger. Even with Luci on it, there's still space for me to choose which of the humans to lie on.

Well, they push me off mostly if I do that, but at least I can lie *against* them. And *on top of* them, if they're not paying attention.

But it's not all wonderful. There's a couple of things that aren't quite right. For instance, Misty the cat thinks he can come and join us. I don't know what gives him that idea. Even when we were living in this house before, he left us alone in the bed at night. And then when we were in the other funny place, where our friend Lina turned up downstairs, well, he wasn't around at all.

Now that we're back, he thinks he can just come and demand that we let him sleep on the bed with us. Like it belongs to him. Really cheeky.

The odd thing is the way the humans behave. When I try to go over and explain to Misty that the bed isn't the place for him, with just a bit of a pounce and a push with my nose, and some moderate barking ("yapping," says Misty, but he would, wouldn't he?), they sometimes grab me and hold me down.

"No, Toffee, don't," they say, as though they thought that it was Misty's bed too.

How on earth can that be right?

Still, I quite often get him off the bed. If the humans aren't quick enough, for instance. And then he goes running downstairs, and that's something I just can't resist. I'm off the bed like a shot and running straight down the stairs after him. I mean, him running downstairs is just like a *game*, isn't it? And why shouldn't I play too?

But then comes trouble. Because, like I said before, the bed's so terribly *high*. And the floor is *terribly* slippery. Jumping *all that height* is horribly difficult because I slip around everywhere when I'm trying to jump.

I run around the bed from one side to the other trying to get the humans to lift me up. But often they don't want to. So then I whimper a bit to try to make them understand.

And they aren't always that nice even when I show them how unhappy I am. They say nasty things.

"That'll teach her not to chase Misty off the bed," human number 1 once said. She's the one who believes in discipline, so it really hurt to hear her say that. After all, what was I doing but teaching Misty a bit of discipline?

"No," said number 2, "she ought to learn that he's part of the family too. Anyway, if she wants to come back up, she can jump."

Well, that was even worse. I mean, he's the soft one. If *he* was getting tough on me, what hope was there?

"After all, she's jumped up before," he said, "she can do it."

Well, it's true that there've been times when I'm not thinking about getting onto the bed, and I just suddenly find I'm there. I can't explain how it happens. Misty says it's because I jump up without even thinking about it.

"Of course, that's why it is, you silly yapping creature," says Misty.

Maybe he's right. About the jumping, that is. He's completely wrong about silly or yapping.

It's just so much harder when I'm thinking about it, though.

I mean, I can't see where I'm jumping and the floor's so slippy, I skid about on it. Can't get a proper runup for a jump.

As for the humans, they're gigantic, aren't they? I don't see how it can be any trouble for them to lift me.

Still, they didn't help, so in the end I had to jump and, to be honest, I managed. It was great being back up on the bed. Without Misty.

But what a pain it was getting there.

Ah, well. It's a great bed, so I suppose I just have to put up with the trouble getting onto it. It's a price worth paying.

After all, you never sleep better than in your own bed.

Misty enjoying proper service renewed

It's good to have proper domestic service re-established after the regrettable recent interruption. You know, when the domestics and the little yappers went away for such a ridiculous time. While lots of drastic things were being done to our house.

To be fair, and I'm always scrupulously fair, the results haven't been all bad. One of the innovations those awful smelly undomesticated domestics made to the house is a glass door to the kitchen. It's quite nice. I can sit inside and look out. Or I can sit outside and look in. Both provide fine relaxing entertainment.

But the really amusing thing is the way domestic number 2 behaves. If he sees me by the door, he comes rushing over to open it for me. To go out. Or to come in. I could use the cat flap, but where's the fun in that? If he's around, I make a point of having him open the door. If nothing else, it's a form of valuable training for him, so he doesn't forget that his main purpose is providing high-quality service, of the kind required by a discriminating cat. That way, serving me becomes a bit more instinctive rather than the kind of hit-and-miss shoddiness I've been getting recently.

That's the real point, isn't it? I don't *need* him to open the door, but it's good practice for him that he does. As well as proper respect for me.

Domestic number 1, who's the sharper tooth in the jaw of the two of them, understands.

"What on earth are you doing?" she asks.

"Well... letting Misty out..." Or, as it might be, "in".

"What do you think the cat flap's for?"

It's so good to hear people talking about the "cat flap" and not what domestic number 2 calls it, "the-cat-and-small-dog-flap" which is quite a mouthful, or just "the flap" which feels a bit dismissive. It's a cat flap that I generously allow the small dogs – and, boy, are they small – to use.

And it's certainly true that my cat flap is rather special. I mean, it's huge. No more of that demeaning squeezing in and all that. Comfortable, too. Cut through the brick. Painted. Just *nice*.

But that still doesn't mean that I'll use it when I can get a domestic to open the door instead.

The best bit? It isn't just at the door I've got service resumed. It's in the bedroom too.

It isn't always easy to sleep on the bed with the domestics, in my rightful place. The presence of the two ghastly canines has rather put a dampener on that pleasant custom of our distant, hallowed past. This bed's bigger than the old one, with more space for us, but there's never enough space anywhere that contains Toffee.

She is *such* a fidget. First, she has to scratch and scratch the duvet to make herself a place she thinks is comfortable.

"It isn't earth, you know," I tell her.

"I *know*," she says, "that's obvious, isn't it? What do you take me for? Dumb?"

There are certain questions that are best left unanswered.

"Well, if it's not earth, but duvet, why do you keep trying to dig it?"

Maybe she takes the same view as I do of leaving some questions unanswered. In any case she didn't reply to that one.

Once she's finished her scratching she'll lie down for a while. Until one of the domestics moves a bit. Infinitesimally even. When she'll go over to get stroked, and when *that's* done, she'll go back to some new place and start scratching again.

When she finally decides to get a bit of shuteye and allow the rest of us to do the same, it'll only take some sound from downstairs – a bit of furniture creaking, a group of domestics chatting in the street outside, a fox jumping a fence three gardens away – for her to leap up, start yapping and rush down the stairs. As though she could actually do anything about it. As though there really was an 'it' to do anything about.

Still, domestic number 2 has kindly taken to making a bit of an extension to the bed for me to sleep on. Very kind and thoughtful of him. I'm happy to take advantage.

Of course, I *know* it isn't really an extension to the bed. And it wasn't made available as an act of generosity. It seems domestic number 2's too much of a wimp to sleep with two pillows, unlike number 1 who has higher aspirations. So now that she's given him two – another innovation with the new bed – he chucks one on the floor. Which suits me just fine, because I can sleep on it.

Perhaps I should care that this isn't as generous a gesture as it looks. But I don't. It suits me much better to believe he's offering me my own special side bed, so why blame me if I do?

In any case, I like having the pillow and I take advantage of it.

A funny thing happened this morning. I came in for a rest at my usual time, just before dawn, and settled down quietly for a kip. Well, not straight away, of course. I did spend a little while walking over the bed and mewing at the domestics, waking up Toffee and batting her down when she got uppity again. But, hey, there simply are certain things you have to do to inculcate a culture of respect, aren't there? If there's one thing I hate it's not being noticed. That's something that walking on the dogs and the domestics has going for it, especially at 6:00 in the morning: it gets you noticed.

After the others, including domestic number 1, had got up and done whatever it is they do in the mornings, when anyone civilised is asleep, domestic number 2 came up to go through those silly rituals he engages in each day, involving splashing a lot of water around in the bathroom (what's wrong with using a tongue, for God's sake, if you want to get clean? And why would you shave your fur off, especially in the winter?) Anyway, after he'd done all that he went back downstairs again, closing the door behind him.

I didn't say anything. I just thought "interesting to see how long it takes him to remember." Sure enough, a couple of hours later he came tearing back up the stairs and flung the door open.

"I'm *so* sorry, Misty," he said, "I didn't mean to lock you in. I hope you've been OK."

Of *course* I'd been OK. What did he think? I couldn't get through a nap for a couple of hours without popping outside? What sort of weakling does he take me, or my bladder, for? So I just lifted my head off the pillow and gave him a look. The kind that says, "what's the panic? What are you so worried about? In fact, just what *is* your problem?"

He got the message, too. Because he said, "well, sorry Misty. Won't happen again. I don't know what came over me. I just wasn't thinking."

So, what else is new? I wanted to ask.

"I'll leave you to it," he went on, "sorry to have disturbed your rest."

I'll say. He really should be. But I drifted off comfortably. All the more contentedly at knowing the door was now open, so I could go out if I ever decided I wanted to.

And, above all, at knowing normal service had been renewed.

At last.

Luci training Toffee

What an interesting challenge it is to train Toffee.

I mean, she's an adult now. Or so the humans say. "A year old – she's an adult."

We have to take their word for things, I suppose, but to me she's just the same puppy she's always been.

She still has that magnet head of hers. Show her a bowl of food, anybody's food, and her head just goes in and seems to stick to the bottom. No way of dislodging it. I've watched even a human trying to get her head out of food bowl and finding it a struggle.

I thought it was quite funny, until it turned out it was *my* food she was sucking up.

I had to take her in hand. In paw. Make a few things clear. Teach her the rules of life.

"You can't just eat my food," I explained to her, patiently.

"I don't know what you mean," she said, "I just have."

"Err. Let me make this clear. That was *my* food. For me to eat. Not *your* food. Which is the only kind you should be eating."

"Food's food," she told me, her silly tail wagging away at full tilt as though we were having some kind of amusing game and not talking about the most serious thing there is.

"No," I continued, as patiently as ever, "there's your food and then there's my food. We each eat our own. It really is that simple."

"You often eat my food," she replied.

Damn. There's some truth in that.

"Only if you leave it behind."

"I only eat yours if *you* leave it behind," she replied, clearly thinking she'd scored a point.

"I like to be able to come back to it and have some more later," I explained. Patiently, I felt.

"How am I to know when you're leaving it for later and not just leaving it?"

"Why don't you just always think that I'm leaving it for later? That way you can't go wrong."

She thought about that, but not for long.

"What if I'm not that worried about going wrong? After all, the main thing is that the food that was in the bowl before, is inside me afterwards. That doesn't feel wrong to me."

I suppose she isn't quite the puppy she was before. She's getting a little too clever. Too clever for her own good. Or for my good, at least.

"Well, anyway, just leave my food alone, will you?" I repeated, though I didn't feel I'd made my case quite as forcefully as I'd planned.

"And you'll leave mine alone?"

See what I mean about needing training? She's becoming horribly cheeky these days. An answer for everything.

The worst of it is when we're playing in the park. Which is my second favourite thing. After food. Sorry, third – third. After food and belly rubs.

She's *too* quick these days. All I used to have to do before was put on a little spurt of speed and I'd lose her completely. Just miles behind.

Not anymore. She comes racing across the ground and catches me up. *And bites my tail*. It's just infuriating, and I can't stop her. Which is even more infuriating.

She also refuses to come to the humans when they call her. Sometimes. Well, any time she's found something to eat. To be fair, I sometimes join her. Just for a moment if she's found something particularly good. Just long enough to get a mouthful or two. But then over I go. Of course. That's what a good dog's supposed to do. Besides, there's usually a treat going, if we do what we're told. Over I go, sit down obediently and get my lead put on.

Then the long wait starts.

"Come on, Toffee," calls human number 2. This doesn't generally happen with human number 1. She just says "goody, goody", which seems to be Toffee-ish for "treat, treat", and Toffee just trots over. But Toffee knows she can get away with whatever she likes with human number 2. So she just keeps her nose to the ground, sniffing round a rubbish bin or whatever.

Near a bin is usually the best place to find really interesting things to eat when we're out on walks.

"Toffee," he calls again, "come here. Now."

Maybe he claps his hands. Maybe she looks up. I don't know what number 2 thinks, but I know what Toffee's up to: she's measuring the distance between him and her.

"Tof-*feee*," he calls again, getting irritated. She's gone back into deaf mode, not hearing a word he says, and still smelling around. Maybe even swallowing a nice bit of mouldy bun or something equally appetising.

Note that in the meantime, I'm still waiting for my good-girl-who-got-her-lead-put-on treat.

Eventually he'll start walking towards her. Then she does one of two things: she trots over towards him looking innocent, like a bit of kebab meat wouldn't melt in her mouth, which means she hasn't found any, or she crouches down until he gets close and then makes a dash for it, which means she has.

It's such a *bore*. What with me waiting for my treat and all.

Eventually she lets herself be caught and have her lead put on. And you know what happens? It's ridiculous.

Number 2 gives us both a treat. *Both of us*. Me that's had to wait for so long *but also* Toffee that made us wait.

Where's the sense in that?

"Were you waiting?" Toffee says, all angelic, afterwards.

"Of course, I was," I reply trying to stay patient.

"Oh, I'm *so* sorry, I won't do that again."

She will, though. At the very next opportunity. She always does. She's a law unto herself. And the law she respects is the call of the food. Hers, mine, anyone's, in a bowl, in a bush, under a rubbish bin. If she gets the chance to dive in, she's straight there, like a flash, magnet-head first.

Nothing the humans do is going to change that.

My training work, it seems, is far from done.

Misty on drawing attention. Or not

When you're a large cat, you have to be a bit careful about how you use your weight. I mean, draw too much attention to it and the domestics start to talk. And what they say isn't what I want to hear.

"Time to put him on a diet," domestic number 1 might say, or perhaps, "should we switch him to the low-calorie version?"

"Oh, but he enjoys his food," says number 2.

His is a slightly more generous view of what's due to me. Or perhaps I've just trained him rather more effectively. She's virtually untrainable. For instance, if I show her my dissatisfaction, perhaps with a small nip, she just chucks me off her lap, sometimes adding insult to bad behaviour by making some unkind statement like "God! What a weight". He, on the other hand, may well complain but he generally does what I ask.

What's his support worth, though, against the real decision maker? She's the one who chooses which lap I lie on or what food I'm served. And she takes a much tougher line when it comes to matters of diet, so I prefer not to have too much discussion of my figure. Fine, sleek, and well-lined as I know it to be, whatever nastier tongues may say, I'd still rather they talked about something else.

Best not to attract too much attention to it, I say.

Still. The quality of domestic service being what it is, I do sometimes have to take steps to make certain wants of mine clear. There is occasionally a need to point out to them that something has been missed. Like filling my bowl.

But I have to find a discreet way of doing it, *without throwing my weight around*.

Fortunately, I have other means.

Obviously, *obviously*, there are teeth and claws. As there ever were. And mews, of course. That's often enough with domestic number 2, if he forgets, say, to open the door when I'm standing by it. If he ignores me, there are more serious measures. For instance, if he's typing on his silly computer at a table instead of the couch – domestic number 1 told him it's better for his posture – that gives me a fantastic opportunity: I can jump up between his legs and administer just a gentle scratch reminder. Does that get his attention? Instantaneously. Completely focused. Obedience is practically immediate.

"OK, OK, OK, so what do you want? More food? More water? To be let out?"

I think he'd do all three just to stop me.

At night, though, I need something a tad subtler. Jumping on his chest isn't a smart move. It would certainly wake him up but I might get them back on to the subject of whether my weight requires attention. And talking about the whole appalling notion of dieting again. That's not a conversation I'm anxious to start.

As for jumping on *her* – domestic number 1 – well, the consequences just don't bear thinking about. So I don't. I mean, I don't even think about it, let alone do it.

Besides, jumping on the bed is no good because of the canine element. They *both* go and sleep there these days. Between the domestics, if they don't spot them. At their feet if they do. Either way, it means that jumping on the bed only triggers a terrible burst of noise and the risk of being pounced back on. While my aim is to wake the domestics, waking them with canine bundles leaping around and drowning us all in a chorus of barks – well, yaps, really, from those two – could be counterproductive. It leaves the domestic help less inclined to be, well, helpful. Or even particularly domesticated.

Fortunately, the domestics have come up with a really good invention. It's called the bedside table. They like to keep things on them. Phones. Kindles. TV remote controls (yes, yes, the new bedroom has a TV in it – pathetic the way they indulge their silly foibles – I mean, what's the point of a TV without a proper couch?). Other things too, sometimes: pens or makeup compacts or whatever.

This makes waking them up not just useful but *fun*. I've always liked gently pushing things with a paw. You know, push a bit. Then another bit. Then maybe a bit more. See it tipping on the edge. Just a tiny push further. And – there she goes! Over the edge slips the pen. The remote control. The mobile phone.

That puts me in mind of a story from way back. From when I was little more than a kitten. The first time, but sadly not the last, when the domestics abandoned me, leaving me behind in France while they headed to England. It was either because I was protesting against what I saw as a completely unnecessary move, or because of some kind of domestic rule about vaccinations, I forget which. The outcome, at any rate, is that they deserted me, drat them.

To be fair, the pair of domestics they left me with turned out pretty satisfactory. Good, even. Why, I was tempted to stay with them long term, since my own domestics have never reached that level of service quality. But you have to stick by your employees, don't you? A certain loyalty is required from a cat with principles. Eventually, I bit the bullet and went to England too. At which point, the French domestics found another cat to serve, seeing how much they'd enjoyed the experience with me.

I hope the new cat appreciates how well I got them trained.

The female domestic had a ring which she used to take off and leave by her bed at night. Oh, that was fun. Nice and easy to push around, all over the top of the bedside table. This way, that way, closer to the edge, away from the edge, and then –

bingo! – over the edge.

Very satisfying.

And the fun went on, because I could push it about even further on the floor. Forwards, backwards, left, right, all over the place. Then out through the door into the bathroom. Where, oddly enough, it rolled about a bit and then simply disappeared. I looked for ages but couldn't find it.

A pity. It had been a lot of fun, and then it was gone.

The domestics were just as sad about that as I was.

"But…," she said, "I put it on the bedside table. It could hardly have disappeared."

They got down on their hands and knees, searching everywhere around the floor, under the bedside table, under the bed.

"Oh, hell," the male domestic said eventually, "we're never going to find it. Did you drop it down the basin plughole?"

"My engagement ring! We can't give up on it. We've got to find it. It can't be far. I really did put it on the bedside table."

Then, suddenly, they both looked up at me, with a bit of a glimmer of suspicion in their eyes. But I can do innocent and stony as well as anyone. Not a word did I say. Not a muscle did I move. Not a hint did I give to confirm or deny my involvement.

"It must be him. And he must know where it is. But he's not telling," she said. And sighed.

Well, he was obviously a nice guy to be engaged to. Nice guy to be married to as well, I expect: they've had the wedding since. He gave her another engagement ring, even more splendid than the first one. All's well as ends better, right?

But the story didn't end there. It went on.

After they got married, they moved to another house. And had to clear out the first one pretty extensively. Cleaning, among other things, the bit behind the washbasin pedestal in the bathroom where no one looks. They told my domestic number 1 on a phone call about what happened.

"No!" I heard my domestic saying, "you found it? Where?"

She said uh-huh a few times as they explained.

"Between two floorboards? Behind the washbasin? Standing up? That's just amazing."

She gave me quite a look after she'd hung up.

"Oh, Misty, Misty," she said, "the chaos you leave behind you."

Oh, well. I had nothing but the warmest feelings for that female domestic. And she was obviously terribly attached to her engagement ring. I like to think she must be pleased she now has two.

While I had a lot of fun with the first one. So there's nothing to complain about, right? Feels like win-win all around.

These days, in the new bedroom in my English home, the great thing is that it's got a wooden floor. That makes a satisfying crack under a mobile phone or a remote control. Quite enough to jerk a domestic out of inattention. Or slumber. Or even, frankly, deep sleep.

It may not leave them in the best of moods but, hey, if I get their attention, I can live with any degree of irritation that stops short of actual fury. By being careful and not knocking too many things on to the floor, that's generally achievable.

"Oh, what the hell's the bloody cat up to," says domestic number 2. "Oh, Lord, is that my phone on the floor?"

He swings his feet out of bed. So who cares what he says? He's getting up, isn't he? That was the aim of the exercise. Words can never hurt me, especially if they're muttered as a preliminary to measures necessary for refilling a bowl.

I generally dash out of the room at this point.

"Look, he knows he's done wrong. He's running away."

You really think so, you poor sap? I'm just showing the direction you need to take. Downstairs. Towards the bowls and cat food pouches. And downstairs he obediently comes.

Well, not always, of course. Not first time anyway. But that's the beauty of the bedside table. There's plenty more lying on it. And nothing at all to stop me sneaking back in.

And starting all over again.

Luci witnesses a disaster

I could see it happening. So could the human. And I couldn't stop it. Nor could he.

Toffee and I had taken human number 2 for a walk. In the park with the lake. It's quite a good place to visit. There are lots of birds to chase, though unfortunately there seem to be a lot of other dogs there to chase us instead. Which is less fun. Though Toffee doesn't seem to mind.

Honestly. I don't get her. She's a bit careful with the really big dogs, but even with them, if they show any kind of friendliness, she just trots over as though they're ready to play with her. Even if their jaws are bigger than her whole head. For a clever little dog, she can be *so* dumb sometimes.

It's like when we get to the lake. A place where all sense seems to desert her. Like she doesn't understand what a railing is. I mean, I never go through the railings down towards the water. OK, obviously it doesn't help that I'm just a bit too big to fit and when I was smaller, I did sometimes slip through. But I learned not to. These days I'm a wiser dog, so I wouldn't even if I could.

Really, really, *really*.

Toffee's not wise. She just goes wandering through the fence anyway. Whenever she feels like it.

Most places there's a bit of shore sloping down to the water. But not where Toffee went the other day. There the sides have been bricked up quite high. Three good strong brick walls forming a sort of open-ended box with water at the bottom and open to the lake on the fourth side. I've decided that it's where the water flows into the lake. I mean, it has to come from somewhere and that looks like as good a place as any.

To be honest, the walls aren't *that* high. Not as high as human number 2, say, and he isn't very big as humans go. But it's still quite high enough. Especially as you wouldn't be standing on anything solid at the bottom. Not land or anything. There's just water. And by the smell of it, cold water these days.

Toffee was on the sort of platform at the top. Wandering around smelling things. Kibble knows what. There were no birds to chase, there was no food to eat. What was the point?

Meanwhile, the human and I had kept on walking down the path. On the right side of the railings. The *out*side.

Of course.

But if you're out with Toffee, you can never walk far without checking up on her. So we'd only gone a few steps before the human looked back. And saw what was going on.

"Oh, Toffee," he said, in his annoyed voice.

Funny how often he has to use it with her.

"What on earth are you doing there?"

Toffee looked up. She gave him that innocent look she does so well. You know, "what me? I'm not doing anything wrong, am I?"

"You know you're not allowed inside the railings. Come out at once," he said.

Not only was she on the other side of the railings, she was still on the far side of the brick-sided box of water. There was her, then the water, then the railings, then us.

All I could think was "don't call her! Don't call her!"

"Come on, Toffee. Come out. Come on Toffee," he called, ignoring me completely.

I knew exactly what was going to happen. When Toffee does her innocent act, she only has eyes for the human she's trying to impress. It's like she actually can't see anything else. Not even what's right in front of her, however awful it may be.

The water was right in front of her. And pretty awful.

He stopped calling, with a great intake of breath. I could see that he too had understood what might be coming next. We both stood there watching. Aghast.

She trotted gaily straight towards us, right to the edge of the wall.

And then she kept on going. Straight over the line of bricks and into the great drop down to the freezing cold water. Into which she neatly fell with a bit of a plop but barely a ripple.

To be fair, it was a pretty nice dive. Though it probably helped that she's so small. And I don't think she was actually trying, she was just super-graceful by accident.

As it happens, most of the snow that had been lying around over the previous days had gone. But there were still odd bits here and there. It was a lot too cold for anyone to want a nice swim or anything.

Her little head came back up to the surface. Toffee doesn't like to complain. Not like me. I make it clear to anyone listening when I'm not happy. But not Toffee. She tried to look determined and purposeful. Like she'd really intended to go for a swim and knew just what she was doing. But I could tell she was panicking, if only because she was swimming round and round in circles. After all, where could she go? The way out into the main lake is blocked by a net. The other end is where the water comes in – through a dark tunnel. And either side is just sheer brick wall.

There was no way out.

The human wasn't doing well either. I mean, he reacted fast. He tore round to the other side of the water where Toffee had been and over the fence even more quickly than Toffee had got through it. But that only left him where she'd been before. You know, *before* falling in. She wasn't there anymore. We'd seen that. There wasn't a lot of point looking around there – he wasn't going to find her where she wasn't.

Meanwhile she was still just swimming around in circles.

I wanted to try to encourage her.

"How are you doing?" I asked her.

"Fine, fine," she said, but her teeth were chattering, so she said it a bit grimly. And the way she was paddling hectically away, she didn't seem that fine.

"Cold?" I asked.

"What does the human always like to say? Bracing?" she replied breathlessly, still thrashing away at the water.

By then, the human had worked out that on the *other* side of the water, near where I was standing, there was a ladder stuck to the wall. He jumped out of the fenced-in bit again in a jiffy, ran back round to my side, and went over the railings once more. I was quite impressed by the speed he went down the ladder, even though at the bottom he must have been getting his paws wet.

"Come on Toffee," he called to the still frantically paddling dog.

She kept going in circles, but at least the circles were getting closer to him each time.

"Over here, Toffee, over here," he kept saying.

Suddenly, she seemed to get it, stopped the circling and swam straight towards him.

He bent down (I couldn't help wondering what would happen if he lost his grip and they both ended up in the water – I couldn't get them out, after all – but fortunately that didn't happen). He hooked a finger in her collar and pulled.

It can be an advantage being small. It took him just one movement to land her back on the platform above him, where she could stand shivering.

Oh, well. No great harm was done. Nothing that couldn't be fixed with a quick trip home, a rub with a towel and then an hour or two under the blanket on the couch to get warm again.

And one more thing – a bath that evening. The water really hadn't smelled that good. And now she smelled like the water. I don't think that's a lake to go swimming in, even in the summer.

As for the middle of winter – well, only Toffee would do it. And only if she was being unusually dumb. Though she claims she's learned her lesson.

"Never again," she told me.

Seems she'd come to her senses. Long may it last, I say. After all, we don't need our walks spoiled, and that kind of thing has a terribly dampening effect, doesn't it?

Luci let down by a false friend

I'm beginning to wonder whether I can entirely trust that Toffee.

She has her look. Wide-eyed and innocent. Like nothing you could begin to think was wrong would ever even occur to her.

And then, and then, you turn your back on her for just a moment and she gets up to the most atrocious things.

Take breakfast, for instance. The humans decided a while back that we should get Kibble in the morning. Don't know why. For a time, they were giving us bits of meat out of a proper tin or pouch. Not that dry, biscuit-stuff. All crunch and no satisfaction.

"We need to balance their diet better," human number 1 said, and what human number 1 says, goes. In our house.

Not that I understand what "balanced" means. As much of the deadly-dull as of the interesting food? As much food we don't like as food we do? As much tedium as enjoyment?

It's a daily disappointment, quite frankly. Because hope wakes eternal in the canine breast, as Misty tells me. So every morning, there's this suspense when it comes close to the time for the humans to wake up.

"Oh, look," one of us will say, "it's number 2 waking up first." And we get all hopeful.

Or, "human number 1's first today," we say, resigning ourselves to another Kibble day.

As it happens, it mostly *is* number 2 who wakes up first.

He stirs and groans a bit and thrashes around in bed. Sometimes he looks like he might fall asleep again, which I find depressing, but to give Toffee her due, she's really good when that happens. She climbs up *on top* of him and then she licks his face. It probably helps that she's so stupidly light: he thinks it's endearing. If I lie on him, he usually pushes me off, sometimes saying something uncomplimentary like:

"She's becoming a bit of a weight, that one, isn't she?"

"She's not *that* big," number 1 will reply.

"Big enough if you're trying to sleep."

"You mean, like I was before you started talking?"

Anyway, because he thinks Toffee's endearing, he just strokes her when she licks his face. So she licks him some more and he strokes her again. By which time he's properly awake.

At this stage he grunts something about "too bloody early" but swings his feet out of bed anyway. Then he heads downstairs and we just shoot down with him.

You *bet* we do.

Because there was this wonderful moment one time. Just once. It's never happened since. But we've never forgotten.

He'd got downstairs but he hadn't drunk that evil-smelling black brew he likes every morning. He decided to feed us straight away. And he must have forgotten about the Kibble order.

So he scooped half a pouch of proper, wet food into each of our bowls. Half a pouch… The stuff of dreams. Not a full pouch or anything, but I always say half a pouch is better than none.

Since that glorious moment, even with him, it's been Kibble every day. But we've never lost hope, even though that's basically meant a daily disappointment. Breakfast *could* mean wonderful soft food, even if generally it just means a miserable bowl of Kibble. Which is a sad moment. A moment that leaves us no choice but to look into our bowls and learn to live with the bleakness that besets the soul.

I'm not sure what that last sentence means. Misty dictated it to me. But it somehow says it all about how gloomy we feel.

"You know," human number 2 sometimes says, "they really don't like the Kibble that much."

"Yes," she replies, "but it gives them things they don't get from their other food. And they always eat it in the end."

That's the thing. She's right. We always do eat it in the end.

Which brings me back to Toffee and how she can be... well... a bit two-faced.

Neither of us is in any doubt over whose bowl's whose. Mine's to the left, hers to the right. And when it's food we really like, we vacuum our bowls pretty much clean in basically one long inhale. With Kibble, on the other hand, when we're not so enthusiastic – to say the least – we might leave a bit behind in our bowls for later.

So then there's a bit of a contest. Neither of us may like the stuff that much, but it's always fun to get a bit of an edge, isn't it? If we can sneak in and quickly snaffle a mouthful or two from the other's bowl, well, it's fair game, isn't it?

If I try to take some of Toffee's Kibble, she comes racing in, yapping like a crazy dog as soon as she hears the first crunch. Honestly, it's enough to give you a headache. And it startles me so much each time than I move away at once, giving Toffee the impression that she's won some kind of easy victory.

And if I hear her crunching Kibble, I go running back into the kitchen too, but not yapping or anything. I just growl in a ladylike way.

"Caught me! You caught me!" Toffee will say before dancing away. But if I keep on growling, she just comes running around behind me and bites my tail, as though I were playing. About food! Would you believe it? Who plays about anything that serious?

And the worst of it? I get so shocked I move away from the bowl to settle my nerves. And I just can't believe what she does next. She moves right in and goes on devouring my share.

At least I have the decency to stop eating from her bowl when she shows up. She'll go right on if she can get away with it. How can that be right?

I suppose the whole thing's a bit funny, though, isn't it? However little we like the Kibble, we like the other one getting some of our share even less. So the battle goes on between us.

Not just between us, as it happens. The worst part is that Misty also sometimes gets involved. He'll wait until we're both out of the room. And then he'll stalk over, oh so dignified and all, and sidle up to a bowl and start crunching away, as though it were his.

I know he does. I've seen him. You can see right into the kitchen from the dining room and sometimes I watch him, even if he doesn't realise it.

And what does Toffee do? Well, she goes rushing in just like she always does, but all quiet. Like she doesn't want to wake anyone. She goes right up to him as though about to say "hey, stop eating! That's my food" or maybe even "That's Luci's food".

He just looks up and gives her a long calm stare. And then turns back to the food and goes on eating.

And, to my amazement, she joins him. Her head in there, into the bowl, right next to his. As though nothing's the matter.

Well, nothing would be the matter if it were *her* kibble she was sharing with him. But as often as not, it isn't. It's mine.

And they make a real meal out of it. *My* food. All gone. Into the bellies of two treacherous friends.

I thought she was on my side.

It's a bit of a sad let down, really.

"She just knows who the boss is around here," says Misty, "and that it pays to get on with him."

Dignity? You can't eat it, can you? What possible use is it?

By Senada Borcilo

Misty and the return of domestic number 2

Domestic number 2 came back. As I knew he would. Of course I knew. He was bound to come back. Wasn't he? People do, don't they? But, though I hate to admit it, sometimes people don't come back. Like the old dog Janka, who vanished all that time ago.

Domestic number 2 always does come back after he goes away. Eventually. Why, the domestics even have a saying for this recurring event: like a bad penny.

I'm not going to admit this to the canine faction in the household, but I don't know exactly what a bad penny is. Still, I suppose the clue's in the name – it can't be good. And, like number 2, it apparently always comes back.

Not that I don't like him or anything. He has his uses. But those uses tend to be much more useful, I've found, if I make him feel like I regard him as a bad penny.

Unlike me, the silly little dogs had given up on him completely. I've met mice who have longer memories than they do. Not that they get a third chance, the mice, if they forget how lucky they were to get away with running around in the open once.

"It'll be good when domestic number 2 comes back," I said to the pathetic poodles on an occasion when number 1 was having trouble getting everything done – you know, the important things like getting us fed and stroking us properly.

"Domestic number 2? Who's he?" said Toffee.

"Oh, don't be silly," I told her, "the funny one who tends to be better at doing what he's told. Like throwing a toy for you."

"I remember," said Luci, though I could see it was an effort for her.

Suddenly a light went on with Toffee too.

"Oh yes! I remember! There was a human who used to lift me back up on the bed, after I got down. And it didn't matter how often I asked. He was quite helpful, wasn't he? But he doesn't seem to be around."

It's sad. The domestics like to use those silly phones of theirs, the ones they carry around with them everywhere, and number 1 was talking to number 2 the other day – I knew it was number 2 because her voice goes all affectionate, with nothing like enough of the "you're just a bad penny" tone. She suddenly decided to put the phone by Toffee's ear and the silly poodle went all demented, as though she'd suddenly remembered about him. How could she forget at all? And how could just hearing his voice bring it all so back to her so vividly? How ridiculous can you get?

It's hard to believe, but Toffee spent the next several minutes looking around everywhere to see if she could see him.

"I can hear him but I can't see him or smell him. How does *that* happen?"

To be honest, it's not entirely clear to me either, how we can hear him and not smell him. But, hey, if I wasted my time trying to understand everything the domestics do, I'd never be able to get around to really important things. Like keeping the population of mice and birds within sensible limits.

And just because I don't understand it doesn't make Toffee any less dumb for not understanding it either.

Anyway, it was obvious what was going to happen when he got home. If those two goldfish-brains had more or less forgotten him, they were going to go absolutely mental when he showed up and they remembered again. Which was exactly what happened.

It was a strange sort of time. Hunting was nearly over and

I'd just headed back indoors – there's no point staying out once the sky starts to lighten. That's when he rang the bell. She, domestic number 1, was still asleep with the silly canines next to her. They went wild, of course. Someone walking past the house gets them barking. Someone knocking has them yapping away furiously. But the doorbell? It's like a whole choir of dogs got started, though there's only two of them.

Down the stairs they rushed, Toffee desperately keeping up with Luci – funny how fast Luci moves when she thinks her territory's being threatened, though kibble only knows what she'd do if there were a real threat, like a proper intruder. When she meets strangers, all she does is yap a lot and back away if they come towards her. I'm not sure that hers the most effective of defence strategies.

Anyway, domestic number 2 has this thing he does when he hears the girls barking. He barks back, from outside. And when I say "bark", I don't really mean "bark". It's a lot more like a domestic saying, "whoof, whoof". But it really gets the girls going. They start jumping up and down and whimpering. Or do I mean simpering? Perhaps they simper whimperishly. In any case, it's a bit of a stomach churner. So soft. So sentimental. So sickly.

Domestic number 1 had to get up to let him in. Seems he hadn't taken a key. Probably just as well, since he'd probably have lost them – I wish I had a pouch of cat food for every time he's lost things. She didn't seem to mind, anyway. She was just as silly about his coming back as the girls were, even though at least she didn't dance around on her back feet and make little whiney noises like they did.

I hung back, of course. I'm not like them. I know dignity matters. I waited till all the rotten raptures were over and then approached him quietly while he was struggling upstairs with a suitcase. Man to man, giving him a civilised greeting with proper restraint. He reacted appropriately.

"Ah, Misty," he said, putting down the suitcase (with relief, I suspect), "good to see you. How are you doing?"

I told him how I was doing, as it happens, but as usual I met a blank wall of incomprehension, as though he couldn't understand me. Honestly, why does he ask me questions if he won't admit I've mastered English?

Anyway, he bent down to stroke me, which was just as things should be. So I gave him a playful bite on the hand, just to re-establish a proper relationship between us.

"Ah, yes," he said, rubbing the hand, "good to be home. Good to have normal service resumed."

My own sentiment exactly. That's what good service needed to be. Resumed. And it was. Though without always being *that* good. Mostly he does feed me when I look at him piteously. And he doesn't generally do anything about it if, having vacated a chair to get something from the kitchen, I move in and sit on it. He just moves to another one. And he opens doors for me, even the one next to the cat flap, when I ask him.

But he can't resist the odd sarky comment, all the same.

"Too tired to open the cat flap, then?" was one, the other day.

I suppose I shouldn't mind. The important thing is that the door gets opened. But that kind of unnecessary remark does rather spoil the good effect, doesn't it?

Ah, well. Normal service resumed, like he said. For better *and* for worse.

Toffee, a trainer without even knowing it

Misty's so clever, you know. He understands things. Things I don't always get until he explains them to me.

Like claws. He keeps telling me just how useful they are.

"They're particularly useful," he says, "when you have to deal with a tedious puppy."

"Really? Really?" I told him, "We have a puppy? Where is she? Where is she?"

"I'm talking to her, you silly fool."

I looked around, a bit confused.

"Where is she? Where is she?"

I said nothing but looked at her, meaningfully, I hope.

"Do you mean me? You don't mean me, do you? Or... do you?"

"It's OK. Getting your mind around an idea's the important thing. It doesn't matter that it takes some time."

It's odd. When he said that, I thought he was being quite kind. But now that I come to write those words down, I'm not sure he was. Not really.

Still, there was an important point to make, even if I wasn't that comfortable about what he'd said.

"But I'm not a puppy. And I'm not tedious. *At all*. I hardly ever annoy you."

"That's the first time I've heard you admit you aren't a puppy anymore," he said. "Congratulations. And I agree, you're not a puppy anymore. Sometimes, though, you behave like one. In fact, not just sometimes. Pretty often really. Which is when you annoy me."

"But I'm only trying to play. Who doesn't like playing?"

He sighed.

"Not everyone likes it that much. Or not all the time. Sometimes some of us reach the point where we need to use our claws just a bit. So you understand that it's time to stop."

"But using your claws… that's not very nice… it hurts…"

"Of course, it hurts. What would be the point if it didn't hurt? You need to understand that things can turn nasty if you don't behave. And unless it hurts a bit you might not realise that it could hurt a lot more."

"But you don't really want to hurt me, do you?"

"I want you to stop annoying me when I've had enough. That's all you need to understand. And you do understand, which is why you stop."

"That's true! It does works, doesn't it? I always go all quiet when you get your claws into my fur. When you do that, I just think how nasty it would be if you stuck them in any further."

"Exactly! Which shows you can be trained. And claws are really good for that."

"Oh, I wish I could do that too!"

"What do you mean?" Misty seemed really surprised. "You *do* have claws. And you use them for training."

Now I was confused again.

"But… but… but… I don't have real claws, like you do. And I don't remember ever using them that way. And I don't train you, anyway."

"Of course, you don't train *me*, you silly girl," he said.

He's often like that, calling me names, but he doesn't mean it. He really, really likes me. Really.

"No one trains cats," he went on, "everyone knows that…" And, before I could say that I didn't know it, he went on, "everyone who knows anything about cats and dogs, at least. You can't train cats."

"So who do I train?"

"Well, it's obvious, isn't it?"

Not to me it wasn't.

He sighed again.

"The domestic, of course."

"The humans?" I asked.

"Well, one of them. Domestic number 2. You train him every evening."

You know, I hadn't noticed. I'd been training one of the humans without knowing it? I was a trainer without thinking about it? That was just wonderful.

"Every evening," he went on, "when he's trying to watch TV. You jump up on the couch with one of your silly toys in your mouth and you get him to throw it for you. And it works, doesn't it?"

"Yes! Yes!" I said, "it does! And that's me training him, is it?"

"Of course, it is. You're getting him to do what you want. Whether or not he wants it. That's what training's all about. And it works all the time, doesn't it? Or does it?"

"Well, no, not all the time. Sometimes he forgets to throw the toy."

"Exactly. And what do you do when that happens?"

"Well, I scratch him a bit. On the arm."

"Hard?"

"Oh, no. Not terribly hard. Just hard enough to get his attention."

"And what do you use to do that?"

"Well, my claws of course."

"There you go! Your claws."

That was just such an amazing thought, I had to stop and think about it a while.

"Wow. You're so right. I *do* use my claws."

"And what does that make you think of?"

"Err... what it makes me think of? I can't think of anything. Because I'm only really thinking about running after my toys. Oh! I really like that game," and that *did* give me a thought: "you couldn't throw one for me, could you?"

But he just scratched me instead of answering. Unless that

was his answer.

"Just stop thinking about playing, for a moment, will you?" he said. "Instead think of what we were talking about before. Claws. Hurting a bit but not a lot. Training. Come on. What does that make you think of?"

I thought and thought because I didn't want him to scratch me again. And then it came to me.

"You! You and me! Training me! With your claws."

"Exactly," he said, "you've got it. I'm a trainer. You're a trainer too.

"I am, I am. I train him to play with me! You're so right."

"Of course, he's training you too."

What? What was he saying now?

"What do you mean?" I asked.

"You annoy him just like you annoy me. By making him play with you when he doesn't want to. And what's more you scratch him if he doesn't. And instead of just giving you a clip and sending you off to behave yourself, he throws the toy for you. Poor sap. He thinks he'll get a bit of peace that way. Instead, he just encourages you to keep doing exactly what you want. So he's training you to go on irritating him."

"But that's just silly…"

"Yep. Who said that you were the only one in this family who's silly? Others can be just as silly. Don't you listen to what domestic number 1 tells him when he does it?"

Frankly, I don't.

"Well, I'm too busy chasing the toy and getting him to throw it again."

"Next time, listen," he said.

I did. That evening. What she said was, "if you keep encouraging her, she'll just come back for more. You've got to learn to say 'no' to her."

He did say "no" to me and for a while he didn't throw the toy anymore. But I waited until he was really wrapped up in whatever he was watching on TV – I wasn't paying attention because there wasn't any barking or mewing or anything else interesting – and then I scratched him on his shoulder.

"Oww," he went. And then, almost like he wasn't thinking about it at all, he picked up the toy and threw it for me.

Fantastic. It worked. Just as Misty explained.

Like I said. He knows his stuff, our cat. He's wise.

A proper trainer. And so am I.

Luci suspects Toffee of cleverness

You know, I'm beginning to wonder about that little Toffee. I mean, she's so obviously silly. Misty always says she is. But then I keep noticing little things about her which make me think, "watch your step. She may not be so dumb after all".

The first hint I got was when we were out for a walk with both humans. We met two other dogs coming up the road, and that's always a bit awkward. I like to get well out of the way but Toffee wants to go jumping at them. That makes for a bit of a tangle. Literally a tangle. Like leads around our legs.

Once the other lot had gone away, human number 1 started untangling my legs. She does that quickly and deftly so I just stand still and let her get on with it. But then human number 2 said something that surprised me.

"Look at Toffee! She's got herself disentangled. All on her own."

We all looked. It was true. Her lead was hanging neatly in front of her and all four legs were free.

Now I know there's a trick you can do. You have to lift one leg and put it down again. Then I think you have to lift another one. But I always get confused at this point and can't remember which leg has to be done next and what has to be done with it. So I give up, especially as it doesn't matter, and one of the humans will sort me out before long anyway.

But Toffee had pulled it off? How did she do that?

"She's a clever dog," said human number 1.

A clever dog? Well, *that* took my breath away. Toffee? Clever? Not silly?

I mean, she walked off a wall into freezing water. But she's clever?

Naturally, I didn't believe it. Just an accident that she'd got herself disentangled. I mean, Misty and I agree that she's silly, and we can't both be wrong. Can we?

Except that... it kept happening. Every time she got entangled, she disentangled herself again. One leg up, jiggle a bit, put it down again and, hey presto, the leg's clear. I watched really carefully but I couldn't see how she was doing it. All I know is that it *worked.*

And that wasn't the end of it. She's always getting into scrapes, that Toffee. That's what I mean by silly. One time we were walking on the common where there are those strange creatures that look like big dogs but are really horses. Because Toffee's small, she can sometimes slip through the holes in the wire fences. She just can't get enough of horse, so as soon as she saw a hole in the fence, through she slipped, to get closer to them.

Human number 2, who we'd taken out for the walk, went mad.

"Toffee! What are you doing? Why are you in there? It's dangerous in there with the horses. They could kick you. And that could kill you. Come here, Toffee. Come out. Come."

Well, she tried. She knows the word 'dangerous' as well as I do. And the word 'come'. So just like the time when she fell in the water from trying to come straight to the human, she ran straight at us – but hit the fence. That wasn't a bit with a hole big enough for her to get through.

Oh, I was so worried. What if one of those horses came over and kicked her? I could see one of them had heard the commotion and was looking in our direction. Oh no, oh no. That little girl was about to get into really bad trouble.

All human number 2 could do was keep repeating, "Come on, Toffee. Come on. Come."

Then something really weird happened. She went running *away*. Completely the wrong direction. Along the fence. Back the way we'd come but much further. She was leaving us *completely*.

And – suddenly she wasn't. She was racing back towards us – no one races quite like Toffee does when she gets started – and on the *right* side of the fence. On our side. But I hadn't even seen her find a hole.

How on Earth did she do that?

"Well done, Toffee," the human was saying, "you found the gate. Well *done.* What a clever dog."

She even got a treat for being so clever. Well, I got one too, because they always give treats to both of us when they're giving out treats at all. Which is only fair. Except when I deserve the treat and Toffee doesn't. And I enjoyed it, of course I did, why wouldn't I? But all I could think of was that one word – "clever". There it was again. And used for Toffee.

But the final thing was to do with the letters. We have a favourite game, Toffee and me. There are these strange people who stick things through the postbox in the front door and into *our* territory. The postbox is a kind of hole in the door and they stick letters through without even asking us whether that's alright. I mean, we always bark at them when we see them outside. But then there's a door between us and them. So we just bark and bark and *bark*. Then we try to get the letters and have a wonderful time tearing them into little bits.

The humans have put a kind of cage on the door which means we can't get at the letters. Which means we just have to keep barking. Then a human takes the letters out of the cage and puts them on the table. We follow barking all the time but once they're on the table, well, they're out of reach so I just go back to the couch and lie down again.

But not Toffee. She came trotting over the other day with one of the letters in her mouth, so we tore it to pieces. But afterwards I asked her:

"How did you get it? Did it fall on the floor?"

"No," she said, "I got it from the table where the human put it."

Now I was really thrown.

"But... you can't jump onto the table. I can't jump onto the table. Only Misty can do that. And you're smaller than I am."

"Well, I jumped onto a chair, and from the chair onto the table."

"You jumped onto a chair? But what's the point of that if you want to jump onto the table?"

"It's easy to get onto the chair. And a lot easier to get onto the table from the chair than from the floor."

I had no idea what she was talking about. It's a bit like the day with the horses. She wants to go to one place and she gets there by going somewhere else.

Beats me how she does that. But I have to admit it works.

That's what makes me feel she's smarter than you might imagine. Which is a bit sneaky, when you think about it. Seeing how most of the time she acts like she was a lot stupider. I need to watch out.

"Oh, Lord," said human number 2 to human number 1, "we need to put the post somewhere else than on the table. Toffee's worked out how to get up onto it."

"She's a cleverer dog than she seems," said human number 1, "we need to learn to be a bit more careful."

See? Just what I was thinking.

Toffee playing and being smart

What a great time we had yesterday!

There's this human who comes round the house from time to time. She's a lot of fun. I mean, Luci always barks at her – fierce, fierce, fierce – but then backs away as quick as she can when the human reaches out to her – scared, scared, scared.

"That's Luci for you," says Misty, "all bark, no bite."

Anyway, we all just wait a bit and then Luci goes all quiet and lets the human stroke her. It never fails. Happens every time. Lots of barking then all calm and tame.

Of course, I don't wait at all. I just go straight up to her and wag my tail when she first turns up. And she's great: she just picks me up as soon as I do that. So I sit in her arms while she strokes me, and we both ignore the Luci chorus. The only thing she doesn't let me do is lick her face but, hey, you can't have everything, can you?

Anyway, yesterday she turned up – and she had her two puppies in tow! I mean, not the doggy type. The human type. Two girls and they were even more fun than the big human.

One of them picked me up, just as soon as her mother put me down. And the puppy was just as good at stroking me in her arms as the Mum was. She wouldn't let me lick her face either but, hey, even with a puppy human, you can't have everything.

The other one just waited for Luci to stop barking. But when Luci finally let the Mum stroke her, the puppy girl decided to be friends with her. So we both had a friend, which was just great,

I suppose. I mean, it's good that we shared the puppies, isn't it? Though, oddly, it didn't feel as good as if they'd both been stroking me.

My puppy had much more fun, of course. Because we did lots of interesting things. I mean, Luci just played her usual game. She just grabs a toy in her teeth and then had her puppy try to drag it away from her. She loves that. She growls and growls and sounds terribly fierce, but no one's fooled, not even the puppy. She just kept pulling back and they both seemed to be enjoying it.

I suppose it might be OK to play that game, but Luci has these *really tough* jaws, and she always grabs the toy from me when we play, so I don't play with her anymore because, hey, where's the fun in having her win all the time?

But I don't get it anyway. I mean, it's hardly the best game, is it? Isn't it silly that anyone can play that game for ages and ages? It's not like having the toy *thrown* for you so you can chase after it. Now *that's* a really good game. A game it's easy to play for hours and hours. Which makes it bizarre that human number 2 just won't. After a stupidly short time he complains that his arm's hurting. His arm? What does that have to do with anything? When you're playing a *really good* game, a bit of pain in the arm shouldn't matter.

Honestly. Pathetic.

With my puppy, we played that kind of proper game. Throwing things for me to fetch – a toy or a ball or whatever. And then, just for a change, sometimes I'd hide it in my little house.

"That isn't your house. It's my house," Misty says. "I really liked it, with its sponge on top and its soft furry stuff underneath. I used to enjoy resting in there till you turned up and interrupted any kind of rest for any of us."

"It's *my* house," I tell him, "I'm the one using it."

It's Toffee's house now
By Senada Borcilo

He sighs. "Well, I suppose it *is* yours now, but only because you don't let anyone else get near it."

So I'd hide, say, the ball in it, and she – the human puppy – would get down on her hands and knees and try to get her head in – while I was in there – to get the ball back. It was *great.* That lovely house – *my* house – smells very nicely of me – and when she stuck her head in, it smelled of her too, and how great is that? The smell of two people who're having fun playing a game, it's just magic.

Then she'd walk around holding a toy in her hand and I'd go wandering around her, doing my walking on my back legs act, which human number 1 calls "dancing dog". I kept trying to grab the toy from her hand and she'd keep pulling it away. Wow, we had *such a good time*. I was really sorry when the mummy human told the puppies they all had to go.

"Gosh, it's so good having the puppies around with her. I hope she'll bring them every time."

"She won't," said Misty.

"How do you know? She *might*."

I tried not to sound too disappointed, but Misty's usually right, so I couldn't help feeling a bit sad.

"The only time adult domestics bring the little domestics with them is when school's out. So it must be out right now. It won't be next time she shows up."

"School?" I said, "What's that?"

He shook his head. "Something you've never had the benefit of and wouldn't understand anyway."

He stalked away. I hate it when he does that, in the middle of a conversation. But I knew better than to go after him. Those teeth of his, you know, and those claws. I think I've mentioned them before.

Still, it had been a good day. Though it got a bit spoiled in the evening.

"Time for your worming treatment," said human number 1, brightly, like she was telling us we had extra food on the way or a really long walk.

But I saw Luci trying to back away, like she does, when she knows she can't escape human number 1 but would like to try anyway. *That* didn't look like more food or a good walk.

The human caught Luci. "Open up," she said.

"Oh, no," said Luci, but that was a mistake, because then her mouth was open. So the human popped something in and then clamped Luci's jaws shut with a hand over her muzzle. With the other hand she was stroking Luci's throat downwards, energetically, not like proper stroking at all.

"There you go, Luci," she said, "good girl. That wasn't so bad, was it?" and she gave her a treat.

Then she grabbed me.

"Your turn, Toffee," she said, "open up."

Well, I wasn't falling for that so I gripped my jaws tight. But the human has strong fingers. She quickly had my mouth open and popped this nasty hard round thing in.

"Now just swallow," she said, going through the same act as with Luci, holding my jaws shut with one hand and stroking my throat – nothing like real stroking – with the other.

"Good girl," she said, and then I got a treat too.

But I'd outsmarted her. I'd made little swallowing movements, but I'd popped the nasty round thing into my cheek. When she wasn't looking, I spat it out again, on the couch.

Unfortunately, later on she saw it.

"Oh, no!" she said, "you naughty girl! You spat out your pill!"

Hmm. Odd, isn't it? How did she know it was me? It could have been Luci, couldn't it?

She tried again. Force, force, force the mouth open. Push, push, push the thing towards my throat. Stroke, stroke, stroke the throat. This time she really thought she'd got it.

"At last," she said, but I noticed I didn't get a treat.

She hadn't noticed that I'd just put the pill back into my cheek again. Maybe she didn't spot it because I used the other cheek. I'm not stupid, whatever Misty says.

This time I spat out the pill under the table in front of our couch.

But she *still* noticed it.

"Oh, no!" she said again. "She's spat it out this time too. Naughty dog."

This time, though, she seemed to have learned her lesson.

"I'm not doing that again," she said and went to the kitchen with the pill. That's where the bin is, so I knew she was going to throw it away and I'd won.

And the odd thing is, this time she gave me a treat. A special treat. A lump of cheese. Quite a big lump. It was delicious. Though, funnily, it was a bit crunchy inside.

When she came back to the couch, she said, "phew. At least that worked. I didn't want to go through all that struggle again."

I'm a bit puzzled. What did she mean? What worked? What was she so pleased about?

Still. Doesn't matter. It was a good day, all in all. First, the human puppies, especially my one. Then dodging the silly pill. And then the wonderful big cheese lump. Crunchy inside or not, it was a great way to end the evening.

I'm not complaining.

Luci ponders
human sayings

Humans have some strange ideas, don't they? Sometimes they even have little sayings they trot out to each other. Perhaps they keep repeating the sayings to make sure they never forget them. Maybe someone should explain that forgetting them is much the best thing for silly ideas like that.

Take "you can have too much of a good thing", for instance. Weird, isn't it? How can you ever have too much of a good thing? I mean, I've often had too *little* of a good thing, but too much? What kind of sense does *that* make?

Still, I almost knew what they meant a while back. I mean, I've said before that it gets on my nerves when outside gets too hot. You know, like when the humans don't put anything on over their shirts when we go for walks. Always a bad sign.

"It's called 'summer', you silly animal," Misty says in that rude way he has when he doesn't want to admit that he likes us lots and lots. I wonder why he does that? We all know dogs are lovable. And you don't get more lovable than me and Toffee.

Well, Toffee some of the time.

"I've told you before," he goes on. "Best time of year. When a cat can lie outside on a warm paving stone and soak up the sun."

"Yes," I replied, remembering, "very uncomfortable. I'm just glad it doesn't happen too often."

"Nothing like often enough," he says with what sounds strangely like a sigh, "and that's called 'England'."

I didn't know that the word for not enough warm weather was 'England', so I'd learned something new.

In any case, he may like it when things are that way, but I prefer it when you can run around in the park without collapsing and panting. Toffee does that collapse-and-pant bit a lot, but then she runs around a lot more than me. Still a puppy, you see, even though the humans say she's an adult.

"I'm so glad you think so," Toffee says.

That's an odd thing to say, isn't it? "I'm glad you think so"? What's that supposed to mean? It sounds like her whole puppy act really is just that. An act.

I don't like acts. They're much too clever for me. And it's a bit uncomfortable to think Toffee may be much cleverer than you'd think from looking at her. But why does she do it? I mean, if anyone thinks I'm going to leave her extra food just because I think she's a puppy, well they need their heads examining. After all, I'm quicker at eating than she is. And anything she leaves, I'll go straight for if I get the chance.

So what's in it for her, this puppy act? If it *is* an act. I watch her really carefully in the evenings, as I sit quietly in the corner of my sofa. She rushes about chasing toys for just as long as human number 2 is silly enough to keep throwing them for her. She lies on human number 1's lap and gets stroked. And sometimes she lies up against human number 2 and has him stroke her instead.

Just what is the act getting her? I can't see what it does for her. It must be something I'm missing. And that's not a comfortable feeling.

Anyway, I like cold better than hot. I like it when the pavement doesn't feel warm to my paws on the way to the park. I like it when the grass in the park is crisp and cool. To be honest, though the humans don't like it when I get home, I enjoy it when the paths are a bit wet and refreshing and I can dip my paws in the puddles or feel the mud ooze around them. Much better than when it's all hard and dry.

Why, I even like that cold white stuff that Misty calls 'snow'.

"Of course I call it snow, you silly creature," snaps Misty, still pretending not to like me all that much, "That's what it *is*. I've told you loads of times. Nasty wet stuff that sticks to the fur and makes my paws sting."

Snow it is, then. But it isn't nasty, like he says. It's cool and soft and you can run in it without getting all pant-y and tired. It's fun to run around in and smell and even eat bits of. Soft and cool and crisp and fun. I can't get enough of it.

Except, well, I *can* get enough of it. Maybe that thing about too much of a good thing isn't quite as silly as I thought. After a while, maybe you can have more than enough snow.

After a few days, when it's there on the ground every time we go out, it starts to get just a little bit annoying. Eventually, we just come back wet and cold. A bit shivery and uncomfortable, if you know what I mean. So maybe in really strange situations, you actually *can* have too much of a good thing. But it's still a lousy idea generally. Normally, there's *never* enough of a good thing.

The other day, Toffee started shivering even while human number 1 was getting her ready to go out.

"Why are you shivering?" I asked, "it's nice and warm. What's the problem?"

"*Here* it's warm," she said, "but we're going outside in a minute. And it's freezing out there."

I couldn't get that at all. "You mean you're shivering now about the cold you're going to feel in a while?"

"Well, yes," she said, "I know what's it going to be like."

It's sort of odd. I can't do that. Work out how I'm going to feel *later*. I know how I feel *now* and if I think about it really hard, sometimes I have a sense of how I felt *before*, but how I'm going to feel *in a while*? How would I know? And what's the point anyway? I mean, particularly if it's a bad feeling, won't it be annoying enough when I actually have to feel it, without making myself feel it already?

The humans do that too, though. They call it "being prepared", which is one of the other strange ideas they have. So when it's really cold they make us put on our silly coats.

I *hate* those coats. They go over our heads, which is OK, though it isn't nice. Then they have to push our front legs through a strange kind of long holes that leave me feeling really weird and uncomfortable, like someone's grabbed my legs. I always whimper when they do that, and to be honest I even try to bite them.

"You mustn't let her do that," says human number 1.

"Well, being bitten by Luci's a bit like being bitten by bubble bath. It doesn't actually hurt or anything."

"Still, she shouldn't do it."

Well, maybe I shouldn't, but I really hate it when they do that thing with the coat.

"But it doesn't hurt," says Toffee, who always lets them put her coat on without a problem.

"I know," I tell her, "but it *might*."

"So you see, you also react to things that haven't happened yet."

Really? I'm doing the same thing as her? Getting upset about what's going to happen but still hasn't? That's an interesting thought. I'll have to think about it. But later – it's too tiring to think about now.

For now, I'm just going to keep complaining about having to put that terrible coat on. I don't like it, whatever Toffee may feel. I think it's all part of another one of the humans' silly sayings: "there's no such thing as bad weather, just bad clothing".

Rubbish, isn't it? There was nothing wrong with the weather. OK, maybe it was just a tad *too* cold. Too much of a good thing, as the humans would claim. But hey, that's still a *good* thing. The bad thing's the ghastly coat. Specially having to put it on. Or take it off, which is painful too. It's just a lousy idea.

Like I said. Weird notions. The humans have far too many.

Toffee and what's fair

He's a bit tricksy, that Misty. I hadn't realised. But he is.

The humans give Luci and me our breakfast in bowls on the kitchen floor. Kibble. We make that last a bit. That's not so hard, making it last. I mean, it isn't meat, is it? Crunchy biscuits. Supposed to be good for us, according to the humans.

"They don't like it as much as the meat, do they?" human number 2 said the other day.

"No," says number 1, "but it's good for them."

Right. OK. If she says it's so, it must be so, mustn't it? Kibble's got to be good for us. After all, it tastes like most things that are supposed to be good for us. You know, at worst really nasty, at best – like the kibble – a bit dull.

Still, it's food, isn't it? Fills you up when you're hungry. We eat it. But, like human number 2 says, we don't just hoover it up. Sometimes it lasts till lunchtime, when they give us a real meal. The odd thing is Misty's attitude. While the kibble's in our bowls, it just seems to draw him to it all the time. He likes to sneak in when we're not looking and help himself.

I don't get it. I mean it's just *kibble*. It's not like it's really good or anything. Why does he want to steal it from us? But if he can get away with it, he does, every time.

Take the other day. I was lying on the couch like I do, nice and close to Luci, minding my own business, when I heard a tell-tale noise from the kitchen. There's a crunch to kibble you can't mistake. I was off the couch like a shot and headed straight for the bowls.

You can't mistake it and I wasn't mistaken. There was Misty, at it again. His head buried in *my* bowl, crunching *my* kibble. The cheek of it!

I wasn't putting up with any of *that*. I moved right in, nose first, and dived into the bowl. Kibble or not, I started positively *hoovering*. I may not have wanted it that much, but it was *my* kibble not his, and I wasn't going to let him have it.

It worked, too. Even though he's twice my size.

"Not twice," Misty points out, "*nearly* twice."

Well, even nearly twice my size makes him quite tough enough. But he knows he can't withstand me when I really care about something. I really care about things being *fair*. And there's nothing fair about eating my food, if you're not me.

Well, *of course* you're not me, because then who would I be? But you know what I mean.

"It's not whether I'm fair or not that matters," says Misty, "it's about whether life's fair. It isn't. So you should be thanking me, not criticising me, because I gave you a really important lesson in life."

Hmm. That *sounds* like it's clever. Misty's good at that – sounding clever. Sometimes he really *is* clever. But this time it was obvious that he wasn't making any sense. I mean, just look at it straight. The food was mine. The mouth it was going into was his. What else mattered? All that stuff about life lessons? Just that. Stuff.

Anyway, he went away which tells you something about what he really thought. I mean, he must have known he was in the wrong or he wouldn't have left off, would he? Not without throwing his weight around a bit first, at least. And he weighs twice as much as me.

"*Nearly* twice as much."

Anyway, I got on with chomping my kibble. But he didn't go far. In fact, he just walked behind me and around to the other side and stuck his face into the *other* bowl, next to mine.

Well, I naturally just reached across with my muzzle and started pushing him away again. A move which, like the first time, was working well at first. He pulled back a moment. Like he knew, again, that he was in the wrong. But then he came up with an argument that made much more sense. None of that nonsense about life lessons or anything. Something much more real.

"What's your problem, Toffee?" he said. "You've got *your* bowl. It's the one you're eating out of. It's because you're eating out of it that we know it's yours. So this one *can't* be yours, can it? Since you're so keen on fairness, how can it be fair to stop me eating out of a bowl that isn't yours?"

Well, he had a point, didn't he? I'd defended *my* bowl. The other bowl had nothing to do with me. Not *my* problem at all.

"You win," I told him, and went on eating my kibble. And he went on eating the kibble in the other bowl.

"Didn't it occur to you that it might be *my* bowl?" Luci asked me later. In a plaintive sort of way. Whiny, nearly.

"Yes, I suppose it might have been," I told her. She might have been right, after all. But then I saw the weak point in her argument: "but doesn't that just make it *your* problem?"

It all made sense to me. It isn't fair to have someone else take your food. It's only fair to stop them doing it. So it's only fair for Luci to stop Misty taking *her* food.

I don't see what else there is to say about it all.

Or, to go back to what I said before, there was a moment where *my* food was going down *Misty's* throat. That was definitely, totally unfair. And then, a bit later, my food was going down *my* throat. Which is definitely, totally fair.

So everything's good, isn't it?

"Depends on your point of view," says Luci.

Misty injured and insulted

Those dratted domestics can be so irritating at times. Despite all my efforts to educate them, they sometimes resort to the most stupid behaviour. I do make my displeasure clear to them – and I'm a bit of a champion when it comes to expressing displeasure – but they nonetheless persist in their unconscionable insolence.

Every month, they insist on grabbing me and sticking some ghastly smelly substance on my back.

"Got to be done," human number 1 says, "it keeps you free of fleas and worms. And you wouldn't want them, would you?"

Doesn't that just add insult to injury? A damn fool question like that? Would I want fleas and worms? What do *you* think?

It's an irrelevant question, isn't it? I mean, the right question is, "have I ever *had* fleas or worms?" Guess the answer to that one.

Yep, that's right. Flea and worm-free my entire life. Eleven years without so much as single insect bite or a single pesky wiggly creature to disturb my peace. And despite all that, despite the clear evidence of my long, eventful but flea-free life, the domestics keep sticking that nasty smelly stuff on my neck.

What's more, last time the domestics imposed that disagreeable experience on me, that pesky little Toffee decided to make things worse with a question of rank insensitivity.

"Hey, Misty, what's the matter, why do you let that silly treatment bother you so much?" she asked me.

We were out in the garden, even though it was cold and

dark. I always go straight out of the cat flap when they inflict that indignity on me. Which is a bit odd because generally I like to stand by the door and let the domestics open it for me, if they're around, but that flea treatment just drives me to distraction. I need to get outside fast, so the cat flap it has to be.

Though being outside doesn't do me any good. They put the ghastly stuff on the back of my neck where I couldn't lick it even if I wanted to, which I don't, since the smell of the stuff suggests the taste would be nothing short of stomach churning. You can still smell it in the garden, but at least out there the smell's a bit less strong.

But there are some irritations you just can't avoid So here was the moronic little orange dog asking me a stupid question. Well, I should say *another* stupid question, because she comes up with plenty of them. At first, I just didn't answer – there's a level of inanity in questions that makes it hard even to imagine an appropriate answer. But that orange dog's one of nature's little bouncers – I don't just mean because she jumps around all over the place, though she does, but because she bounces back from just about anything: a growl, a well-aimed paw, even a stinging rebuff. So obviously my cold contemptuous silence failed to cut her down to size.

It occurs to me that, since her bounciness often gets me bouncing off the walls, it may be infectious.

Anyway, the little bouncer just kept on asking.

"Misty, Misty, Misty, why, why, why do you let it bother you?"

I decided I had to come up with some kind of answer.

"Because it's irritating."

She stopped to think about that for a bit. I could see I'd got her with my devastating argument but then, tricksy creature that she is, she came back with a response that did, I have to admit, surprise me. Just a little.

"But isn't irritating just the same kind of thing as bothering? Isn't saying it's irritating just the same as saying it bothers you? Isn't it like saying it bothers you because it bothers you? Doesn't that make it a pretty useless answer? Doesn't it, Misty?

I mean, doesn't it, when you think about it?"

Well, that had me thinking a bit too.

"Not really. I suppose you can be bothered by things that don't irritate you... though maybe you can't really be irritated by something that doesn't bother you..."

"OK, Misty, Misty, Misty. Why do you let it irritate you so much? What's so irritating about it?"

See what I mean about *bouncing*? You think you've shut her up, but she just comes back with more of her prattling.

"Come on, Misty, Misty, Misty. It doesn't hurt, does it? They put it on my neck too, and it doesn't hurt a bit. So why does it irritate you, why, why, why?"

It's true that it doesn't actually hurt. A bit cold but, to be honest, that doesn't last long. It's wet, and I don't like wet on my skin, but that doesn't last long either.

"It smells bad," I said, conscious that it seemed a bit of a feeble explanation of why I reacted so intensely to the awful stuff. But I couldn't think of anything better.

"Oh, well, that doesn't bother me much. It's not that bad. And it soon smells less anyway. Besides, I've smelled a lot worse."

"So have I," I assured her, more comfortable now that I was able to take control of the conversation again, "especially when you come home after having rolled yourself in something awful."

"Oh, that's not smelling bad. That's smelling really *interesting*."

"Some of us have better taste. We know what smelling good is really like. And, let me tell you, it isn't how you smell after you've been out making yourself 'interesting'. Where 'interesting', I assume, is just another word for 'repellent'. And 'repellent' is how this flea and worm stuff smells to me."

She looked at me as though she wasn't sure of my common sense. Which is ironic, because I'm completely sure she long ago lost touch with any of her own.

"Oh well," she said, "suit yourself. You can stay out here if you want, if it bothers you that much to be inside after this easy little treatment. I'm going back in. They're on the couch and I want to sit on a lap."

With that, she was gone. Straight back through the cat flap. The one she calls the small dog flap.

"Of course, I call it that," she tells me, "that's what it is."

See what I mean? Always got a cheeky retort ready, the little bouncer. And I didn't even realise she was reading over my shoulder.

"Please yourself," she says, "if you don't want me reading over your shoulder I'm heading to the kitchen. There's still some breakfast kibble left."

And off she goes. Honestly, it makes me tired – breathless, even – just to watch her.

Anyway, back then, I didn't follow her in from the garden. I waited a bit, until they called me in. Not that they *did* call me in. But I knew they wanted me to come back in because I'd been out there for minutes and minutes. The little orange thing was on number 1's lap, and barked at me when I tried to get up on the sofa. But number 1 got all stern with her.

"*No*, Toffee," she said, "Misty can come up if he wants."

"Huh," said Toffee, "I thought you were staying outside."

Once I'd settled down, domestic number 2 tried to stroke me.

"No," said number 1, "they've just been treated. It's poisonous. No stroking till tomorrow."

Insult to injury again, you see. No stroking. And then injury heaped on insult: the stuff's actually poisonous. *Poisonous*. And they think I ought to be OK with it?

The worst of it?

I still don't have worms or fleas. I never have had. I'm sure I never will.

But you can bet your bottom dollar that next month they'll put some more of that product on my neck again.

Even though everything says I don't need it.

Luci tries to understand her own weirdness

Some things in life are a bit strange, aren't they? A bit weird. Which is bad enough generally, but particularly bad when the thing that's weird is yourself.

See, I really, really like my humans. Even human number 2. I mean, I know human number 1's the one that matters, the one who really knows how to look after me properly and all that, and even when she's telling me off – oh, that is just *so* dreadful – I know it's really for my own good. And I always do what she says *really, really* quickly, because I don't want any more dreadfulness. Which usually works out for the best because, like I said, she tends to know what's best.

But human number 2's nice too. He's a bit more easy-going. He doesn't always watch too carefully. I can sometimes get a bite of a bit of mouldy bread in the park before he notices. Whereas she just seems to know that's what I'm trying to do and stops me before I can even start.

"No, Luci" she says, very quietly but *so* threateningly, "don't. Drop that."

Amazing. It's not even in my mouth. How does she know?

Of course, none of that works with Toffee. Once she's spotted something to eat, no one's going to stop her getting it. Poor old number 2. He was chasing her all around the park the other day, trying to get her to drop a piece of meat she'd found and wasn't going to leave. It was too big for her mouth, really, and she couldn't eat it, but that didn't mean she wasn't going to try to get it home and work on it there.

In fact, that's what turned the whole thing a bit nasty. Because she got so focused on keeping away from human number 2 that she actually *ran out of the park*. I haven't done that since I was, oh, such a little puppy! And I got into *so much* trouble. I've never done it since.

That made it all the more terrible that Toffee was doing something so awful. I mean, she had to cross *two* streets without having a lead on! Bad, bad, bad.

Though I've got to admit that it was quite funny. All the way up the street, we – human number 2 and me – were rushing along trying to catch the little orange figure in front of us. Even when she was looking straight ahead we could see the lump of meat, because it stuck out either side of her head, it was so big. And every now and then she'd look back at us, I guess to see if we were catching up, and then we could see the whole piece.

"Like a kind of extended grin on her mouth," he told human number 1 later. Grimly. He wasn't pleased at all.

Toffee knew exactly how fast to go to keep ahead of us, however fast poor old number 2 tried to walk. All the way up the street she went, crossing another road, until she got to our front door.

You know, I don't think she'd thought about what would happen then. We caught up with her, looking a bit forlorn, standing outside the door with no way of getting in. She was still gripping the meat which was sticking out either side of her head and, my, she looked so silly.

Oh, boy. Things turned nasty then. I'm not going to describe what happened because it's too painful to write it down. Even if it was happening to another dog, it was terrible to watch such anger from a human. So I'll just say that he made it very, very clear to Toffee that he wasn't at all happy with her. I mean he didn't hit her or anything, but it might have been better if he had. The things he said were just awful. Why, he even called her a *bad girl*. And then explained why.

"Funny, that," Misty said when I told him, "since he just

knows we don't understand him."

We got inside eventually, with a very unhappy little orange blob making straight for the sofa, treatless, to lie there feeling sorry for herself. The piece of meat, meanwhile, went straight in the bin. The one outside the house. No way of recovering it. Making it a bit pointless to have brought it back from the park in the first place.

Anyway, I felt sorry for number 2. More than for Toffee – she'd had it coming to her, what with running away like that. She'd made him look horribly silly.

"Made a right fool of me, running away as I ran after her," he said later.

"No point. I just walk away from her," said number 1, "because she eventually comes after you."

"Yes, sounds like a good idea. I wish I'd thought of it this morning."

Poor old him. I couldn't help but sympathise. I like him. I'd never want to do anything nasty to him. Which leads me to the weird bit about myself, the bit I don't understand

Why do I keep growling at him?

It only happens when we go to bed. If he comes last and I have to move over to let him in, I just can't help it, I get annoyed. And I *growl* at him. Well, not so much growl as grumble. A kind of low, quiet sort of growl. But still not exactly affectionate.

Human number 1 gets all upset when I do that. She startles me every time when she ticks me off, her tone's so sharp.

"No, Luci," she says, "No! You're not to do that. Behave yourself."

I wouldn't mind if I didn't know she was right. I shouldn't grumble at him like I do. Of course I shouldn't. I know that. So why do I?

It's not really because I want to just have number 1 with me, to myself. Well, to myself and Toffee. I mean, I'm perfectly happy when he's there. He's just as good to lie next to, and a lot better to lie on top of, because he doesn't shake me off.

She does, of course. She pushes me around something dreadful. Why, she'll even pick me up and chuck me down to the end of the bed at her feet if the mood takes her. And I don't grumble, far less growl.

So you see, it can't be because I just don't like being moved on the bed. I get moved lots. It's only when *he* does it that it gets to me. That's when I growl.

I can only think that it may be something to do with the humans' reactions. I mean, she tells me off, which isn't nice. But he *laughs.*

"You growling at me, Luci?" he says, like he thinks it's a huge joke. And then he strokes me with his nose. Which a really angry growling dog might bite off. Something I could do too, you know. And growling suggests I might, doesn't it? Even if it *is* only a grumble.

Number 1 does warn him.

"Don't!" she tells him, "when a dog growls, you've got to be careful!"

"With Luci?" he says, laughs, and sticks his nose back in my fur.

Could that be it? I growl because he treats me like a joke? Which, frankly, is pretty irritating.

Number 1 thinks it's all down to some terrible thing that happened to me in the first family where I lived.

"Or it might be the simple fact of having moved from her first family to ours," she wonders. "That may just have been too stressful for a sensitive soul like hers."

Misty doesn't agree that I'm sensitive.

"Sensitive?" says Misty, "you mean highly strung, don't you?"

Well, maybe highly-strung, then. But the highly-strung don't like being laughed at, do they? Maybe he could start taking me a bit more seriously. I mean, people have to show you some respect, don't they? Otherwise a small dog doesn't have a lot to rely on, does she?

"I'm an even smaller dog," says Toffee, "and I swap half a treat for a bagful of respect."

Oh, what the heck. It takes all sorts. Maybe I just have to settle for being a tad weird. And see it as part of my charm.

Companionable silence, on the stairs

By Senada Borcilo

Toffee not even trying to understand hers

Steps to get up on the bed! What a great idea. Human number 1 has set up some nice furry steps for me to get up on the bed at night, so that I don't have to make that horrible big jump on to it myself.

"They're not just for you," Luci tells me, which may be right, but she always jumps anyway, so I can't see how they can be for her.

"I keep forgetting there are steps," she reckons, but I think she just doesn't understand what the steps are for. When I used them the first time, human number 1 said, "clever dog!" and, turning to number 2, "see how clever she is? She's learned to use the steps immediately."

Well, Luci didn't, did she? I learned quickly and she didn't learn at all.

"I just forget!" she says, "I just jump because I'm used to it and I keep forgetting that there are steps now."

Yeah. Right. That's what she would say, isn't it?

"Well, you jump sometimes too, don't you?"

Now, that *is* an odd thing. Like I said once before, I'm beginning to suspect that sometimes I just jump up without even knowing it, even though it's obvious I can't. I don't know how it happens, it just does.

It's a mystery.

Anyway, now that I have my nice furry steps, I don't need to jump anymore and that's great. Though it doesn't stop me wandering around whimpering sometimes, because being lifted is quite nice, really, isn't it?

"What are you doing?" says human number 2, "you've got steps now. You don't need helping up. You're a clever dog who learned to use the steps as soon as we put them there. So be a clever dog and climb up them."

But if I whimper long enough, he usually gives in anyway.

"Oh, come on," he says, "come over here and I'll pick you up."

So he leans out of bed. But, funnily enough, something odd happens then. As soon as he reaches for me, I back away. Like at the last moment I don't want to be grabbed. Like I was frightened of him. Which I'm really, really not.

"Oh, do make up your mind," he says, sounding a bit irritated.

So I move closer again. And he reaches for me a second time. And, weirdly, I back off again. No idea why.

"Toffee! If you don't let me get you, how can I help? And if you don't let me help you, I'll let you get up on your own. Or not at all, if that's what you want."

So finally I let him catch me. And I actually jump a bit, as far as his hand, like I wanted to help him grab me after all, and then he lifts me the rest of the way, which is a good way of mixing things, isn't it? I jump a bit and he lifts a bit, and we get me onto the bed together. It saves my legs without making him get out of bed. I reckon that's a good arrangement.

"I don't get it," he tells human number 1, "we know she's a clever little dog and she understood the steps really quickly. So why doesn't she use them?"

Honestly. He's supposed to be even cleverer than me, and he doesn't understand that? I'll just spell it out for him so maybe he can get his fine brain round the idea.

The steps are a great help. Practical. Convenient. Time saving. Energy saving.

But they're just steps. *Just* practical.

A hand onto the bed says "you belong up here. I want you here. We like having you lying next to us."

Steps can never do that. Steps, even furry ones, don't say "we love you" the way a hand does. Steps don't show affection.

And affection matters to us little dogs.

Now do you get it?

Just please don't ask me to explain why I sometimes back away when you're trying to help me up.

Because I don't get that any more than you do.

Luci and the pain of Spain

Oh, Lord. It was back to the ghastly place with all the animals yesterday. The one I call the house of pain. That's the place that smells funny, and has humans in strange blue coats, poking us about and sometimes sticking horrible things like needles into us.

Which was exactly what happened. They put me on that nasty, smelly table and then one of my humans held me while one of the blue-coated ones stuck a *huge* needle into me. Massive, pointy, cruel thing. It hurt and *hurt*.

"I didn't mind," Toffee said later, "just a prick. It was over straight away and then there were treats. What's to complain about?"

"I wasn't complaining about the treats. I was happy with the treats. If we could have jumped straight to the treats I'd have been just fine."

"Here's what I think," said Toffee, and she really *did* look thoughtful. "What I reckon is going on is, that we only get the treat because we let them do something that we don't much like to us first. There's a link. You get the good thing after you've put up with the horrible one."

I'd never noticed that. I'm not sure she's right, mind, but there may be something in it. Human number 2 always gives us a treat when he puts us on our leads before leaving the park. I always thought it was just part of the process of leaving the park, but maybe it's just a way to get us to put our leads on. Toffee seems convinced of it.

"Cunning, isn't it? Even if I'm doing something important,

like playing, I mostly come running over when he starts putting your lead on. I know he's going to give you a treat, see, so I come over to get my treat too. Even though it means he's going to put me on my lead too and put an end to the massively important game I'm playing. And he does. On goes the lead. So, bye, bye, playing, right? A clever trick. It fools us. And even though I know what he's doing, it fools me anyway."

Well, if they're giving us treats to stop us complaining when they stick needles into us, in the house of pain, then it doesn't work that well. In fact, with me it doesn't work at all. I made it *very* clear I wasn't pleased with that needle.

"Good God," said the man in the blue coat. I've never heard a dog scream like that over a rabies shot."

Scream? I thought it was more of a big whimper. Still, human number 1 looked a bit shocked, and even Toffee, come to think of it, didn't seem her usual completely calm self. Maybe I was just a tad louder than I'd intended.

"Don't be so silly, Luci," human number 1 told me, "it's worth it. That way we can travel together. You know, it's Pain we want to go to."

Pain? She didn't need to tell me that. I'd felt it. All the pain I ever wanted and then some. Without going anywhere to get more.

"Not Pain, you silly muppet," Misty told me, "Spain. You remember the two younger domestics who come and see us sometimes?"

I looked a bit blank so he hurried on.

"Well, you like them a lot. They usually come at Christmas. And they live in Spain. Once you've had a rabies shot you can go and see them there."

I didn't like the idea at all. If some young humans want to come and see us, that's great. I couldn't be happier. But what's wrong with coming to our place? We're all comfortable here. Why would we go somewhere with a name like Pain? It can't be nice.

"Spain. It's called Spain."

"Still sounds like Pain, though, doesn't it? That can't be good."

"What is it, anyway?" asked Toffee, "what is this Spain thing?'

"It's a country," Misty said. He was looking a bit apprehensive. Like someone worried he was about to get sucked into giving a much longer explanation of something than he really wanted to.

"And what's a country?" asked Toffee.

Misty sighed. "I was afraid you'd ask. And I'd have to explain."

"Well? Well?"

"It's like this. Domestics – not just our domestics but all domestics – like to divide places up into countries. The domestics from different countries speak in different ways and their food smells different too. They prefer to live in their own country."

"Like a house, then?" I asked.

"Bigger than that."

"Like a very big house?"

"I think he means much bigger than that," said Toffee.

"The house. All the houses around it. All the way to the park. All the houses beyond that. That's a town. Then no houses for a while then lots more houses, in another town. And then on and on and on – more and more towns with houses, more bits without houses, and so on."

"Like when we're in the car for ages," Toffee suggested.

"Yes. That's a country. But things go on even further. To other countries. Where the domestics sound different. And the food smells different."

"Yeah, right," I said, "I don't believe any of it. I mean, how do you even know about all this?"

"I was born in one of those places, which the domestics call France, and then lived in another one, called Germany, before coming here. And, believe me, it's a real pain changing from one to the other. I wouldn't wish it on my worst enemy. Not even an enemy like you."

Good old Misty. Always pretending not to like us. And inventing strange stories to make us feel just a teensy bit scared.

Still. What if there was some truth to what he was saying? All this nonsense about countries – towns beyond towns beyond towns and then more, even further beyond? What a ghastly idea. And we might have to go there? Just the thought makes me feel queasy.

I don't want to go anywhere. I'm perfectly happy here. And I certainly don't want nasty needle shots, especially if they're just to make us go. Spain? Pain? None of it appeals to me at all.

The needle was quite spainful enough.

Misty ready to enjoy good weather

At long last! The domestics have got their act together. They've arranged a bit of sun for us. A bit of warmth. But so late this year. After so much lousy weather. I don't know what got into them.

Winter, I've learned, is one of those necessary evils you have to learn to put up with, like noisy canines. But only for so long. There comes a point when it has to be told that even painful things come to an end. I expect good domestic staff to see that happens at a reasonable time each year. But then, as anyone who ever reads this diary of mine will no doubt have worked out by now, I've been cursed with indifferent domestic service since I was a mere kitten.

What should have happened is that, once winter had been around for a reasonable time, they'd have let us have summer again, perhaps with a bit of spring in between. But this year they've been horribly lax about getting it all to happen to anything like a sensible schedule.

Could it be age that's catching up with them? That they're frankly getting a little old for this kind of careful planning and, even more important, for timely execution of the plan? If so, it's a bit ironic that they go on about *my* age.

"You know, he's 64 in human years," said domestic number 1 the other day, reading off one of those silly charts they get sent from time to time by the vet's surgery.

That's the place Luci calls the 'house of pain', and she's not entirely wrong. But most of the time it seems to be the house of business acumen. They send out these silly puff pieces, like charts to convert cat years to human years or whatever, so the domestics can buy 'age-appropriate' cat food. At an 'appropriate' price.

For the avoidance of confusion, let me say that an 'appropriate price' is the kind of price that allows a business to do a bit of appropriation.

That's something the domestics never seem to ask themselves. Those special brands of cat food – what do they think the manufacturers are doing to make sure the vets keep boosting them? It never seems to occur to them that the stuff they get from the supermarket isn't just cheaper, it can even taste a lot better too.

Pathetic to see how easily they fall into the marketing traps.

So, they were going on about my *great age* the other day as though the vet's conversion table meant anything. Which it didn't. After all, it didn't consider that I have nine lives. How do you convert *that* into human years?

As for *their* age, it clearly keeps advancing in a way that does them no good at all, if their depressing slowness in getting summer going this year is any indication. I mean, a couple of weeks ago it even looked like winter had finally stopped. The skies were blue. The sun was shining. I was able to go out into the garden with plenty of pleasurable expectation.

First, I jumped up onto the roof of one of the sheds (I've no idea why they have several sheds but, hey, I'm not complaining: it gives me a choice of roofs to lie on). It was ecstasy, absorbing the effect of the early sun, feeling the fur getting warm for the first time since wretched winter started months and *months* ago.

Later, after a while on the shed roof, I wandered over to the patio, once the sun had got onto it and cooked the paving slabs to a pleasant temperature. Ah, the bliss. Feeling the warmth coming from underneath just as it flows over me from above.

And then – next day – there we were back in winter again!

Rain. Cold. Grey skies. Dire.

I expect better of the domestics than that. I mean, once they've called the winter off, quite late enough if you ask me, the least they could do was keep it away for a while. Give summer a chance. I mean, what we got for that one day didn't even feel like spring. It was like we'd jumped straight to summer. Even after sunset, that night, it still felt mild. It was great.

So what were they thinking of, letting winter back in again so easily and so quickly? It's got to be their age, hasn't it? Maybe they're just so old, they've lost all control over conditions.

Still, at least they've finally got their act together. The last couple of days have been fine again. Quite summery. Again, with no hint of a spring, probably because with winter so long there was no time for one. Which might be a pity, since spring's the time when the young birds appear. I wouldn't want to miss that.

Then again, I'm beginning to get the impression I may not have to. I've been keeping a close eye on the adult birds, as you can imagine, and some of them seem to be behaving in that slightly soppy, slightly aggressive way they do just before they produce their young.

I very much hope there'll be a few fledglings around before long. I'm certainly going to keep an eye out for any of the poor dear little things who are so unfortunate as to fall out of their nests. After all, we don't want any of them to go to waste now, do we?

In the meantime, I'm just enjoying the warmth being back. So I can bask in it again. And I'm keeping the domestics under close observation. To try to understand why they let things drift so badly this year.

Which takes me to another, far worse concern. It may have been deliberate. The silly canines were chatting the other day. One of them mentioned 'Spain'.

"Spain?" I said, "what do you know about Spain?"

"We're going there, we're going there," said Toffee. "Do you know what it is?"

Well, I *do* know what Spain is. Not that I've been there or anything. France, Germany, Britain, yes. But Spain no.

I thought I'd travelled enough. Another move? I'm not sure I'm keen. On the other hand – well, Spain has the reputation of being *warm* at least. Maybe there's a case for going there despite the hassle.

Though I'd like to have been consulted first. Rather than learning about it from the silly little girls.

Which gives me a bad feeling. A terrible idea. They're not going to clear off there and leave me behind – again? They did that before I came to live in England. I know they were getting the place ready and everything, but I resented kicking my heels out there on my own, even if I was with nice people.

It'd be even worse if they took the silly girls with them and not me. Like when they moved away and left me here while those terrible men were doing horrible things to my house. Doing something like that again would be just too awful.

Could that be what they're planning? The girls were moaning a while back about having gone to the 'house of pain' and having needles stuck in them. At the time, I just thought how glad I was to have escaped that fate. But now they're saying the domestics were talking about how it was necessary for going to Spain. If they've been through something that prepares them to go to Spain and I haven't, what does that say about what the domestics are scheming?

It all sounds suspicious. If not downright sinister. I may have to make it clear to them that I'm not in favour. That it might not be in their interests to consider such a poor idea. That I might take punitive action to teach them discipline. Again.

Still, all in due time. Right now, the fledglings are just about to start appearing. Spain – that's just an irritating problem that may or may not arise sometime in the future.

Worries for another day. For now, I'll just enjoy nature's bounty. Sun. Blue skies. Birds falling out of the blue sky when the sun does its shining. Good times that make the living easy.

Toffee goes to Scotland again. Probably

Trains! They're *so* dull. And we've been in two in two days. Such a pain. We rattle along. Getting shaken about. With nearly nothing to do but lie on the chair and bark from time to time at the other dog further back in the carriage.

"Quiet, Toffee," says human number 1 every time I do, "whatever's got into you?"

So I go all quiet for a while until I hear the other dog grumble a bit. So I bark and number 1 has another go at me. Which is a *little bit* fun and a bit of a break in the boringness. Though not much of one.

The only other fun was when the human across the aisle go all soppy about me. Which she did every now and then. Especially if I did my puppy dog eyes at her.

"She got soppy about me too," says Luci.

"She only stroked me," I tell her.

"That's because I don't like strangers stroking me."

"Stranger? You're the one's that's stranger! What's stranger than not letting yourself be stroked even if you don't know the person stroking you?"

That shut Luci up. I reckon Misty would call that "a telling argument". And he'd say so if he were here, but he stayed at home.

"Not because they didn't want me to come," he explained before we left, "but because somebody has to look after the place while you lot are away."

"But what if we don't come back?" I asked. I didn't like the idea but sometimes you just have to say these things, don't you? "Imagine if we never saw each other again, Misty."

"A sad fate for you, little one," he said. I could see he was trying to put a brave face on the idea but wasn't succeeding. "Still. We shouldn't paint things too black."

I was impressed that he didn't want me to overstate things, about how we'd miss him and all that, so obviously I needed to say something more accurate, that gave things their real weight. I didn't want him to think I was going over the top or anything. So I picked my words with more care.

"We'd miss you. That would be sad. On the other hand, I guess we'd adapt in time, I suppose we'd learn to get by. But how about you? How would you cope?"

"Ah. Now isn't that you through and through? You say something which sounds quite nice. And then you spoil it."

Well, that was strange. I was trying not to paint things too black, just like he asked. But when I got more realistic, he didn't seem to appreciate it. It was almost as though he didn't enjoy accuracy as much as I thought he was claiming.

Odd.

"Anyway, you'll be back in no time," he went on.

He had that air of confidence he usually has, except this time it sort of faded a bit into the background, and I noticed something that doesn't often happen with him. He seemed worried.

"At least, the domestics have always come back before. This time can't be different. Can it?"

Then he turned to me looking all serious.

"No one's mentioned anything about going to Spain, have they? You haven't heard them talking about Spain, have you?"

"What's Spain?" I asked him, "and why does it matter so much to you?"

"Never you mind. You just tell me if you hear them talking about going there. Particularly if they talk about going there without me."

Spain, eh? Misty makes it sound like a place. But I don't think it's where we went this time. They kept talking about Scotland, which *is* a place. And last time they were talking about Scotland, that's where we ended up, so I reckon it probably *was* Scotland we went to this time too.

"Was it cold?" asks Luci.

"Was it cold? Well, you tell me. You were there too."

"It wasn't *that* cold."

"No. It wasn't."

"Well, Scotland's cold. Maybe it *was* Spain, after all."

"I don't know. It had the same people in it as when we went to Scotland before. And it felt like the same place, didn't it?"

That was one of the best things about going there. It had that nice human puppy we met before. The one that's still a puppy even though she's bigger than my humans. She picks me up all the time and carries me around. Very nice it is too. She has a nice length of forearm, so I fit in well, with my bum against her elbow. Also, she remembers to keep stroking me, which the adults aren't so good at – they eventually get distracted by one of their silly phones or some boring conversation with another adult. She knows how to focus on what matters, which is how to keep an armful of dog happy.

We went to a show, too. I didn't know what a show was, but it turned out to be fun. It was in a park, with lots of female humans. They were wearing odd-looking dresses which one of the humans said were very old, which is peculiar, isn't it? My humans keep throwing out clothes they think are old. But this lot were wearing theirs.

"They were showing them off," says Luci, "it was an old dress show."

Well, that may be so, and anyway it hardly matters whether I understood what the point of the whole thing was or not, because it doesn't make any difference to the fact that it was just great. Who cares about dresses when you've got lots of humans sitting around on the grass and you can go and lick them a bit? They mostly seemed to like it too, which is the right thing for humans, though some of them went all horrified and tried to shoo me away, which is completely the wrong thing. The fun ones picked me and stroked me, or wrapped their dresses around me, or passed me from one to the other. It was magic. Not that Luci took advantage of it.

"That's because I don't like to let strangers touch…"

"I know, I know," I interrupted her, "*so* silly."

She grumbled a bit. "All very well and fine but you never know what a stranger might do and *you*'d look silly if one day one of these strangers turned round and did something nasty to you and then…"

I couldn't hear the rest because she was walking away from me and mumbling a bit by then.

Anyway, I had a *lot* of fun. I *like* Scotland. Even if it's Spain.

But I don't think it was Spain. It *was* a bit cold. Now that I come to think of it.

Rest is something to take seriously

By Senada Borcilo

Misty aspiring to boredom

Who knew life had a sense of humour?

That's the only explanation I can find for my being forced to share my house with a noisy, smelly, irritatingly excitable little bundle of orange fluff. Or the other one, the scared, excitable bundle of black fluff. In the household I endeavour so untiringly to civilise, to force into some kind of compliance with decent standards: training the domestics, ensuring a sufficiency of food, insisting on the availability of a wide range of comfortable resting places. All undermined by canine saboteurs.

That's life's little joke, isn't it? Not a pleasant joke, you understand. A twisted, sadistic trick. With me as victim.

Toffee overthrows all my carefully laid plans for calm and order. She just seems to live for excitement. She apparently likes nothing better than chasing around all over the place. Or getting all worked up about anything that goes by outside. Barking at it.

Yapping, I mean.

Yapping until she drives the rest of us barking.

Lots of excitement. And a real pain in the hindquarters.

Talking about excitement, why does anyone think it's that great? Whenever I hear domestics saying something like, "Isn't that exciting?", it's in a tone of voice which says as clearly as anything could, that they think it's a good thing.

Really? What's so wonderful about being excited? Or is that a question they even bother to ask themselves? Because they should.

OK, maybe when I was a kitten, I had a bit of a hankering for excitement. But thirteen years on? Well, you have to grow out of these things, don't you? These years, I'm more than happy with simple normality. In fact, to be perfectly honest, even normal strikes me as dangerously close to thrilling. I aspire to plain boring.

Not that *I* find it boring. Lying around on the domestics' bed all day? I know some might find that uninspiring. It strikes me as much the best way of passing the daytime. The same food each and every day? Never understood what people find to object in that – if you like the stuff, I can't see why you wouldn't want it all the time. Patrolling my territory night after night and stalking the occasional reckless field mouse? That's all the excitement I feel I need. And even then, most of the excitement is felt by the field mouse. Briefly, at least.

That's why I don't like all the commotion that engulfs our household every so often. In particular, when the domestics clear off, as they do from time to time. Honestly, they really have the most awful notion of service. Appallingly casual. They wander off, sometimes for days at a time, without even consulting me first.

It's true they get domestic number 3 to look after us, and that's not that bad. Actually, it isn't bad at all. She doesn't always stay the night or anything but sometimes she watches TV which provides a lap for a bit of relaxation, and that suits me fine. Plus she feeds me, so what's to complain about?

But, however satisfied I may be with the substitute they lay on, it *is* still just a substitute. I'm not inclined to forgive my domestics for clearing off in the first place. I resent it. And not even excitement disturbs a sense of feline calm so painfully as resentment.

Still, at least I don't take things as badly as that little Luci does. Oh, boy, does she whinge and whimper when the domestics clear off.

"Oh no, oh no," she goes, "don't go away. Or don't leave me behind. Stay or take me with you!"

Reduced to a pathetic jelly of self-pity, she is. "Separation anxiety," domestic number 1 calls it. "Separation panic" strikes me as nearer the mark.

Funnily enough, Luci and Toffee often don't stay at home when the domestics clear off, even if it's for a long time. They go round to number 3's home. Or so they tell me. There's another dog there, much bigger than them, but older.

"Luci's great," Toffee tells me, "she's taken charge completely. Luci keeps the dog from there right out of the bedroom at night. Just dashes up to her and barks and the other dog *goes*. During the day, too. I've never seen anyone getting driven away as effectively as when Luci's doing the driving. The human's taken to feeding us in a different room, which is a pity, because we used to get the other dog's food too. That was *great*."

"Not for her," I point out, trying to inject a little maturity into the conversation.

"Well, no, not for *her*," says Toffee, "but it was great for us, wasn't it?"

They seem to like going there. It wouldn't be my bowl of cat food, though. I mean – *a new place? Another dog?* Who needs any of that? More excitement, I suppose – great if you like that kind of thing, but no good for someone like me who prefers plain normal. Or even good old boring.

Still, I'm glad for Luci. If she can have some fun despite the domestics' absence. I mean, if it helps recover from that whimpering mess their departure reduces her to. And, in any case, I'm glad she goes off to that other place. I mean, if she has to do all that separation-panic wining, I'd rather she did it somewhere else. It isn't much fun, and it does very little for a proper sense of quiet during the day, to have *that* racket going on in the house.

I mean, I know I like boring, but Luci's whining's another kind of boring. It's boring with a lot of exasperation mixed in. A lot of grating, you might say. Grating on the ears. Nothing like the kind of peaceful boring I'm after.

The worst moment was the time before last that the

domestics went away.

"It was heartbreaking the way Luci was crying after I dropped her off with you," Domestic number 1 told number 3.

"She went on for a while afterwards too. In the end she was fine, but it took a good twenty minutes. Miserable to hear her like that."

So number 1 decided to be a bit clever the next time they cleared off. Instead of dropping the dogs off at number 3's house, she left them at home, and asked number 3 to come and fetch them. That meant when number 1 left, she was doing what she does most days: heading out of the door, as though she was going to work. We all know she comes back a while later. Although, it has to be said I'm the only one who knows she's going to work: the other two just think she's disappearing for a while, which they find upsetting, and they have to make an effort to stay calm in the face of what they see as a completely unnecessary interruption to their enjoyment of the day.

"It *is* a completely unnecessary interruption," Toffee tells me.

"What do you mean unnecessary? They have to work. What do you think keeps your bowl filled with kibble?"

"Well, I don't know about this work thing, but I know that what keeps *my* bowl filled is having the humans around to fill it for me. If they've gone away, they can hardly do that, can they?"

She gave me a sort of triumphant look, like she knew she'd come up with an unanswerable argument. And it's true I found her logic so outrageous that I couldn't immediately think of a reply.

"Look," she went on, "my bowl's still got the remains of my breakfast kibble in it right now. And the humans are here. Which proves my point. There's kibble in my bowl when they're around."

She went over towards her bowl to finish her brilliant demonstration of irrefutable logic. And found it was empty.

"What! What!" she snapped, "there was kibble in it just a

minute ago."

She rounded on me.

"You've eaten it, haven't you? You have! You've eaten my kibble."

"Could have been Luci."

"But it wasn't, was it? It was you. It always is."

"Well, you shouldn't leave it lying around, should you? If you want your food, eat it. Leave it and it tends to evaporate."

Anyway, as I was saying, as the domestics were leaving this time, number 1 sort of sneaked out, hoping Luci wouldn't mind if she just saw her going out of the door like she does most days. Except that she doesn't normally go out with a suitcase, does she? Just as soon as Luci saw that suitcase, all hell broke out. Oh, the crying, the whimpering, the begging. It would have broken my heart if it hadn't been wrecking my ears.

You see, underneath it all, Luci's like me. She may pretend to like excitement and change. Going for walks in new places. New smells, new tastes, bits of rotting food she can gobble up if the domestics don't stop her. Variety is what life's about, she thinks.

Until she meets real change. Like the domestics going away. When she's reduced to a sobbing jelly.

She prefers things to stay the same, like I do. Boring: we've got nothing against it. It's comforting. You know what's happening. Nasty events don't spring out and ambush you.

What's not to like about that?

Toffee, big steps and bad foxes

It was excellent when the humans got me a little set of stairs to get up onto my bed at night.

That's the bed I let the humans share with me.

They're nice steps. Sort of furry-covered. And when you get to the top step, it's just a little hop onto the bed itself. Easy-peasy. Even for a nice-sized animal like me. It's great.

Getting off the bed isn't a problem. One quick jump. It means that if I hear something suspicious happening downstairs – like a fox crossing the garden or Misty eating food – I can be off the bed like a flash and straight downstairs, barking all the way to the ground floor.

Barking's a really good idea because it means the foxes go away. I don't really know what foxes are, but Misty tells me they're *big*. Obviously, I have to drive them away, and I'm prepared to do whatever it takes, but I'd rather that what it takes doesn't actually involve me meeting them face-to-face or anything.

Not if they're *big*.

My barking doesn't frighten Misty away. Of course, it doesn't. He's used to me. He's my friend. He doesn't frighten easy. He just stands there, way up on that high place where his food is, and looks at me like I'm a funny, noisy, little thing.

"Which is what you are," he says.

But he only says that because he's my friend.

"I'm glad you think that," he tells me.

Which is good. Right?

When I come running down in the middle of the night, he stands there looking at me. Looking at me... in a way I don't know how to describe... there must be a word.

"Superciliously?"

I suppose that must be the right word, or he wouldn't have suggested it. So let's go with it. Superciliously. That's how he looks at me.

Then he says things like:

"Why are you making such a noise?"

"To keep the foxes away."

"Do you see a fox out there?"

"No. Of course not. I was barking. That's very effective against foxes. Whatever foxes are."

He sighed.

"Did you hear what the domestics were saying?"

He calls the humans domestics. You won't catch me doing that. But, anyway, I had an easy answer

"No. Of course not. I was barking."

Though to be honest I do remember they were saying something. Something a bit angry, I thought. But what was it?

"They're not pleased at being woken up in the middle of the night."

"But... but... they can't want foxes wandering around the garden."

"I think they could cope with that. Better than being woken up anyway."

Strange thought, isn't it? Not barking at the foxes. Where's the fun in that?

Anyway, the nice thing is that I can go straight upstairs afterwards and up the three furry steps onto the bed again. And go and lick human number 2's face, which he always enjoys, even if he does splutter a bit when I do it while he's asleep. He always wakes up enough to stroke me a bit though, which is nice. Isn't it?

"He's just trying to stop you licking him," says Misty.

It's funny. I never lick human number 1's face. I wonder why that is? I mean, she's the important one. It seems unfair not to show how much I care about her too.

"Are you crazy?" asks Misty.

"No. Why?"

"Well, if you want to know why you never lick her face, I suggest you try it just once. You'll soon discover that it's for just the same reason I only ever bite domestic number 2. Never number 1."

Lick her face? I suppose I could. But I don't know why, the idea gives me a kind of cold feeling inside. You know, I don't think I will try, actually. Something tells me it might not work out well for me if I did.

The odd thing about the furry steps is that Luci doesn't seem to have mastered them. She seems to have got stuck with the old way of doing things. She just goes trotting around the bed, first one way, then the other, and whimpering a bit, until one of the humans gets up and lifts her onto the bed.

"Why don't you use the steps?" I asked her.

"Well, it isn't because I haven't mastered them," she replied, "I just don't like them."

"But why not?"

"I just don't."

"But it can take ages for the humans to realise you need lifting and help you up."

"That's all right. I can wait."

It doesn't make any sense to me. It's so easy. And you get up and down as much as you want without having to ask anyone for anything. Why wouldn't you?

"Maybe she really hasn't mastered them," says Misty.

"She told me she had."

"Ah," says Misty, "and how many people have admitted to you that they're not clever enough to learn something?"

"Well, none. But then I've never met anyone who isn't clever enough to learn to get up some stairs."

"Haven't you?" he says, "are you sure?"

He gets that way, sometimes, Misty. Saying things which I think must be clever, though I don't understand what they mean. Misty the mysterious, I say.

I'll have to go away and think about it a bit. See if I can work out what he was getting at. I can't have it beat me.

Anyway. I like the stairs on to the bed. Like I enjoy running around the house barking to drive the foxes away. Or any other strange, *big* animals.

No one seems to mind, really. After all, they always give me a stroke once they're completely awake.

Which is good. Isn't it?

Luci and summertime

It's getting really hot out there. But I'm not surprised. I've just realised that this is something that happens again and again or, as Misty explained to me, every year.

"Misty, I've got it!" I told him.

"What have you got?" he asked, strangely eager.

"I've understood something you told me once."

"Oh," he said, looking disappointed, "I thought you'd found that bit of fish Toffee was talking about. I can't find it."

"She ate it," I explained.

I think he said something like, "fat lot of use you are then," but I couldn't hear him properly, and I didn't ask him to repeat it, because if it really was that, it would have been unkind, and why ask him to be unkind twice?

Besides, I was much too keen to tell him my good news, anyway.

So I told him, "I've got it! This whole idea of years. The way things keep coming round and round and all that. You know, it's hot again now, and it was before wasn't it? Before it got cold again. That's like – a year, isn't it?"

"Wow," he said, "she can be trained after all."

"What do you mean? Of course, I can be trained. The humans are training me all the time. Or they think they are. *You* know. To sit down. To come and have my lead put on. To eat my food – though that doesn't take a lot of training. That sort of thing, anyway. All it takes is the occasional treat."

"To *think*. You can even be trained to think. But don't expect a treat from me. You won't be getting one."

"Oh, it doesn't have to be a treat I can eat. Just a kind word will do me fine."

"A kind word? How about 'get out of my face and I won't bite you?'"

He doesn't mean that kind of thing. He's much nicer than that. So I'm fine, really.

I've just realised he's right behind me now.

"How long has it been?" he's asking. With a kind of distant, thinking look.

He likes to read my diary.

"The word you want for that distant thinking look – which is really a deep thinking look – is 'ruminatively'," he tells me. Helpfully. It must be helpful because he wouldn't tell me if it wasn't helpful, would he?

He kept on ruminating so I asked him, "how long since when?"

"How long since I first tried to get you to understand what a year was. I mean, you've had three of them already, haven't you? This is your fourth summer, for God's sake. You'd think you'd have grasped the notion before now."

But I didn't answer that. He'd said an important word. "Summer". That was what we were having. We know we are, because it's hot and all that. And the days go on and on into the evening.

I'd heard the word before, actually. Human number 2 uses it quite a bit. As in, "call this a bloody summer? It's raining again", or "summer! Huh. I needed a coat *and* a jumper. I remember 1976. Now, *that* was a summer."

"Or do you mean 1876, dear?" said number 1.

"Very funny," he said, which surprised me, because it didn't strike me as all that funny, and the way he said it made it sound like he didn't think it was all that funny either.

Anyway, that's what it is, this time of year (see how I did that? Like I've really got my mind around the idea and can just drop it into conversation when I want). When it's hot and the evenings are light – summer.

It's funny because the humans seem to like it. Even number 2's stopped complaining. And we get longer and longer walks, as if he enjoys being out when out's like this.

Which is odd, really. Because it's not that comfortable. I mean, I like the long evenings. In the winter I get a bit scared in those tree-y places, where the long shadows hide and things jump out at you from them.

"They don't really jump out at you, do they?" says Misty.

"They haven't *yet*, but they could. And I don't like that. It makes me nervous."

"Huh," he says. He says that quite a lot so I don't pay much attention to it.

Anyway, it's nice having the long evenings, because it makes walks much less scary. But all that hot – that's not so good. It makes me feel all heavy, or at least a bit heavy, and not so much like running around.

And it's even worse for Toffee. She can't stop herself racing all over the place. Especially if the human throws a ball for her. She just can't resist. She has to take off after it. I sometimes make a pretence of going for it too, but I don't really care about it. Not like she does. She really, really wants to get to it first. So I let her.

But then it catches up with her. We were out the other day, and did a bit of ball-chasing. But then she just had to lie down. In the shade under a tree, where it's nice and cold. Well, not cold. But a bit less hot.

In fact, I joined her there. It *was* nice.

"I thought you didn't like shade by trees," says Misty.

Well, well. It's not often I get one over Misty about words. But he'd got that one wrong.

"Shade's fine. It's *shadows* I don't like."

"Huh," he said and stalked off.

So Toffee has started doing this thing of lying down in the shade. And the other day, she didn't do it just once or twice but three times on one walk.

To be honest, I don't mind. Because when she's got so tired

chasing a ball or whatever that she has to go and lie down, at least she can't chase me. It gets her off my back.

What's specially nice about that is it means I get the chance to hunt around for bits of food without her nosing in on anything I find. That's something else about the summer – there's lots more food because lots and lots of humans go out and eat food on the grass and they're *so* stupid that they don't make sure to eat absolutely everything (like us) that they leave lots of wonderful bits behind (not at all like us).

Still, I feel sorry for poor little Toffee. The summer's no good for her and gets her totally exhausted. Which is sad to see.

Except that, well, I'm not sorry about her leaving bits of food alone, though. That just means there's more for me. Which isn't sad at all.

Quite the opposite.

Misty and the replacement domestics

I've got to hand it the domestics. They're making quite good arrangements for service continuity these days.

Don't get me wrong. I wish they'd drop this stupid habit of going away without so much as consulting me. But if they must keep behaving in that irresponsible manner, the least they can do is to set things up properly for me in advance. And they've got quite good at doing that now.

First there's domestic number 3. She's always been highly satisfactory. She comes in and gives me food and she's good at providing a lap too – she doesn't move, doesn't suddenly get up to go somewhere else, tipping me off with no thought to my dignity when she does. That's domestic number 2's trick. He apparently can't sit still. Ants in his pants is the expression and, though I've never actually seen any of those ants, it fits him perfectly. Domestic number 3 knows how to sit still and give a weary cat a proper rest. And she remembers to keep stroking me, too. At least until she goes to her own home, but that's OK, because it doesn't generally happen until mousing time, and she's back in the morning to give me breakfast anyway.

In fact, the only downside with her is that she has this dog. She – the dog, not the domestic – barks at me. Now, I know she just wants to play. The domestic even says so. But it's one of the stupid things about dogs: just because they want to play, why do they assume anyone else wants to join them? And what makes them think that barking at someone is going to make them more rather than less inclined to provide the romp, or whatever, they're after?

Personally, it just puts me off.

The domestic keeps that dog on a lead, which is just as well. I don't know what would happen if she came running at me. She might end up seriously injured.

Anyway, it would be a lot more comfortable – for the dog too – if the domestic didn't bring her. Mainly because it would mean she could focus her visits more fully on me.

But, to my surprise, I discovered that this time it wasn't going to be her coming around to see to me. Instead, I got two new domestics. I mean, not completely new. I'd met them before. But they'd never been charged with providing me domestic services before.

There are two of them. I don't know which is domestic 4 and which domestic 5 but since first one of them would come and then the other, I just thought of them jointly as domestic 4/5. At first it worried me to see them instead of her, but I must confess, in the end they turned out to be quite good. Not in the same way as domestic 3 but still more than adequate. They didn't just come and feed me and go. They'd sit down, like domestic 3, and give me a lap for a while.

In the past, when they visited while domestics 1 and 2 were home, they'd bring a dog too. But they had the good sense not to bring her with them when they were supposed to be delivering me service to the standard I've come to expect. They concentrated on me. Very sensible. Very appropriate. Very acceptable.

That still leaves one nagging question, though. Why on earth did the domestics have to go away in the first place? And why did they have to stay away so long? As usual, they took Toffee and Luci with them and left me behind, which I'm not sure I'm happy about, even though I don't much like travelling. Cars? Hate the damn things. Home? If you're happy there, I don't see why you'd leave.

Toffee did try to tell me how things went.

"We got into that noisy rattly-about thing."

"Do you mean the car?"

"Yes, yes, that's the one. And then we were in it for a long time. Like we have been quite a lot recently. Very boring and a bit hard on the stomach."

"OK, but where did you go?"

"A place with buildings and a big field behind."

"A field with buildings around it? That can't be a proper field. Do you mean a park?"

"Yes, yes, a park. And it was that place that had another human in, the one who moves around slowly and sits down a lot but likes it if we sit on her lap so she can stroke us."

I was racking my brain to understand. Could she be talking about the old lady my domestics used to visit sometimes?

"Were you in Oxford?" I asked.

"Yes, yes, that's right, Oxford."

Well, OK, but did she really mean that? I decided to test her.

"Or was it Edinburgh?"

"That's right, Edinburgh."

"Do you really not discriminate at all?"

"No, no, not in the least bit. I don't know what discriminating is, so I can't be doing it, can I?"

I think it must have been Oxford. The one with the slow domestic who's too old to be a domestic at all anymore. I don't understand all these relations between domestics, but there seems to be some kind of link between her and domestic number 2. We stayed with her a couple of times when she wasn't quite so slow. One time was memorable because somebody started letting off fireworks nearby, and I don't like fireworks, so I cleared off and didn't come back for two nights. That was a bit tiresome, though it was quite funny when I came back, because domestic number 1 was all over me, stroking me lots and even giving me loads of proper cat food, none of that boring biscuit stuff.

It was like I'd really disappeared. Which, from her point of view, I suppose I had. I mean, it wasn't like I was really lost. I always knew where I was, which is what mattered, and I could hear her banging a food bowl in the garden and going "Misty, Misty, Misty, psst, psst, psst," so I knew where she was too. Which meant there was never a problem, that I could see. I just waited for the fireworks to stop and then let a bit of time go by, to make the point that I don't like being exposed to that kind of annoyance, until I really needed some of the food in that bowl, so I came back. But the situation was never out of control.

Maybe she didn't know that, which is why she made such a fuss.

Anyway, it seemed quite likely the domestics had gone to Oxford with the dogs. After all, I often hear them talking about going to see that superannuated domestic – "I know it's a pain going all that way," they say, "but the poor old girl needs the company".

Except that the way Toffee told the story, that didn't sound right either.

"We didn't see the human we went to see."

"What do you mean?"

"Well, we went to this place where the slow human used to be."

"How can you be so sure? I mean, you don't know what city you were in."

"I know the place. I know the bed. I know the chair. I know the smells."

Well, that was fair enough. Dogs don't usually get smells wrong. Most other things, especially if it's Toffee, but not generally smells.

"And you didn't see her?"

"No. She never showed up."

"Didn't that strike you as odd?"

"No. You think it should have? Was it odd?"

I sighed.

"So, let me get this straight. You went to a place but you don't know where it was. And you went to visit someone but she wasn't there. And you don't know why."

"Yes. Yes. I suppose that's right. But our humans were there, so what does it matter?"

Ah, well. Sounds like a perfectly useless trip. Pointless. I don't see why they didn't just stay home.

Still. Let's be fair and give credit where it's due. At least they did lay on some decent service for me while they were away. For that, at least, let us be grateful.

Toffee and the mystery of the old human

Exciting! Exciting! Exciting!

The humans took us to a place with *lots of water*. The kind that trundles along slowly. No waves. Though it isn't still either. Just moving along smoothly in one direction, if you can imagine that. And the humans threw a stick in so we could go and get it. It was *so exciting*.

"What do you mean *we* could go and get it?" says Luci. "You didn't get it even *once*. It was me every time."

"Well, I went in too, didn't I? We both chased the stick, didn't we? You weren't alone, were you?"

"No. You were there too. But you only went in as far as you could stand. You didn't actually swim."

"Well, I didn't feel like swimming. I felt like splashing about a bit and then going back to the side. Where the earth was all sandy and there was yellow grass instead of the usual green stuff."

"Don't try to change the subject. You were scared. You didn't swim which is why I had to do all the work swimming out to the stick and bringing it back."

"No, no, no, I wasn't scared at all. I just didn't feel like swimming."

"Of course you were scared. What's more, you only went in a short way, let me fetch the stick, and then tried to grab it off me as I came out. Which wasn't very nice."

"It was a game, Luci, a game. I was just *playing*."

I'm not sure what Luci said then. Something like "Humph – *playing*" in a nasty, sarcastic kind of way, and maybe "yeah, right". Which is a funny thing to say, because it doesn't really mean she thinks I'm right. It's just sarcastic again. Which is mean, really. Specially as I don't understand sarcasm.

I didn't recognise the place with the water at first because the grass was all yellow and the ground was all dry. But I realised later that we'd been there before, several times, when the grass was greener and the ground wetter. We used to come with this really old human that my humans would push along the path in a chair with wheels on.

"A wheelchair," says Misty.

"Isn't that what I said?"

We've been spending some time in the home of that old human. It's a bit of a tall building with a lift that creeps slowly up to her floor. Sometimes our humans take the stairs, and I think we do the four floors more quickly than the lift goes. But then most of the humans in that place are a bit on the slow side themselves, to say nothing of *the* old human, our one, who always walks terribly slowly if she gets out of her wheelchair.

She was nice, though. I saw her just a while ago, in a place where there were lots of old humans, mostly lying in beds. We went out with her in the garden of the place, with her in a wheelchair. I sat on her lap some of the time and I licked her.

"Oh, look," she said, "she's kissing me!"

And she stroked me a lot. I liked that. It was fun being with her.

This time it was strange being in her place. First of all, she wasn't even present. I don't think I've ever been there when she wasn't. And, almost as though they were just being naughty while she's gone, our humans made a terrible mess. They piled things on the chairs that used to be really comfortable to lie on. Luci and me really liked them.

"Luci and I," says Misty.

"But you weren't there."

Now the chairs had stacks of plates or old photos or clothes on them. And the humans keep having strange conversations.

"Yes, that lot can go to the charity shop."

"We ought to keep this. It meant a lot to her: it came from my grandma."

"Do you think your brother might like that?"

Every now and then, human number 2 would disappear with a big bag of things and come back with it empty.

Luci and me just lay on the bed and watched. It wasn't very nice. The smell said "grim mood" all round the humans, as though they were doing something they didn't really like but felt they had to. That's something I just don't get. I mean, why do anything if you don't really want to? If I don't like something, I just stop doing it, unless the humans tell me really, really firmly that I have to.

Actually, not even then, or at least not always.

Fortunately, we didn't actually stay the night in the old human's home. That was good, because I didn't like the atmosphere there. It seemed to make our humans sad and that made us sad too.

Instead we stayed in what they called the "guest room". Which is odd, because we didn't have any guests. In fact, when somebody else did try to come in, we gave him the bark treatment, good and proper, so he knew it was our place, not his.

The strange thing about the guest room is that it doesn't have a proper sized bed. Not a real wide bed where we can all sleep. What I like to call a pack bed, for the whole pack. Instead it's got two silly thin beds, so the humans take one each. Obviously, Luci and I joined human number 1 on her bed the first night, but the second night I just absent-mindedly got onto human number 2's bed instead. In the morning, number 1 seemed all pleased.

"Look, you see – Toffee spent the whole night with you – she really *is* your dog now."

I'm not quite sure what that means. After all, we all know who the pack leader is. It certainly isn't number 2.

On the other hand, he did seem terribly happy I'd slept on his bed, so I did the same the other nights. I got a lot of stroking. Also, he has a looser hand when it comes to giving out treats than number 1, and thinking he's a kind of secondary pack leader helps him hand them out, and that's fine with me.

"Besides," says Luci, "there's more space with you on his bed."

"Yes, that's true."

"And there's no such thing as a secondary pack leader, you know."

"Oh, I know that," I assured her. There are certain things we just all understand, don't we? As dogs, I mean. "It doesn't do any harm, though, if he thinks there is, and that he's it, does it?"

"No," says Luci, "just as long as you don't start to believe it too."

After breakfast, we went back to the old human's place. She still wasn't there. And our humans just went right on with piling things up and taking them away, and having more of their dismal conversations.

"At least it was merciful. Quiet and peaceful."

"Just how she'd always wanted."

I don't know what any of that means but it sounded bad. I was glad to get away. And delighted to be home with our proper bed again.

And it was so exciting that we stopped at the place with all the water on the way home! So Luci and me could have a swim. Well, more of a dip than a swim when it came to me. But not because I was scared – just because I wasn't in the mood.

And I had just as much fun as Luci did.

Looking endearing just comes naturally to some
By Senada Borcilo

Luci on friends

Wow, what a good time we've had! The house has been just full of people. Nice people. People I know. People who've been here before. People my humans like. Which means people I like.

We had more humans than I have paws.

"There were six domestics," says Misty.

"Is that more than I have paws?"

"It's two more."

It's amazing how he can know that kind of thing. I mean, it wasn't as if it was his paws we were talking about.

So there were nearly as many humans as Toffee and me have paws.

With that many humans, there's almost always someone sitting down. Which means there's almost always a lap to get on or someone to snuggle up against on the sofa. Though, actually, when I'm on the sofa, I prefer lying at the top of the back. I like the fur the humans keep on top of their heads. And with more-humans-than-paws, there was somebody I could lie behind pretty much all the time, on top of the sofa, with the fur-on-their-heads near me.

The other nice thing when there's lots of humans is that we get to go out to fun places. Like a place we go to sometimes, with lots of trees, and lovely smells, and sometimes you catch the smell of some other animal you can track without any danger of actually catching up with them.

"And lots of other people and other dogs," says Toffee, with her tail whipping from side to side. Like she was really happy about it.

"Yuck," say I.

I mean, who wants strange humans? Who's to know they won't be nasty? That's the thing about strangers. You don't know them. They might be strange. And strange dogs are even worse.

"What do you mean? What do you mean?" says Toffee, "they're just friends we haven't met before."

"Well, I've seen you back away from a few of them. Even barking at them, which is pretty damned stupid. That's just *provoking* them. Making them nasty even if they aren't."

She looked a bit sheepish. Even though she remained completely doggish. She's much more dog than sheep, really. Hardly sheep at all. Dog quite a lot, to be fair. But sheepish just then.

"Oh, do stop rambling, Luci," says Misty.

Honestly, having them both hang around while I'm trying to write my diary isn't fair. And what's wrong with rambling? That's exactly what we were doing in that place with all the trees.

Anyway, Toffee got a bit embarrassed when she read what I'd written about her. Which serves her right. She got embarrassed. Sheepishly or maybe doggishly. One way or the other. Definitely embarrassed.

"Rambling again..."

Misty can get quite frightening when he growls like that. So let's just say that she got a bit embarrassed in a perfectly Toffee way.

"Sometimes friends you haven't met are mostly great, but sometimes they aren't quite as friendly as you might like," she tried to explain. "So, it can pay to back away a bit, just to be safe. But not like you: you back away all the time, from everyone."

"If it's safer to back away sometimes, it has to be safer to back away every time. That's just common sense, isn't it?"

Toffee didn't have an answer for that. I was quite proud. The number of times I've reduced her to silence is... Well, small... Less than all my paws put together... Quite a lot less...

One of the other things I liked about having all those humans around is that one of them was sleeping in my favourite place, the couch. That meant I could sleep on it close to him. What could be better? My favourite place – and someone to sleep next to. About as close to perfection as things get, I reckon.

Toffee, of course, has to go over the top. In the morning, we mostly come downstairs with human number 2 – he sort of crawls down like he was still mostly asleep and makes himself some of that strong-smelling black stuff he drinks.

"Coffee," says Misty.

"Her name is Toffee."

"No, not the dog. The stuff he drinks… oh, never mind."

The drink smells revolting, but generally he makes up for the nastiness by giving us our breakfast while he's waiting. Which is how things should be.

But while all the humans were here, we didn't get straight down to where our bowls are. Or not straight away, at least. There was a distraction on our way downstairs. A different bedroom. One where the door's usually closed. But this time it was open. Toffee couldn't resist it, so in she shot and jumped up on the bed. Two nice humans were sleeping there and you could hear them soon afterwards.

"No, no, Toffee," I heard, "just lie down and keep quiet."

"Oh, yuck! No. Don't lick my face. Stop it, stop it."

"Lie *down*, Toffee. And we can wash our own faces. Stop licking!"

Oh, well. At least with Toffee distracted I can get down to breakfast first. Which is important because it means she doesn't get a chance to nick any of mine. In fact, I may even take a little bit of hers, just for the fun of it.

"Hey! That's nicking too, isn't it?" she asks.

"No, not really. Just sampling."

"Well, that's what I do with your bowl. Just sampling a bit."

"Yeah, right. *Your* sampling's hard to tell apart from gobbling."

"With your sampling," she said, a bit nastily I think, "the bowl ends up empty."

"Rubbish. I just sample in a ladylike kind of way," I told her, stung.

"Yeah, right," Toffee had the cheek to reply, "a bowl is just as bare if it's been emptied in a ladylike way, you know."

Oh, well. She's incorrigible. Which is a good word, but a bad thing.

"And who taught you that?"

OK, OK. So Misty taught me the word. *And* what it meant.

Anyway, we all had a great time. Even Misty. He always had someone to stroke him, which is nearly his favourite thing. And one of the humans had left his suitcase right in the middle of the floor, nice and conveniently. That's just Misty's size. Bigger than the basket he used to sleep in, smaller than... well, a bigger suitcase than that one. He just took it over every day and slept in it until the evening.

He must have been pleased. Not many things fit him like that any more.

"What are you saying, young lady? What are you saying about my size?"

"Just that you're... well, you know... you *know* what I mean, don't you?"

"No. Please explain."

But he said it in a tone that suggested that, if I did explain, things might not turn out as pleasant as I generally like. The thought made me quite jittery. But, oddly enough, that made the words all come out right, after all.

"Well, you know, now that you're the proper size for a cat of your importance, it takes a certain kind of container to, well, contain you."

"Hmm," he said. He didn't sound convinced. But at least he kept his claws to himself.

Ah, yes. A great time. We all enjoyed it. They've gone now, which is a bit sad. But I hope they'll come back soon. It was fun having them here. It was fun having the house nice and full.

And now there's a pitter-patter of little paws again. Toffee's back.

"I've got it, I've got it." She's looking pleased with herself, like a cat who's got at the cream. And I know what that looks like, because one time I saw Misty after he'd got his nose into a whole bowlful… That growl of his. Really worrying.

"You're doing it again, girl. Rambling. Don't make a habit of it now."

Well, Toffee was looking jolly pleased with herself.

"I've worked out why you shouldn't back away from all dogs you don't know."

"Oh? Why?"

"Because you miss out on a lot of new friends!"

She seemed to think she'd won some kind of victory.

"Hmm. Small price to pay for safety. And don't forget: you can't enjoy a friend if you're not safe, can you?"

"How can you *say* that?" she asked, as though it was difficult to say something like that. Which it wasn't. After all, I'd just said it. It was really quite easy.

But, of course that isn't what Toffee meant. What she was finding hard was understanding what I'd said. But that's only hard for her.

Just wait till a new "friend" bites her…

Luci and the ethics of food

I was terribly worried about Misty the other day. He seemed to be off his food. I heard Human number 1 talking about it.

"Misty's not finishing his wet food. And he doesn't seem to be eating any dry food at all. Do you think he's unwell?"

Misty didn't think so himself.

"I was just carrying an injury," he told me.

"An injury? What from?"

"Oh, you know," he said airily, "the bloody Tom from up the road. Napoleon. He thought he could wander around my garden at will."

"Your garden? Don't you mean our garden?"

"My garden. That I allow you to use."

I thought I'd let that pass.

"So Napoleon from up the road beat you up?"

"Beat me up? I came out with a minor injury. But you should have seen *him*."

"Oh, Misty, you shouldn't do that. What's the point of getting hurt over silly things like who can come into the garden and who can't?"

I bark at invaders of my territory. But I don't fight them.

"Ah. But to me, there's a point of principle at stake. We're a pride, we are, you, Toffee, me and the domestics. A pride defends its territory. You little dogs don't understand that. So it falls on me. And you'll see – Napoleon won't be back."

"I saw him in the garden this morning."

I've got to give Misty credit. He headed for the garden straight away after I'd said that. Not perhaps all that fast. And it was a bit late – the Tom was long gone – but at least Misty went out to look. You can't really fault his dedication. Which is why I didn't tell him that when I saw the Tom from up the road, he didn't seem injured at all. I wasn't sure Misty would be pleased to know that.

Human number 2 hadn't noticed anything wrong with Misty in the first place.

"I didn't realise he wasn't eating. But maybe you're right. Maybe he *is* leaving a bit more in his bowl than he usually does. But it hasn't stopped him trying to eat the dogs' biscuits. I have to keep shooing him away. His appetite seems fine to me, seeing how fast he empties their bowls if he gets a chance."

That's certainly true. He might have been off his food but he wasn't off ours. We don't always finish off our breakfast in the morning – after all, it's biscuits instead of meat or rice, so we're not half as inclined to hoover it all up as soon as we can. I mean, lumps of meat we'll wolf in no time. Biscuits? Not so much.

Problem is, we like going back and eating another mouthful every now and then, but Misty just zooms right in and helps himself.

"Well, you shouldn't leave it in your bowls, then should you?" he says. "Bowls. With food in them. Meant to be eaten. What do you expect?"

"You leave food in your bowl sometimes, don't you?"

"Yes," he agreed, "sometimes. To eat later. Most days, actually."

"Well, we don't eat it, do we?"

"Only because it's up on a kitchen cabinet. Too high for you to get at."

"Well, *of course* we can't eat it if it's up high. Stands to reason. You *know* we can't jump up there."

"So you should put your food up high too. Somewhere I can't get at."

"Now you're just being nasty. You know if it was too high for you to reach, it'd be *far* too high for us."

"It's hardly my fault if I'm a better jumper than you are."

I looked at him. There was an air about him. Smugness, I'd call it.

Then he looked back. And I could actually smell the smugness.

"Tell you what," he suggested, "you can have as much of my food as you can get at, and I'll have as much of yours."

Toffee wasn't impressed by the fairness of his suggestion.

"We'll see about that," she said.

She meant it.

She's become much louder recently. I mean, I don't like people having the gall to walk past the house on what is clearly our part of the street, and I bark warnings at them when they do. But I've noticed recently that I'm not the loudest voice in the house anymore. When Toffee gets going, she just drowns out the rest of us. She may be a bit shriller, but that doesn't make her any less deafening, just more painful.

This is all part of her being simply more assertive than she used to be. Take dinner time. We both know when our dinner's due. But I don't like to be pushy. I just stay on the couch. At most, I might look at one of the humans a bit sadly from time to time.

Not so with Toffee. She just goes trotting over to one or other of them and stands up with her paws on their knees. And after doing that a couple of times without getting them to react, she makes a point of scraping their legs with her claws on the way down. And if that doesn't work with one human she tries the other. Eventually, one or other gives in and give us our food.

It's a good tactic. A tactic that works. But – scratching the humans to get their attention? I'm not sure I'd ever dare do that. The most I can do is lick their faces to remind them they need to give me my breakfast, if they haven't got out of bed yet. And I only do that with human number 2 – human number 1 would just chuck us across the bed if we tried to lick *her* face.

Having a go at number 2 has become our thing every morning. I don't know how he does it, but Misty always knows when number 2's going to wake up. So he comes up from downstairs and jumps on the bed. Then Toffee jumps on *him*.

Come to think of it, maybe Misty doesn't really know when human number 2's going to wake up. He just knows that Toffee will wake number 2 up just as soon as Misty appears. No one can sleep through Toffee jumping on Misty. Even number 1 wakes up, though all she does is say, angrily, "Toffee! Stop it. Leave Misty alone." And then goes back to sleep.

But number 2 starts to move, and that's his mistake. Because then Misty moves in to be stroked and Toffee and I move in to lick his face. For breakfast at least, that works just as well as Toffee's scratching for dinner. In next to no time, he'll be downstairs and feeding us.

The other thing about Toffee is that she's even more annoyed by Misty eating our food than I am. So now every time she hears him moving towards our bowls, she's out there like a shot. And barking! No wonder he can't stand it. He actually moves away from our bowls as she barks in his ear. Then she just settles right into it, eating food as fast as she can to stop him getting any more.

It's pretty impressive.

"Bloody little pipsqueak," Misty grunts, "thinks she can push me around."

"Maybe because she can," I answer.

That feels like a good reply. Like it's my turn to be a bit smug.

As it happens, I reckon Toffee is only able to drive Misty off because he knows he shouldn't be there in the first place. She's much too small to drive him away by simple force. It's his guilty conscience that gives her the advantage, letting a much smaller animal get the better of him.

"I don't have a guilty conscience," Misty grunts again, but the way he wanders away after saying it tells me he doesn't believe it himself.

The one who never has a guilty conscience, as far as I can tell, is Toffee herself. It's great that she stops Misty eating our food, but I have to say that doesn't stop her eating someone else's food. Namely mine.

At one time, she'd at least wait until she'd finished her bowl before starting on mine, but that's all in the past now. These days she eats half her bowl and then comes nosing over to where I am. Literally nosing: she pushes her nose into my bowl, *while I'm actually trying to eat from it.*

I don't know why but somehow I always let her. It's as though when that little thrusting nose shows up, I just have to back away and let her get on with it. I mean, I'm as bad as Misty, letting a tiny creature boss me around. The worst of it? I don't even have a guilty conscience. I've got nothing to feel guilty about.

"You what?"

It's funny how Misty and Toffee managed to say that at exactly the same time.

"What's the problem?" I asked.

"You honestly think you've never nicked anyone else's food?" asks Toffee.

Misty shook his head in that superior way of his.

"Of course, she has, and that's not what she's saying. She just doesn't feel guilty about it. No conscience at all."

Whatever. Anyway. I reckon human number 2's right. If Misty's eating our food, he can't be that ill. I'm not going to worry about him anymore.

Misty on Toffee in pain.
But still quite funny

Oh, how I laughed!

The joke was that little tyke Toffee. Of course. Nearly always, if we're laughing in this household, it's because of her. She just never stops being laughable.

It was all because of her latest vet trip. Not that she thinks of it as the vet's. To her it's "that place where there's always lots of cats and dogs and they give me treats". I suppose it was time for her to learn, as I had to learn years ago, that not everything at the vet's is a treat.

Far from it.

Luci's understood that. She calls the vet's "the house of pain", which at least has the merit of being more accurate than Toffee's silly description.

Well, when she came back from her latest visit to the house of pain, Toffee was in a terrible state. Completely exhausted. Out of it. And hurting. Nobody could ask for a firmer object lesson in vets-not-being-nice-ness.

I'm not without sympathy, and I was sorry for her pain, but I couldn't help feeling she'd had a salutary experience. A much-needed lesson. But no laughing matter. I'm not so nasty as to laugh about someone else's pain. Not even Toffee's.

Well, not unless I'm causing it myself, with my claws. That's pain enough to make a point, but no more than a small dog can take. But pain inflicted by a vet? Wouldn't wish it on anyone.

Well, she got more than she could take the other day.

"What's happened to me? I was in this nice place with lots of nice people, cats and dogs, and then suddenly – bang – I was waking up though I couldn't remember going to sleep and, oh, it hurt so much! And it still hurts so much! What's happened to me?"

"It's so you don't have puppies," I explained to her.

"What do you mean don't have puppies? I wasn't planning on having puppies. I wouldn't know where to look for any."

"They'd come out of you."

"Oh, don't be silly. I'm feeling much too bad to be listening to your jokes."

"It's true. That's how it happens."

Luci chimed in here.

"That's what they told me too. And they did the same thing to me to make sure I couldn't have any. And, you're right, it was nasty and painful."

"Oh, go away," said Toffee, "you're both talking rubbish. How would anybody get puppies inside me in the first place? What would be the point if I'm only going to get them out again? Anyway, I don't want puppies. *I'm* the puppy in this pack."

"Well," I explained, trying to stay patient, "in that case, maybe it's just as well you can't have puppies yourself anymore."

"And for that I have to go through all this pain? For something I never wanted to do? Something I haven't the faintest idea how to do and don't even think I could have done? What a stupid idea."

Oh, well. She's pretty clever, Toffee, but only for a dog. There are some things you just can't explain to her. Though, to be fair, explaining anything to someone who's sick is never easy. Besides, explaining how a puppy's made seems a bit pointless to someone who's just had an operation to make sure she can't.

Anyway, none of this was the funny bit. That didn't start until nearly mousing time. Which, for strange reasons known only to the domestic staff with their weird habits, is when they decide to go to bed. I was just having a stretch after a hard day's resting, ready to pop out for a rodent or two, when I heard the number 1 domestic talking to number 2.

"I'm a bit worried about Toffee."

"Well, she does seem miserable, I know. But she'll get better. Just give her time."

"Yes, I know, but the vet was clear: she mustn't do any running or jumping in the meantime. I don't like the idea of her coming upstairs. You know, she's so small she jumps up from step to step. And getting onto the bed's even worse, even with the steps, because they're even bigger jumps. She could do herself some harm, so soon after the operation."

"Ah," he said. In a tone that suggested he could see something coming and didn't like what it was going to be.

"And what if she decides she needs a pee? She'd be jumping off the bed again, going down all those steps, through the cat flap and out into the garden. Then she'd have to come all the way back up. It really could be very bad for her."

"You want me to carry her up and down the stairs each time?"

"Oh, no," she replied, "It might be better if I slept down here on the couch. That way she can sleep next to me and if she needs to go out, I can take her into the garden myself."

"Well, it won't be super comfortable," he told her with apparent sympathy but, I felt, relief too.

"Oh, I'll be fine. I'm sure there'll be no problem."

Well, there wasn't a problem for quite a time. All three of them, domestic number 1, Toffee and Luci, who decided to join them, were asleep on the couch. It was only at the very height of my hunting time, unfortunately, that things went wrong. Suddenly, domestic number 1 appeared in the garden. She looked funny, with a coat over her nightdress, and she sounded distraught. She had a light in her hand and she was peering behind every leaf and bush in the garden.

"Toffee! Toffee!" she kept calling miserably, "don't crawl away and die somewhere! Come to me. I can make you feel better."

Well, she'd spoiled any hope of my getting a mouse, what

with the light and the noise, and she'd got me feeling curious, so when she went back into the house I followed.

She rushed upstairs into the bedroom. Domestic number 2 was sound asleep (of course). But not for long. She burst in through the door with a great clatter. And turned the light on.

"What? What? What's happening?" he said.

"Oh, I'm so worried, I've lost Toffee," number 1 started, and then suddenly cried out, "oh, thank God! There she is."

And, indeed, there she was. Lying on the bed. She, like number 2, had clearly been fast asleep until all the commotion broke out. She was curled up in a ball pressed against the back of his legs. Now she was looking up, all innocence awakened and bemused. As though to say, "what's all the noise about? What's the matter? Everything's fine."

"Actually," Toffee told me later, "that's exactly what I was thinking. I couldn't understand all the racket. We were sleeping quietly and disturbing no one."

"You weren't supposed to get off the couch while you were still hurting."

"Nonsense. Didn't hurt at all."

"You weren't supposed to come up the stairs."

"Felt a couple of twinges. Nothing I couldn't cope with."

"You weren't supposed to climb up on the bed."

"Listen, Misty, the couch is just fine for sleeping on during the day. Or lying on with the humans when they're watching TV in the evening. But it's not where I spend the night. At night, I sleep on the bed. Preferably with both of them, but if one of them doesn't come up, I'll sleep with the other. That's the way things are. That's the way things ought to be."

Anyway, domestic number 1 might not have been that pleased about what Toffee had done, but she was so relieved to find her again that she didn't do anything about it.

"Well," she said, "if she's upstairs anyway, I'm not going to sleep on the couch. I'm coming to bed, after all."

"Sounds like a good idea," said number 2, "you do that."

And she did.

After a while, Luci worked out that she was all alone downstairs, so she came up too. And since it was obvious the mousing was over for the night, I just climbed up on the bed as well and curled up in a space I found for myself, only slightly biting number 2's feet to make him budge a bit.

That way we all slept together on the bed and no one slept on the couch. Which, as Toffee said, is how things ought to be. No one had anything to complain about.

She knows what she wants, that Toffee. She knows how to get it. Sometimes she's cleverer than you might think.

"You haven't seen the half of it," she told me later.

I'm a bit afraid I haven't. I just hope she never gets around to showing me.

You think I spend a lot of time resting? So?

By Senada Borcilo

Toffee dealing with pain

Gosh, they hurt me so badly in that place! Which is really unfair. I used to like it so much, what with all the other dogs and cats there, and the humans with treats. How could they suddenly turn around and be so mean, in a place like that?

"The vet's, Toffee. It's called the vet's," Misty tells me.

"Whatever."

Usually when I go there a nice human gives me a treat or two and then they take me into a back room where they pummel me a bit, which I don't like, or stick needles in me, which I like even less, but they give me more treats, so it's basically OK.

On balance.

This time it was different. And *much* worse.

First of all, I somehow managed to fall asleep. That's never happened to me before when I've been there. In fact, it's never happened to me anywhere – falling asleep when I haven't decided I'm going to. Usually, I like to scratch the place a bit and worry it until it's just right for lying down, before I decide that I'm ready to fall asleep. Instead, this time I just went from being awake to not being awake. Just like that.

And it was even worse when I woke up. Just *awful*. Everything hurt. Worse than I've ever hurt. More-than-treat-curing worse.

In fact, I wasn't pleased at all, and nothing anyone tried could get me pleased. Food didn't do the trick. Being stroked didn't do the trick. I just felt *lousy*.

All for no reason. I hadn't been naughty. I hadn't done anything to anyone. Anything nasty, anyway.

"It was to stop you having puppies, silly," says Misty, "I've told you before."

"Whatever."

"It *was*. It really was."

"Oh, stop it. I'm not in a mood for silly stories. No one's put puppies inside me, so how are they getting to get them out? And if they want to get them out, why would they put them in?"

"I can explain…"

"Oh, look! The postman's coming! Luci – let's go and bark at him."

I know Misty's a good explainer, but sometimes, well, I don't feel I need quite so much explanation.

Anyway. It's not hurting so much anymore. But they still keep putting me in this silly coat. They say it's to stop me licking the wound.

Hey, if they don't want me to lick a wound, why give me a wound in the first place?

It doesn't make sense.

"I can explain…"

Oh, Lord. He's back again.

"Whatever. Do you know, I think I left some dog biscuits in my bowl…"

That got rid of him. Not of course that he shot straight off to the bowl or anything. Oh, no. He's far too devious for that. He slunk off towards the kitchen, but stopped before he got there, to lie down for a while on my nice furry mat, as though he'd never planned to go any further.

"*My* furry mat," he claims, "And I'm not devious."

Well, no. Perhaps he's not all that devious. Except that the mat's near the kitchen door with a good view of my bowl, allowing him to check whether anyone else is around. Which does suggest, just a bit, that he might be after my bowl.

After a few minutes, he sat up and licked a paw. Pensively, you know. As though he had all the time in the world. And then licked the other paw.

Then he stretched and quietly stepped off the mat. He looked around as though he was trying to decide where to go next. Out of the front door? Upstairs? The kitchen?

He chose the kitchen. Which, coincidentally, is where my bowl is. Not sure who was meant to be surprised.

He wandered across the kitchen in a calm sort of way. At his leisure. No hurry. And then – well, isn't this a surprise? – he ended up by the bowls.

He looked in Luci's.

He looked in mine.

And – shock! Horror! – there was nothing in either of them!

Hee, hee, hee.

Like taking kibble from a kitten, tricking Misty, if there's food involved.

Anyway, back to what we were talking about, before I so rudely interrupted myself. I have to wear this coat. And it's warm these days. Last thing I want is a coat. Specially indoors.

"It's much better than those silly cones," I heard human number 1 tell human number 2.

"The cones? Oh, the lampshade things dogs wear round their necks? After surgery?"

"Yes. They keep banging their heads. They must be uncomfortable. Painful, in fact."

Well, I'm glad it's better than a cone. Not that I know what a cone is. All I know is that, if it's even worse than the coat, then I really don't want to try one, thank you very much. And, as for being less painful, the coat's a real pain, I can tell you.

At first, they didn't take me out on walks at all. Luci went out but I'd be left behind. The furthest they'd take me was round the block, so I could have a pee. Not much fun there. I got quite depressed. Fortunately, human number 1 noticed.

"I think poor Toffee's getting demoralised by not going out on walks."

Well, I don't know what demoralised is, but it doesn't sound good, and that's just how I felt.

"Maybe we should take her out after all."

So they did. But, hey, they kept me on a lead! A long lead but a lead all the same. It meant I couldn't play with other dogs and they didn't throw the ball for me.

That, apparently, is the point. According to human number 1, I "mustn't run around," at least "until the wound's healed entirely. It'll be a little while yet."

A little while yet? How long's that? It's been long enough already.

Tedious bloody business. Lots of pain. A silly coat. Always on the lead. If I'm even taken out at all. And all for no good reason. To stop me having puppies, they claim. But what makes them think I wanted puppies in the first place? I didn't want puppies. To stop me having puppies I didn't want anyway, they had to spoil my visits to that place with the dogs and cats and treats – to the *vet's* as Misty always tells me? That's just crazy.

What on Earth was the point?

"Ah I can explain that…"

Oh, no! He's caught up with me again.

What are they planning now?
By Senada Borcilo

Luci enjoys the water

It's really amazing what's been happening to us.

Well, to be honest I don't really understand what *has* been happening. But it's *still* amazing.

First of all, we spent ages and ages *and ages* in that awful shaky, wobbly, smelly car thing the humans make us get into from time to time. On and on. For hours and hours.

But now and then we'd stop. And there'd be lots of new smells to smell and bushes to explore or water to investigate. Lots of curious and exciting stuff.

New streets, new woods, new people. There were other dogs, too, and not like the ones I already know. I can't put my paw on exactly what the difference is, but they don't sound quite the same or smell quite the same. I know that's not necessarily a bad thing, but I always find it's better to be a bit suspicious of things when you don't know them, and that includes dogs with smells you don't recognise.

I kept out of their way whenever I could.

"You *always* keep out of the way of dogs you don't know," Toffee tells me.

Well, that's true. But this time I was even more careful than usual about keeping out of their way. Because they smelled strange.

The odd thing was that it wasn't just the dogs that were different. The humans sounded different too. And, when our humans were talking to the other humans, they didn't sound the same either. I mean, I couldn't even understand what they were saying.

"That's because they weren't talking English anymore. They were talking French."

Honestly, sometimes Toffee just amazes me.

"How do you know that?"

"Because I heard them talking about how funny it was to be talking French again. Human number 1 said it was like going home."

"But we're *not* home," I told her.

"I'm just telling you what she said. I don't know what it means to be talking French. And I don't know what human number 1 meant about being home when we're not home. Sometimes, humans say the oddest things."

"OK. So, what you're telling me isn't all that helpful, is it?"

I know that it wasn't nice of me to say that, but she really wasn't being helpful. I mean, I didn't understand any better what was happening after her explanation than before. Once we had someone who would explain things like that to us. That was our cat, Misty. He was good at explaining things, even if he sometimes went on a bit too long. But he's not with us, and I was starting to forget him, until just now when I remembered his explanations, and realised there was a Misty-shaped hole in my life. And not enough explanations, unless you count Toffee's, and you can't really count hers.

Not that she seemed upset about my cutting remark. But then nothing much upsets her.

"Well, it doesn't make a lot of difference to me, you know," she told me. "Or you, really. Don't you listen to *how* they say things, more than *what* they say? How they smell when they say what they're saying? How they move or stand still?"

"It's nice to understand what they're saying, though."

"Yes, but it doesn't matter much, does it? You know how they feel. You know when they've stopped the car but are going to start again in a moment, or stopped the car because they're getting out, don't you? You don't need *words* for that."

Well, I suppose she's right. And, in any case, it all changed again a while later. Suddenly they were speaking something else which wasn't English either, but the way it wasn't English was different from before.

"That's because it's Spanish," said Toffee.

"All right, thank you Toffee, you can stop just there," I told her. I didn't want another of her clever explanations that just left me more confused than before.

One thing we saw lots of was water. I've really started to enjoy water more and more. I mean I always did, really, but now it's better than ever.

The first water we came across was moving quite fast, but smoothly. I liked it. I mean, you could drink it and everything. I went in right up to where my legs were completely covered, but Toffee just paddled her paws and danced around barking at me.

But that was only the first time. Afterwards we got back in the car and spent a long time in it, and when we got out again, we went to see some of that really strange kind of water we've visited a few times before. The kind of water that keeps getting up and attacking us. You know, bunching up and sort of throwing itself at us. Toffee got quite frightened and ran away but I *quite* liked it. It was a bit fun, in a scary sort of way.

"A *very* scary way," said Toffee.

Very scary, then, fair enough. And it wasn't good to drink. It was *salty*. And there was lots more of it.

"That's because it was the sea," Toffee explained.

Oh, Lord, I thought, here comes another Toffee explanation. But this time what she was saying did vaguely remind me about something I'd heard before. I remember the other times we saw really strange water we talked about sea, and the water had been salty then too.

"But how did it become sea?" I asked, "it wasn't in the morning."

"That's because we weren't in the same place."

Now *that* made sense. All that time in the wobbly, shaky car. We'd probably gone somewhere else. The water was different water.

I think that explains what's happened since. I think we must be in yet another new place. You know, now we've got Spanish instead of French, where before we had French instead of English, if you know what I mean.

This place has got some nice green quiet warm water. And I've discovered it's *real* fun. I can swim right out into it. Quite a long way from the land. And then come back. And then go out again.

When I'm on land I can chase birds into the water. Like I always did. The difference, now that I've learned to swim a lot more, is that I don't have to stop near the water's edge. I can just keep going and swim after the birds. There was a silly little bird that thought it could get away from me in the water so I swam up quite close to it. That taught it a thing or two. It flew away at the end. Which is just as well. I thought I was going to get *right* up to it, which means I would have been able to catch it, and I have no idea what I would have done then. But it flew away, so I didn't have to do anything.

Anyway, I like this water. I wish the humans would take me there every day. Because it's so much fun to go in and chase the birds.

And we *can* go every day. Because now we hardly ever get into the car. Instead we're in a house which seems quite nice, except it doesn't have a dog flap and you have to go up lots of stairs to get there. Still, you know what it *does* have? A couch. We can lie on it, Toffee and me, while the humans watch TV. Like at home.

"It *is* home," says Toffee.

"How do you mean home?"

"Well, we're staying here. Which makes it home."

A different home? That's a weird idea. Though I vaguely remember something from a long, long time ago. A place with a human and two human puppies. I don't remember it well except that I think I thought it was home, until I came to the home I share with my human number 1, where I met human number 2. I think that means I had to learn to live in a new home once before. So maybe this is another new home and I can learn to live in it too.

But that gives me a terrible thought. Because something isn't right about this home.

"There's something missing..." I said.

"Misty," said Toffee.

Of course. I'd forgotten again, but now I remember. Our great big furry cat with his nice smell. I liked how he used to let us lie with him. Or chase him, sometimes. At other times, he would beat us up a bit, but that wasn't *so* bad. He did it in quite a friendly way. I remember all about him now.

"Yes," I said, "Misty. He isn't here. And I miss him."

"So do I," said Toffee. "Maybe he'll come here too."

"That would be nice."

"Yes. In the meantime, it's a pretty good place though, isn't it?"

I thought of all the water again.

"Yes. It's great. Specially that big patch of water. Let's see whether we can get the humans to take us there again."

The right kind of water is great to stop me feeling sad. Even though I *do* miss Misty. At least, until I get into the water. Then I can't think of anything else.

Togetherness
By Senada Borcilo

Toffee, water and friends

It's funny watching Luci doing all that swimming.

Don't get me wrong. I like this water we have near where we seem to be living these days. I like it a lot. I like going in as much as Luci does.

No, no, that's not what I mean, exactly.

I mean that when I go in, I like it as much as Luci does. Not that I go in as much as Luci does. Not as far, anyway. I prefer just wandering in a bit of a way. It just seems sensible to keep my feet on solid ground. Water up to my belly is quite fun. But when it gets to my neck, well I just have to swim, and I'm not so sure about that. I don't feel so *anchored* if I can't get my paws on the bottom.

Not that I actually *mind* swimming. I mean, I can do it. It takes a bit of an incentive, though. Something like a ball. Or even a stick.

Have you ever chased a ball? Because you're letting what's best in life slide past you if you haven't. It's odd to think about it now, but there was a time when I really didn't care about it all that much. But recently it's become my favourite thing.

Well, second favourite thing. After food.

And belly rubs. Third favourite thing.

Which is still really, really good, isn't it? I mean, there are lots and lots of things bigger than three. Like as many things as I have paws and then more. So third favourite is pretty good.

The thing about balls is that if you throw them in the water, they sometimes go below the surface. When that happens, I like to dive down after them, which always amazes Luci who just won't get her head into the water. It frightens human number 1 when I do it, though. She says things like "she's going to drown! I know she's going to drown, how are we going to get her out of there?", which is quite funny, so I try to do it more often.

Sticks do the same thing too, sometimes, and that's a bit irritating, because while I don't mind getting water up my nose for a ball, it's annoying for just a stick. When the humans throw sticks instead of a ball, I prefer to stay near the edge, with water only on my legs, jumping up and down and barking a bit. That's quite fun. And I get the stick anyway, because by the time Luci has come panting back with it in her mouth, she's too tired to stop me taking it from her. That means I can run up to the humans and give it to them. Which is the most important bit, because it's what gets you congratulations. Though, to be honest, they don't congratulate me as much as I might expect for going to such lengths to bring them a stick, but humans aren't always properly grateful, are they?

Funnily enough, I've noticed that before. Like when I go off into the bushes because I've smelled a nice piece of mouldy sandwich or something, and they keep shouting for me to come back. Obviously, I can't go back straight away as I have to finish the mouldy thing first. But then I race back, really, really fast. They don't always seem glad though. However quickly I run. They don't give me a treat. It's enough to make me think I shouldn't hurry even if they are calling me over and over.

Anyway, playing around in the water in our new park is fun, whether I swim or not. And watching Luci's fun too. Even more, if I take a stick off her after she's swum for it.

But that's not the only fun thing that's happened since we got here.

We went somewhere *else* too.

Getting there was a pain. First, we took one of those train things. They shake you around and make a terrible noise, but at least Luci and I can lie on the floor by the humans' feet and wait for it to be over.

Then we got in a car. That's worse, because they shake you about even more, pushing you one way then the other, going faster and slower for no good reason that I can see, and just being plain uncomfortable. But this time it wasn't so nasty because we had friends with us: people from the other home, where we lived before, and which I'd almost forgotten about what with the new park and the water and everything. Two big humans I remember from before. Nice friendly humans.

We were in the back as usual, but human number 2 came and sat with us instead of staying in the front, which was nice because it meant we could lie on him instead of just on the seat. That makes the whole business much more bearable. For us of course, but for him too: what's not to like about two toy poodles crawling over you on a car journey?

Finally, we turned up at this new place we were going to and it was just amazing! There were lots and lots and lots of friendly humans there. And loads of them I knew already. The girl-human who likes to make a fuss of us. The female-human we usually see with her, who picks me up and cradles me in her arms for ages and ages, because she understands that if you're doing something that feels good, you should just keep doing it and there's no reason to stop.

And lots of other humans, who generally come and see us just one or two at a time, but this time they were all there. All at once. Like a big pile of treats instead of just one like we usually get. Far, far more of them than I have paws. More than my paws and Luci's paws together, I reckon, or even Misty's too. And Misty wasn't even there, which was sad. Not that I had time to be sad. There were just so many friends there that I couldn't think about anything else.

And that was just the people we already knew. Luci prefers being with people she knows, and it's true that I like it too, but sometimes it's good to meet other people because then they can become people you know, too. And almost all of them become friends. Not many of them go "oh, oh, oh, get the doggy away from me", like someone did a few days ago in the park.

Except that she didn't say that, she made different words, the way most people around here do, but I could see – and smell – what she was trying to say.

No one did that in this place we were at. They were all really pleased to see us. Specially to see me. And the really nice thing was that they kept eating things, so there were always bits of food on the floor for me to swallow quickly. I had to make sure that my humans didn't see me, but I'm getting quite good at that. And it's easier when there's lots of legs to wander in and out of, and lots of tables to hide under.

People kept saying what a great wedding it was. I've no idea what a wedding is, but I agree with human number 1, who said it was the best wedding she'd ever been to. It was certainly the best wedding I've ever been to. And I'd never been to one before. Maybe the next one will be even better, though it's hard to see how.

Bring it on, I say. You can't have too many weddings, Lots of old friends, lots of new friends, lots to eat. What's not to like about a wedding?

But they didn't keep it going like they ought to have. Why do humans stop things that are good? You'd think they'd understand that, if they like it, they should just keep doing it. Instead, they made us get back into a car. And a train. And then we were back in our new home again.

Still. That's where the new park is. With the water. So all the pain of the car and the train were worth it.

Can't wait to go in again. Let's hope they take us on a walk up there. Because then, there'll be no stopping me…

All the way in I'll go. Well, up to my paws. At least.

.

Luci does some thinking

Well, well, well. Or rather, bad, bad, bad. The humans put us through another dose of horrible horribleness. Or should that be horribility? They stuck us back in the car. And then bumped us along for hours and hours and hours. Again and again and again. Taking us to another lot of new places. Odd places. With strange people and even stranger dogs. On and on. It's almost as though they *enjoyed* being that weird. Which wouldn't bother me so much if they didn't also seem to think that we'd enjoy it too.

"What's the alternative?" says Toffee. "You'd prefer it if they left us behind?"

She's becoming rather too much of a smartarse these days. I often find the best thing to do is just not to answer that kind of dumb remark. Well, not exactly dumb. Too damn smart for her own good, I suppose. Far too smart for mine.

One of the places we went was completely new to us. Never been there. Never even smelled it before. But when the door opened, we found people inside we'd seen before. At first, I couldn't think where. But then I remembered.

"You mean I reminded you," says Toffee.

Well, yes, she may have jogged my memory just a bit. But it was my memory that got jogged. So it was me remembering, wasn't it?

We'd seen them in our old home. You know what I mean? The home from before we went to the new home. The old home with the park, not the new home with the green lake. I know this is confusing, but hey, how do you think I feel?

Anyway, it was nice to see people we knew. Even in a strange place. It was a nice change.

"Sameness makes you like a change?" says Toffee, but I think she's just being smartarsey again.

Thinking about the old home got me thinking about other things too. Like old friends. Especially one old friend. Furry. Smelling good. A bit fierce sometimes but nice all the same.

"You mean Misty, don't you?" says Toffee.

Misty! Yes. I mean Misty. Our cat.

I kept thinking how nice it would be to see him again. And you know what? After more being bumped around in the car, I suddenly felt like I knew where I was. And when I looked out when we stopped, and smelled the smells, well it all came back to me.

We were in that old home again. It was the weirdest thing in all that weirdishness. Amazing. I have no idea how that happened but, boy, it was just great to see it all again.

And then we went inside and everything was just the same. The sitting room. The kitchen. The small dog flap. The garden. And when we got out there, Misty was there! Not a memory. Real, cat-smelling, live Misty. He was there to welcome us back. And seemed really, really pleased to see me. The others too, I'm sure, but me particularly. Which was an odd thing. Because I had to remember all over again how to get used to having him around. And Toffee was worse. She kept trying to chase him away.

"That's Misty," I told her, "leave him alone."

"That's Misty," human number 1 told her, "he's your friend. Don't be nasty to him."

Toffee told me later that it was just all a bit too freakish for her.

"Of course, I *know* it's Misty," she told me, "he looks like Misty, he sounds like Misty, he smells like Misty. But is Misty in our family at all anymore? He left us, didn't he? What do we do now – just let him back?"

"Well," I said, "it wasn't really him who left us, was it? It was us who left him. He's been here the whole time."

She thought about that a bit.

"I suppose you're right. We've been moving around a lot, haven't we? But, and this is a really important but, we've been with the humans the whole time. Where they are is home, isn't it? And he wasn't there. He wasn't at home with us. So... I don't know... it feels like he was the one who left home."

She's got a point. It's quite confusing and I don't claim to have completely mastered the whole thing. But it's a bit like this: the humans are where home is. On the other hand, we went with them to lots of places we didn't know. And meanwhile Misty was in this place that we know really well and where we are again now. And the humans too. So if home is where the humans are then home is here again now. Where it used to be before. But in between it wasn't.

Maybe the answer is that Misty's part of that place we know so well. Now – and this is where it gets complicated – home is where the humans are, so when they're in that place too, then Misty's part of our home. But when they're somewhere else, then he isn't.

I don't pretend to understand all this. I'm just telling it like I see it.

"That's too complicated for me," says Toffee. "I'm just going to get on with enjoying being here. I'm getting used to Misty already so I don't see why I should be worrying about all these difficult things. You're overthinking things, Luci."

"Maybe. But it still worries me a bit."

"Well, stop worrying. Remember the park that's part of this place. Let's just hope we can keep going there. That'll be fun and you'll stop making such a fuss about things that we can't change and which don't matter."

The park. Yes. That much was true, and Toffee was right. We've been going there quite a lot since we got back, and it's as nice as ever. But I'd forgotten that we don't go near any water. I mean, there is a place with water, but that's where Toffee fell in ages ago, and it was terribly, terribly cold, she says, not like when we've gone swimming together in that other place, which is lovely and warm.

I suppose it was the cold that stopped me realising how much fun swimming is. When we were living here, it probably wasn't all that great, what with the cold and everything. But now that we've been swimming in a place where the water's really nice, I miss it. A bit. When I think about it.

Not that Toffee apparently does. The thing about the park here is that, even if we can't do any swimming, it does have food. Really good stuff. You know, bits of sandwich that have been there a day or two, old chicken bones, little piles of soggy rice. That's the problem with the other park: there's these annoying people in it who wander around with carts and brooms and shovels picking up all the mouldy snacks we'd like. I don't know what's so special about the cart people, but they seem to think they should have all that food and we shouldn't.

Of course, I don't eat the snacks we find unless whichever human's with us can't see me. You know, if the wonderful food's behind a bush or something. But Toffee's not like that. She'll eat anything anywhere.

"Well, of course I do," she says, "I mean, what am I supposed to do? Walk past food? Without eating it? Are you crazy?"

So she has this whole way of doing things, where she gets something in her mouth and then watches the human while she tries to bolt it down. She lets them get quite close sometimes, almost close enough to catch her collar. But then she dashes away and stops somewhere else to go on eating. So the human tries to catch her again.

She thinks it's quite funny, but I don't think they do.

"Of course, they do," she says, "who could miss the joke? After all, they keep playing the game with me, so they must be enjoying it, mustn't they? They'd stop otherwise."

Well, I'm not sure. I mean, I can smell irritation on a human, even if Toffee can't. And I think they both get a bit irritated chasing Toffee around when she doesn't come to them.

I can't behave that way. I try to eat what I can, if I find

something really good, and maybe I don't come first time they call me. But second time? I can't ignore them that long.

Toffee does. She runs away. And I'm sure I can feel them getting more and more irritated. Someday, they might just punish her.

"Punish me? What do you mean?"

"Well, I don't know. They might hit you?"

"*Hit* me? Hit *me*? I don't think so. I mean, they never have, have they? Why would they start now? I'm the adorable little orange one, don't forget."

"I don't think I've ever known them as irritated as they got last time."

"Oh," she says, smelling a bit puzzled. But she brightens up again quickly. "Well, they haven't hit me yet, and I like the food, and I like it when they chase me. So I'll just keep going, I reckon. Let's see what happens."

That's Toffee for you. Happy go lucky. And maybe that's not such a bad idea. Maybe she's right and I worry too much about things.

Sill. I've noticed one point she seems to have missed. They may not have hit her, but they put her on the lead a lot more than me. Park walks these days seem to involve more staying on the lead than before, but her specially. Maybe if she hadn't been having so much fun and getting them so irritated, she might be able to run about with me a bit more.

Makes you think, doesn't it? Even if they don't punish you, the humans can make sure you get less fun than you used to, if you take too much fun to start with.

That feels like something else I need to think about. Which Toffee could maybe learn from too, I suppose, if she doesn't just say I'm being too complicated again. Personally, I think it's quite fun that thinking about things can give you new ideas, some of them quite valuable.

Though it's tiring, isn't it? I think I'll go and lie on the couch a bit.

More togetherness

By Senada Borcilo

Misty's foreboding

So, they came back. The domestics. Not before time. They were away for weeks and weeks. No idea what they were thinking of.

They left some strange domestic behind. Never heard of her before. She just showed up one day out of the blue, with a suitcase, and talking French. Oh, yes, I still recognise the language of the domestics of my childhood. But I also recognise good domestic service, and what she provided simply wasn't. Getting her up in the morning proved absolute hell. I had to poke and push her to get out of bed. And sometimes she'd shut her door so that I couldn't even get in to do that. When that happened, I could wait hours and *hours* for my breakfast.

In the evening, she'd sometimes forget my dinner too, unless I reminded her. Occasionally, the reminder had to be a bit sharp too, to get her attention. I don't like having to use teeth or claws on someone with the power to deprive me of my meal, and she liked it even less, but if a domestic won't do her work, what choice does one have?

Domestic number 3 popped in from time to time. So did the couple of domestics we got to know in recent months, the ones I call 4 and 5 though I don't know which is which. That was a boon because they like to be helpful and are good at providing a lap in the evening. Still, that hardly makes up for the inadequate service I was getting most of the time. After all, they weren't live-in domestics, which meant laps were only available on a temporary basis. And once I've settled down with a domestic under me, I don't like the arrangement being disrupted just because they choose to leave.

Why do they do that, anyway? Leave, I mean? Once we've settled down, with one of them on the couch and me on their lap, all comfortable and easy, why do they get up and clear off? After all, what's the point of going somewhere else, if we're enjoying ourselves where we are?

Domestics who keep going away. The bane of a respectable feline's life.

Besides, domestics 4 and 5 have an animal of the canine persuasion living with them. They have the sense not to bring her around all the time but sometimes they do and what a pain *that* is. I mean, she has this tendency to go positively ballistic. You know, racing around the room and yapping like a lunatic. She's even crazier than my own dogs. A bit rough, isn't it? I mean my dogs go away, without so much as a by-your-leave, and even the one benefit of that shameless behaviour of theirs – a bit of peace and quiet – gets wrecked by this yappy lunatic instead.

And there's one other major inconvenience with this dog creature. Lina, they call her, but she's certainly no leaner than my two.

Ha, ha. That's called a pun. I bet you didn't know cats could do them.

Not really a successful pun, though. I've just remembered that her name's really Nina. Which is annoying, since I quite like my little joke. And it hardly matters what her name is, because she doesn't answer to it anyway. Not, at least, when she wants to be doing something else.

"Nina, Nina," her domestics call, while she's eating my food, but she heeds them not.

Anyway. This Nina. She's just as noisy as my two but she's bigger, which makes it far worse. In fact, she's a *lot* bigger. A *bit* bigger than me, even. It makes me miss that little Toffee, who's half my size. Well, a bit more than half, but not much.

Not that I'm intimidated by Nina, or anything. I mean, it takes a lot more than a little yapper to scare *me*. But still. It pays to be a bit careful, doesn't it? I mean, it's easy to pin down Toffee and teach her a lesson in respect. But Nina? Maybe not

Don't get me wrong. I'm not saying I *couldn't* pin her down too. In fact, I'm sure I could. Of *course*, I could. I reckon. But, well, what would be the point of trying? After all, she wouldn't like it. Her domestics probably wouldn't like it. And I certainly don't want to upset them. So when she came visiting and went chasing around everywhere, I always gave her a wide berth. No point in precipitating unnecessary conflict. Her domestics have understood that what I needed was a lap, so I just settled down on one as soon as I could, for as long as he deigned to stay, while they kept the yapper under control.

It was actually quite fun lying on the lap and looking down at her yapping ineffectually.

"Come down here," she'd say, "just come down here and play with me."

"Why?" I'd reply, "I'd only have to pin you to the ground to shut you up."

"You? You? I dare you! Come down and try."

"Noooo," I sneered and watched her going completely mad, until her domestic said, "stop it Nina! Lie down and be quiet" and pulled on her lead.

Yes, they put her back on her lead after a while chasing around in my house. That struck me as an excellent call. It was the deference due to the senior animal of the household. I decided to train my domestics to do the same when they came back.

If they came back. For all I knew, they weren't going to. And these hopelessly unsatisfactory arrangements were going to continue indefinitely. Chaotic. Messy. With different people in at different times, with a most unsatisfactory level of service as a result. A nightmare.

But then, then nightmare ended! Normal service was resumed. The domestics finally did come back! With the yappers in tow. What a relief. Even the yappers. It was the end of a long and painful tunnel, getting the permanent staff back in the house. With a hope of a return to normality. Though the yappers did keep prattling on about some nonsense I couldn't even begin to comprehend.

"We've been trying out your new home, Misty," Toffee explained.

I don't have a new home.

But are you thinking what I'm thinking? They're not going to do that again, are they? Another bloody move, excuse my French? Not that it is French, and I know what French is.

Still, that's just one of my bugbears at the moment. I've got bigger fish to fry. Or smaller dogs to train. Luci was OK. She came back like she went, a bit timid and retiring. But Toffee – oh boy, I had to start my hard work all over again. It was like she'd forgotten how the hierarchy works at home. Or even who I was. She kept rushing at me and yapping, as though it was me who was the intruder. Teeth and claws, teeth and claws – a cat's best friends and I've had to use them a lot just to start knocking her back into shape.

Though, to be fair, sometimes her yapping's quite useful. Napoleon, the cat from up the road, had again taken to behaving like my garden was open to all comers. He'd wander in whenever he felt like it. Especially at night. Which is a pain because it means I had to do some serious growling and howling to put him off. We don't actually tangle or anything because we both know that neither of us comes out of a fight any better for it. But it takes a lot of threatening behaviour to make sure that proper order is respected.

And that's where Toffee's of such unexpected value. Because she comes rushing downstairs and straight out into the garden, through my cat flap, and flies at Napoleon without a thought about what he might do to her if he was minded to.

To my amazement, it works. Where my growling just gets him replying in kind, that bundle of yapping fur drives him right out of the garden. Funny, isn't it? Just because it says "dog" loudly enough, that works, even though it's tiny.

"Quite the little policeman," said human number 2, when he

came down to see what was happening.

"Thank God," said number 1, "all that shrieking was horrible. At 3:00 in the morning. What *did* you mean by it, Misty?"

Me! She was blaming *me*. When all I was doing was protecting the place against an interloper. I was expecting proper gratitude. But what I got was an accusation. Honestly, even with the permanent staff back in place, the standards of domestic service just aren't what they were when I was a kitten.

I've got plenty to do to get this house back in order. Lots of work for a cat who appreciates efficiency and high standards. Plenty of tasks on my to-do list.

And yet, and yet. At the back of my mind there's that thing about a "new home". Just what do they mean by that?

What new disaster is waiting for me just around the corner?

What does life have in store for me next?
By Senada Borcilo

ABOUT THE AUTHOR

David Beeson

A long-term servant to various animals, who learned only from years of experience the depth of my initial mistake. I had honestly assumed that the pets we shared the house with really were pets, and that we owned them.

Fortunately, I eventually realised that the reality was different. Domestic animals expect domestic service. Our presence is tolerated, and our contribution evaluated, only in terms of how we provide for the cat and entertain the dogs.

I now treat all three with the respect they know they deserve.

BOOKS BY THIS AUTHOR

Good Company

When a young teacher follows his new and exciting girlfriend's advice to plunge into the world of business, an inspiring new world opens for him.

And everything goes swimmingly until people starting dying around him.

Random Views: The First Five Years

A collection of blog posts on any imaginable subject under the sun, from family and pets to politics and fun.

Printed in Great Britain
by Amazon